THE FURTHER MEMOIRS

OF

SHERLOCK HOLMES

The Further Memoirs of Sherlock Holmes

CAIDEN COOPER MYLES

MX Publishing

Hardback ISBN 978-1-80424-255-1
Paperback ISBN 978-1-80424-256-8
ePub ISBN 978-1-80424-257-5
PDF ISBN 978-1-80424-258-2

Published by MX Publishing
335 Princess Park Manor, Royal Drive,
London, N11 3GX
www.mxpublishing.co.uk

Cover design by Brian Belanger

For Iain

I believe you would have enjoyed these stories

Contents

Prologue

have remarked in my other published accounts how I always sought my friend's permission to lay any record of his adventures before the public. Some he would permit immediately; with others he would demur. On those occasions, his reason was often a desire not to cause embarrassment either to the police, who had, with his permission, taken the credit for success; or it was to spare his client whose life might be adversely affected by the full truth becoming known. His opposition would occasionally be rescinded if enough time had elapsed, those concerned had passed away, or I was able to effectively conceal both identities and locations.

The accounts that follow are all examples of the above. I trust that you will find them of interest.

John H. Watson, M.D.
London, 1919.

"He lifted the contents out of the box. I recognised it at once."

The Adventure of the Sinister Correspondent

(Mid-1899)

R. SHERLOCK HOLMES was, for the entirety of our association, a man of contradictions. A man who would not set foot outside in anything other than the correct attire but who was perfectly willing to empty a revolver into his wall and store his tobacco in a slipper.

It was this fastidiousness that led to me accompanying him to Savile Row in search of a new frock coat. The previous evening, we had dined at the Café Royal on Regent Street and had left a little after eleven o'clock. Holmes had expressed the desire to walk which, given the distance to Baker Street, I had been less than pleased about. Furthermore, he had elected to take several back streets in an effort to keep his knowledge of the West End fresh.

We had been passing through Manchester Square when we had become the object of interest for a couple of roughs who had clearly fallen out of a public house only minutes earlier. Thanks to their lack of sobriety, they had been less than coherent about who they were endeavouring to avenge but it had become abundantly clear that an ally of theirs was presently incarcerated courtesy of the efforts of my friend. Regrettably, this surfeit of alcohol had not impeded their coordination to the extent we had hoped and the ensuing confrontation had taken longer to win than either of us had anticipated.

Holmes thrived on these bouts of exercise and his experience in all manners of defence had stood him in good stead. I had relied upon my limited experience in the ring whereas, he later informed me, he had drawn on his single-stick experience to, as he succinctly put it, acquaint our adversaries with the pavement. We had eventually walked away, leaving them bloodied and, hopefully, a little wiser, in our wake.

It was just before midnight when we arrived back in Baker Street. I had immediately headed upstairs to attend to my bruised knuckles. I had barely removed my jacket and opened the iodine bottle when I had heard Holmes's voice raised in frustration.

I ran downstairs to find him holding his frock coat. There was a large tear in the left sleeve, no doubt gained in our earlier confrontation.

"It will not do, Watson," he had said. "Would you care to accompany me to Savile Row tomorrow?"

The prospect had not filled me with joy but I had acquiesced in order to get to bed. The next morning, I found myself in a cab en route to that epicentre of sartorial elegance and the door of Holmes's favourite tailor.

Upon entering the establishment, we had been greeted by the proprietor, Mr. Cundey. Holmes had explained his predicament and been led away to be measured. In a short space of time, Holmes was informed that there had been no change since his last visit. Holmes had known this of course, but I believe it had given him a degree of satisfaction to hear it from another party.

Order placed, Holmes and I had headed back to Baker Street. Upon our arrival we discovered a giant of a man standing outside our front door. He was in excess of six feet, well-built with broad shoulders. I could not decide whether he had come from the army or a circus. With a decidedly limited vocabulary, he declined Holmes's invitation to enter and informed us that his mistress awaited us. We stepped inside, leaving our enigmatic guard on duty. Mrs. Hudson approached us and made plain her unhappiness with the situation. She handed Holmes a card upon which was written the name Adelia Walker. Judging by his expression, the name meant nothing to Holmes. We headed upstairs to the sitting room to see what story our visitor had to tell.

"Thank you for seeing me, Mr. Holmes," said Miss Walker after the initial introductions. "I have endured just over two years of unsettling events and decided to place it all before you for your opinion."

"As you can see, Miss Walker," said Holmes, "you have caught Dr. Watson and I midstride. Please resume your seat and I will be with you presently."

He disappeared into his room and Miss Walker tried hard not to appear curious about the noises that she heard. She was a little over five feet in height and was wearing a pastel blue dress. As she sat down, I watched her survey the room, her warm hazel eyes taking in the unusual domestic scene of pipes and test tubes. Her expression was one of both curiosity and barely suppressed sadness. She was anywhere between eighteen and twenty-five and her beautiful auburn hair, although up, was clearly of considerable length.

Holmes returned and took his seat. I took my seat opposite him. "Please begin, Miss Walker," I said, when Holmes remained silent.

The young lady looked down at the envelopes she was holding before looking up at Holmes. "My father, Edgar Walker, was a successful banker and stockbroker. He began his career in India in the 1850s, although I do not know much about it. He returned to England in the 1870s where he met and married my mother. I was born towards the end of that same decade.

"My mother sadly died when I was eleven and this badly

affected my father who distanced himself from most society, channelling all his energies into work and my upbringing. We lived in a sizeable house in Putney and my father maintained a staff of three who looked after us.

"Events started to take a strange turn a little over two years ago. We were at breakfast when the maid, Lucy, brought in the post that had arrived. As was his custom, my father sat at the table opening each letter with his butter knife. Most were swiftly read and put down without a word but the one before last had a terrible effect on my father. As he read it, he paled. Despite the effect it was having on him, he finished the letter, which was two pages long, before walking over to the fireplace and casting it into the flames."

"Do you have any clue as to the contents of the letter?" asked Holmes.

Miss Walker shifted in her seat. Her discomfort was that of a student sitting an exam and realising her preparation was inadequate. "Beyond the fact that it was handwritten, I can tell you nothing. However, I did look at the envelope. It had been posted in central London as I saw the Charing Cross post mark.

"My father noticed me looking at the envelope and snatched it away. 'Pay no attention,' he said. 'Stuff and nonsense.' Without a further word, he threw the envelope into the fire."

Holmes nodded. "What occurred next?"

"Nothing for a few weeks," replied Miss Walker. "Then, one evening, I was at the theatre with my godmother."

"Her name please?" asked Holmes.

Miss Walker looked frustrated at the interruption. "Her name is Mrs. Florence Markham."

"Thank you. Please continue."

"Despite being a long-standing friend of my father, I saw little of her prior to my mother's death. My godmother travels a good deal, spending a lot of her life abroad, and I looked forward to her visits when she would regale me with tales of her adventures. She was not a letter writer, and never brought me souvenirs of her travels, so her visits to England were my only opportunity to learn about a world beyond my limited experience.

"On this occasion, she was back in town for only a week before heading abroad once more. After the performance, she dropped me at home. I remained on the street to wave her off in her cab. I had turned to go in when I noticed a man emerge from the fog, staring in my direction."

"Try to describe him," said Holmes.

Miss Walker clearly had no trouble recalling the moment as her response was immediate. "I would say he was about five foot six. He had black or brown hair, was shabbily dressed, and around thirty years of age."

"You are sure you were the object of his attention?" asked Holmes.

"Initially no, but he spoke to me."

"And what did he say?"

"I shall never forget it. He remained at least ten yards from me and produced an unusual knife. I was frozen to the spot in terror. He toyed with it and smiled before saying, 'Tell Jaichand we are watching.' He put the knife away and calmly walked off into the darkness chuckling to himself. I continued to hear the chuckling long after I could no longer see him."

"Presumably you told your father?" said Holmes.

"Yes, and the blood drained from his face."

"Did you quote the message verbatim?" asked Holmes.

"Oh yes. He seemed to visibly shrink in stature. He said nothing and went into his study. I wanted to ask what was happening but the look on his face told me I would get nothing from him. My father had never been one to share his problems."

Holmes rubbed his hands. He was clearly intrigued. "So, what followed?"

"Within two days my father received an unusual letter."

"Unusual, how?"

"Again, it was handwritten but the paper itself contained a number of holes."

Holmes raised his eyebrows. "How did your father react?"

"With resignation, Mr. Holmes. That is the only way I can put it. He placed it into its envelope and into his pocket. He ordered the butler to bring him a pot of coffee to his study. I remember him saying to the butler that it had to be piping hot.

"He was in there for about thirty minutes. He then emerged and immediately announced his intention to go for a walk. This was unusual. When I asked if I might accompany him, he snapped at me that he wished to be alone.

"He returned about an hour later, carrying his stick and a newspaper, looking out of breath, and went back into his study."

"Was this out of character?" asked Holmes.

"There was nothing about it in character," she replied, with a degree of frustration. "He had not gone for an afternoon walk that I had ever witnessed. He had never bought a newspaper in the afternoon before, and he had never ordered coffee in his study. He always feared it spilling onto his papers.

"The next morning, he announced that he had to go into town. He went out a little after eight o'clock and was back about two hours later. He seemed more relaxed but it was short-lived."

"Please go on."

"The following month, upon the same day, a similar letter arrived in the afternoon post containing a handwritten piece of paper with holes in it. My father immediately ordered a pot of hot coffee and disappeared into his study before going out for a walk. Again, he returned with a newspaper and went directly back to his study."

"I presume you are going to inform us that he made an early trip out the next day?" said Holmes.

"Yes. Later that evening he asked to speak to me. I was hopeful that he was going to explain matters to me."

"Yet he did not, I assume?" said Holmes.

"No. Instead he said that he was concerned for my safety and had engaged a man to guard me."

"I take it that is the formidable sentinel outside our front door?" asked Holmes.

"Yes. My apologies if he startled you. His name is Evans, and he has been my shadow for almost two years now. I am not stupid, Mr. Holmes. It was clear that my father considered me under threat. I demanded to know the nature of the danger but he simply begged me to trust him."

Holmes stood and reached for a pipe from the rack. He filled it and lit it before resuming his seat. I saw at once he had chosen the pipe he always chose when he was digesting information. Miss Walker clearly did not like the aroma of his tobacco but said nothing. Through the smoke, Holmes fixed her with a stare. "I can see that the letters continued and that your father is dead."

Miss Walker was as stunned as I was by this sudden assessment. She pulled out a handkerchief and began to sob. Not so much because what Holmes had said was upsetting but because she was already so close to tears. That had been apparent from the moment we had set eyes upon her. Holmes waited patiently for her to stop. "It is no great mystery, miss. Your father was clearly secretive and yet here you are in possession of what can only be further examples of these letters. He would not let you have them willingly so you have either appropriated them or he is no longer able to object. Given what little I have learned of your father's character, and the fact that you began by referring to him in the past tense, his death seems the most likely. The fact that you are not wearing mourning attire suggests that his death was over a year ago."

Miss Walker recovered herself. "Yes, Mr. Holmes. My father died fourteen months ago, a few days after Her Majesty's Diamond Jubilee. He had received a similar letter the afternoon before he died and had gone out for a walk about an hour afterwards. I had been particularly concerned on this occasion as it was raining heavily, and I knew he would be soaked to the skin, even with his umbrella. My father's health had never been the most robust, which was the result of an illness he had experienced in India, and I feared what prolonged exposure to such weather would do to him. On this occasion he came back much later. He was in a terrible state and had to be supported into the house by one of our neighbours who had found him wandering unsteadily in the street.

"My father was incoherent and constantly said, 'There were none left.' He must have said it half a dozen times before I had his valet take him to his room."

"Did you ascertain to what he was referring?" asked Holmes.

"No, and my father was discovered dead in his bed the following morning. The doctor said from a heart attack.

"I was devastated, as you might imagine, but had no time to grieve as I had to arrange everything. That same morning, I was about to head out to see my solicitor when there was a ring at the bell.

"The maid showed in our neighbour, Mr. Hartley. I remember it so clearly, he strolled into the room casually, newspaper tucked under his arm. Although I did not know him well, I did know he was an early riser who always took a morning walk. He looked pleased with himself. He asked to see my father. He was both shocked and embarrassed when I explained my father had died."

"Was this Mr. Hartley a friend of your father's?" asked Holmes.

"More of an acquaintance," replied Miss Walker. "I asked if I could help him but he said that, under the circumstances, it did not matter. He wished me his best and said that I was to contact him if I needed anything. With that, he took his leave."

"This was the same man who brought your father back the previous night?"

"No. That was Mr. Brewer; another neighbour."

"Please go on."

"A week passed with nothing untoward happening. Then, an envelope arrived in the afternoon post addressed to my father. I cannot say I was entirely shocked when I found it contained a letter with holes in it.

"I was tempted to throw it away but decided to retain it. One of the reasons I did so was that I had no other examples. My father had presumably destroyed them including the one he received immediately before his death."

"You are certain that he destroyed them," said Holmes. "They could not possibly be hidden in the house?"

"It is possible, Mr. Holmes, but I consider it unlikely."

Holmes looked disappointed.

Miss Walker continued. "The following week another letter arrived. In total I received a further five. Then they stopped."

"If they stopped what brings you here today?"

Miss Walker frowned. "The letters stopped, Mr. Holmes, but other strange events took their place. About two days after the last letter, I was sitting in the front parlour reading. It was after nine in the evening and I decided to close the curtains. As I advanced towards the window a man appeared looking in at me. At once, I recognised him as the man with the knife from all those months earlier. I screamed and he immediately fled. Evans burst into the room, ascertained what had happened, and went out the front door in pursuit, despite my plea that he should remain.

"I sat down to gather myself. Lucy fetched me a brandy. As I sipped it, Evans returned. He apologised for not being able to catch the intruder but presented something the man had dropped."

When Holmes and I had walked into the room earlier I had been most struck by Miss Walker herself but the simple box beside her on the settee had not escaped my notice. She now turned to it and picked it up. Holmes leant forward as she presented it to him. He rested the box on his knees and gently opened it. "How singular," he said.

He lifted the contents out of the box. I recognised it at once. It was an elegant Indian curved dagger. Made with a steel known as wootz and often referred to as a tiger-tooth dagger. The handle was blue with gold inlay. I had seen many a similar knife in my army days but had rarely seen one in England.

"Presumably, this is the same knife you were threatened with at the beginning of these events?" asked Holmes.

"I strongly suspect so," said Miss Walker. "Although I could not swear to it."

"May I retain this?" asked Holmes.

"Please do."

"Now, please continue with your story as there is clearly more to come."

Miss Walker nodded. "I was pleased that the letters had come to an end and turned my attention towards the future. Thanks to my father's lack of interest in society, I had not experienced much of a social life. I now found myself very much on my own and I had no desire to be. My only confidant was my godmother, who returned to England a few days after the appearance of my unwanted visitor. She was sad but not surprised when I told her of my father's death."

"Did you telegraph her with the news?" asked Holmes.

"No," replied Miss Walker. "My godmother was always on the move and we never had an address for her when she was out of the country. I was able to inform her when she was back in London and came to call."

"I see," said Holmes.

"My godmother is an independent woman and not one for following convention. Although I was still in mourning for my father, she encouraged me to attend a limited number of social events. I had hoped for theatre but she had said that balls were better for meeting people.

"With her help, I attended several such events. It was good to get out amongst people – especially people of my own age." She stared into the distance. "It was at one such ball that I met Arthur."

Holmes glanced down. I followed his gaze to Miss Walker's left hand. "I presume that he now occupies the position of fiancé?"

Miss Walker also gazed at her hand and flushed red. "Yes, I know it is foolish to become engaged so swiftly but it seemed right. He was introduced to me by my godmother. She later told me he had approached her seeking an introduction. I do not wish to appear unduly modest but I was flattered that he had singled me out when there were so many attractive ladies present."

Miss Walker was being modest. I could easily see how she would turn heads.

"We started walking out on a regular basis. There was something so familiar and comforting about Arthur. It felt as though I had known him all my life. I cannot explain it. Within a few months, he had nervously proposed. I accepted but we agreed that we could not possibly marry before I had completed my mourning. We eventually agreed on a date which is now but two weeks away. In the interim, I told him all about the mysterious letters as I did not wish to have any secrets."

"And how did he react?" asked Holmes.

"He was alarmed, and when I later suggested dispensing with Evans' services, he was full-square against it. He asked for every detail, and I even showed him some of the letters. He asked if I wanted him to try and figure out what they meant. I said to him that there was no need for him to worry himself about it. I distinctly remember him breaking into a broad grin when I said that and he congratulated himself on becoming engaged to such an intelligent woman."

Holmes leant back in his seat. "With your life set so fair, I am wondering what specifically has led you here."

"I am here for two reasons. Two days ago, Arthur failed to meet me for dinner at our favourite restaurant. I called at his home only for his housekeeper to say that he was away. I was worried as being out of contact was not in his nature. I called again the next day and received a similar response. Today, I decided to come to you."

Her gaze returned to the envelopes in her lap. She picked out one and toyed with it. "The postman called as I was about to leave. Amongst the many letters was this one."

She handed the envelope to Holmes.

"Please read the letter," she said.

Holmes took out the enclosure and looked at it. "It says 'You will kindly continue the arrangement.' What do you draw from this?"

"Mr. Holmes, I am forced to conclude that my fiancé has been taken by whoever had been harassing my father. In order to save him I need to do something but I do not know what that is."

Holmes rapped his fingers on the arms of his chair. Miss Walker, her story done, sipped some water which I had placed at her side earlier. She stared at Holmes as if she were willing him to respond. Eventually she turned to me with a rather desperate expression. I had to act.

"Holmes, do you think we can assist Miss Walker?"

"Undoubtedly," he replied. "As you have brought those envelopes, I assume you are prepared to leave them with us?"

"Yes, I am."

"Thank you, Miss Walker," said Holmes. "I will commence my investigation into this matter and will advise you as to my progress."

Miss Walker rose, a little unsteadily, and headed to the door. At the threshold she turned. "Am I in any danger, Mr. Holmes?"

Holmes looked up. "I do not believe so, Miss Walker. Not for the moment."

"And what about my Arthur?"

"His situation I cannot swear to but I would point out that there is currently no evidence that your fiancé has been abducted. He is not mentioned in your latest letter. His disappearance and the resumption of the letters could be coincidence."

"I wish I could believe that, Mr. Holmes. I am sick with worry." With that she left the room.

I escorted Miss Walker to the front door where she was met by

Evans. I watched them climb into a cab and waved as they departed. I returned to the sitting room to find Holmes sitting cross-legged on the carpet, magnifying glass in hand, with the letters and envelopes spread about him.

"Anything?" I asked.

"All the letters carry the Charing Cross postmark," he said. "So, our sinister correspondent either lives in the area or travels there deliberately to post his letters – perhaps with the aim of hiding his location."

"The latter, surely?" I suggested.

"Very likely; but the former cannot be ruled out."

"What else have you deduced?"

He stood and walked to the window. Once there, he spun round to face me.

"The late Mr. Walker's past had clearly caught up with him. If I am reading it right, the first letter contained instructions on what was to follow and possibly hinted at threats against Miss Walker in the event of non-compliance."

He gestured to Miss Walker's box which was sitting on his chair. "I would further suggest that Mr. Walker dismissed the threat initially and that prompted the visit of our menacing friend with the blade. His use of the name 'Jaichand' was a mistake."

"Why a mistake?"

"Because it tells us a lot. Firstly, it anchors the origins of this story in India, where we know Mr. Walker began his career. Secondly, it provides motive."

"It does?"

Holmes walked to his bookshelves. His hand scanned across the many spines. "After the Sholto affair, I decided to purchase more volumes about that great nation." He seized a formidable book and began to flick through its pages. After a minute he found what he sought. He tapped the page repeatedly with his finger. "The name 'Jaichand' refers to a twelfth-century king of northern India. A poem, written many years afterwards, and probably fictional, describes him allying himself with a non-Hindu nation with the aim of bringing about the downfall of a rival."

"Sorry, Holmes. I fail to see the connection."

Holmes slammed the book shut and replaced it on the shelf. "The connection, Watson, is that the name 'Jaichand' has, as result of this poem, become another word for traitor in parts of India. I would venture to suggest that Mr. Walker betrayed someone in India and this person has tracked him down to England to punish him."

"Why punish?"

"Well, he surely had more than enough time to kill Walker had he so wished. Instead, he sent him regular letters which Walker presumably acted on for his daughter's sake. Then Walker did something unexpected."

"He hired Evans?"

"No, Watson. He died. At that point the letter frequency increased. We may assume that those letters were in response to the lack of action. When the lack of response continued the letters stopped and someone was sent to investigate."

"The man at the window!" I exclaimed.

"Yes, Watson. He turned up and, unless he is a fool, he immediately understood."

"What did he understand?"

"He saw Miss Walker on her own and in mourning. After evading the formidable Evans, he presumably understood that Mr. Walker had died. This man, or likely men, delayed while deciding what to do. The traitor was now dead. Whatever he was doing for them could not continue."

"You think more than one person is involved?"

"Yes. The man who menaced her at her own front door is clearly too young to be a former associate of her father. Walker's principal antagonist is likely to be someone of his own age or older. I strongly suspect we are dealing with at least two people."

I nodded. The logic was sound. Holmes continued.

"In the meantime, Miss Walker is moving on with her life. With her godmother's help she meets a man to whom she becomes engaged. Two weeks before their wedding he vanishes and she receives a letter telling her to continue with the arrangement."

"I do not understand, Holmes."

"Neither do I, Watson. Someone is clearly convinced that Mr. Walker shared details with his daughter and that she can therefore pick up where her father left off. The question is why?"

"Have you looked at the letters?" I asked.

Holmes smiled and turned to the papers on the carpet. "I have, Watson, and they are fascinating." He bent down and retrieved one. "Take a look at this one."

I began to read the letter. I got no more than half a page in. "Holmes. This simply describes a recent spell of weather."

He chuckled and handed me another. I read it. "Bizarre. This one is an account of proceedings in parliament."

"Wonderful, is it not?" said Holmes. "Each letter covers a different topic. Another one talks about livestock prices. Do you see what they all have in common?"

"Yes," I replied. "The holes."

He looked disappointed. "Apart from that."

I looked but had to admit defeat. He snatched the letter I was holding from me. "You can see at once, Watson, that the letters were written before the holes were made. Our correspondent did not write on paper with holes. If he had done so he would have navigated his words around the holes. You can clearly see that holes are removing parts of words."

"So, he deliberately made his letters less legible?"

"It would appear so," said Holmes. He bent down and scooped up one of the envelopes. "You will also notice that none of the letters are dated. The only clue to that is the postmark on the envelopes in which they arrived. The handwriting is of a high standard. The author is clearly educated. One thing we can see is that this gang is discerning."

"Discerning, Holmes?"

Holmes held the envelope up to the light. "Yes indeed. The notepaper and envelopes are of the best quality. Paper of this thickness is normally to be found in the homes of the wealthy and the top-end hotels."

"Why did you tell Miss Walker she was not in danger?"

"Because she is clearly expected to do something. Hence, she is unlikely to be harmed. Her fiancé, on the other hand, may be another matter. Time is short."

The next day Holmes requested solitude in order to quietly analyse the information we were in possession of and to carry out some research. Once I was promised he would take no serious steps without me, I decamped to my club and its more sociable air. It was after five o'clock when I managed to get back to Baker Street. I found Holmes cross-legged in his chair, pipe stem clamped between his teeth. He looked up and gestured towards the vacant chair.

I sat down. "So, Holmes. Anything?"

"Yes and no," he replied through gritted teeth. "Using Miss Walker's information, I paid a series of long visits to the offices of the various passenger ship companies. Not one of them carried a Mr. Edgar Walker into England in the 1870s."

"So, he came via another route?"

"Either that or he came under another name. Given that he was fleeing something or someone, a pseudonym seems likely. He was forced to travel under his true name, which is how the gang traced him here, but he changed it as soon as he was able which made the trail cold."

"He did well to evade them for almost twenty years," I said.

"We do not know that it was that long. They may not have been hunting him from the beginning."

"What then?"

Holmes removed his pipe from his mouth, knocked it out on the mantelpiece, and returned it to the rack. "The two most likely scenarios are that they have, as you say, been hunting him from the start and have taken this long to locate him. Alternatively, they started more recently because they were prevented from doing so earlier. I have wired my police contacts in India with some basic particulars to test that theory."

"When do you expect a response?"

"I hope not more than a few days."

"Miss Walker's fiancé may not have a few days."

"I am aware of that, Watson. So, we will pursue other avenues while we wait. Miss Walker is expecting us at her home in a little under two hours."

Mrs. Hudson rustled me up a formidable sandwich and some coffee. Holmes spoke no more of the Walker affair and instead told me of some his more recent experiments in connection with other cases. As soon as he deemed it time, we donned our overcoats and made our way out into the evening. There was damp in the air, although it was not yet raining, and there were wisps of fog. We climbed into a cab and headed for Putney.

"What is the purpose of this visit?" I asked, as we rattled along the gaslit streets.

"I wish to examine the Walker home first-hand," said Holmes. "I also wish to interview the staff."

It was not long before we arrived at the impressive town house. Similar houses were round about it. Holmes advanced to the door and rang the bell. The door was opened, not by the butler, but by the formidable Evans. He greeted us, in his concise fashion, and entered. As we did so, the butler advanced to take our hats and coats. He was a man in his late-forties or early-fifties. He stood at just under six feet and, despite being shorter, looked down on Evans. You did not have to be a detective to see that.

We were shown into the front parlour where Miss Walker greeted us. She bade us to sit and ordered tea. I could see that she was unsettled and had high hopes of us.

"Any news, Mr. Holmes?" she asked, her eyes wide with anticipation.

"It is a little early for that, Miss Walker," replied Holmes. "My purpose in coming here this evening is to take a look at the various rooms you described in your earlier narrative and to interview your staff."

Miss Walker seemed disappointed. This was not lost on Holmes but he ignored it. "Before I begin on that score, can you tell me if your neighbours will be available to interview?"

Miss Walker fidgeted. "Mr. Brewer will likely be. He is a night owl but I am afraid you cannot speak to Mr. Hartley."

"Why not?" I asked.

"Because, Dr. Watson, he died about a month ago."

"What were the circumstances?" asked Holmes.

"Nothing alarming. He succumbed to influenza. He was over seventy. His widow is still alive and may be available to speak to you."

"Later," said Holmes. "Much centred around your father's

study. May we see it and interview the staff there?"

"You may do so here."

"I would rather you were not present," said Holmes. "They are more likely to talk freely when their employer is not listening."

Miss Walker looked mildly offended but I gave her a reassuring smile which appeared to calm her. She rang the bell.

"Incidentally," said Holmes, "it seems your butler and Evans do not enjoy a cordial relationship. Do you know why?"

Miss Walker immediately looked frustrated. "My butler has given notice. He believes that Evans has intruded upon his domain. It was one of the reasons I had considered letting Evans go. The danger seemed to have passed and I could not see the need to retain him. But things got worse between them after Arthur convinced me to keep Evans. I consider it a childish dispute."

The butler entered the room and was given his instructions. He led us to the study and Holmes dismissed him. The study was typical. A formidable desk, chair, bookshelves, and fireplace. Holmes went over the room carefully, checking every drawer, every book, and every shelf. After some little time, he sighed.

"Although we are yet to see Mr. Walker's bedroom, I believe that his daughter is correct. I doubt we will find any examples of letters that pre-date his death. It is a pity. I would have preferred more data."

"You have checked only this one room," I observed.

"Yes, but Mr. Walker was clearly determined that no one else would see the letters. He was, therefore, likely to either destroy them or keep them in a place where his daughter and staff had limited, if any, access. For a gentleman like Mr. Walker, those two places would be his study and bedroom. We will check the latter presently."

He opened the door and called out for the butler. The surly man agreed to fetch the maid for the first interview. Holmes took a seat behind the desk, and I stood to his left.

The maid, Lucy, entered the room. "Yes, sir?" she said, as she curtsied. Her apron was slightly stained and damp which suggested she had been interrupted during a task in the kitchen – likely the preparation of the tea.

"Good evening, Lucy," said Holmes. "What do you know about the letters your late master received?"

"Not much, sir," Lucy replied. "I remember the to-do they caused but I never saw what they said."

"What do you recall of the night your master died?"

"Oh, it was dreadful, sir. Mr. Walker was back so much later than usual. He was out at least twice as long. He was missing his umbrella and was soaked to the skin. I heard a commotion and ran to the front of the house to find Mr. Walker being held upright by Jones, the valet, and Mr. Brewer from just down the road."

"Did he say anything?"

"Err. Something about there being nothing left, sir. I couldn't swear to it though."

After a few questions about the household routine, Holmes dismissed Lucy and asked her to send in the valet, Jones. Jones, unlike the butler, seemed quite amiable. He was young, in his mid to late twenties, and seemed very self-assured.

"Yes, sir," he said. "There was a ring at the bell that night and Wilkins answered the door. Mr. Brewer stood there just about managing to hold up Mr. Walker. If you asked me for first impressions, sir, I would have said Mr. Walker was drunk. I do not mean to be disrespectful but that's just how he looked."

"I understand you helped him up to his room?"

"Yes, sir. He recovered some of his senses on the way upstairs. I tried to assist him with his clothes but he shrugged me off and said he would attend to himself. He ordered that I get the fire lit in his room. This was not normally my duty but something Lucy would do. So, I fetched her to do it. She is a good girl, sir, and got the fire going quickly. By this time, Mr. Walker had changed his clothes and was wearing a dressing gown. He was shivering like he had fever sir. He was also pale. He moved towards the fire and sat down. I watched him take a sopping wet envelope out of his jacket pocket. He held it out to the fire."

"To burn it?" I asked.

"No," said Jones. "He was trying to dry it. I watched him hold it out and turn it to dry it evenly. He held his hands out so long that they must have started to get hot. He suddenly dropped the envelope."

"Then what happened?" asked Holmes.

"He looked terrified," said Jones. "He picked it up quickly but it was still wet and began to fall apart in his hands. He was in such a state of despair that I think he had forgotten I was there. I coughed and he looked up, tears in his eyes, and ordered me out. The next day he was dead."

"And the letter?"

"Nowhere to be found."

"Can you tell me anything about it?"

"I only saw the envelope, sir. Good quality paper it was. The rain had ruined it though. There were rips in it, the address was blurred, the franking had run and the stamps had long since disappeared."

Holmes again looked disappointed and asked Jones to fetch Wilkins.

"Jones is both observant and ambitious," said Holmes. "He clearly has his eye on the soon to be vacant position of butler."

There was a knock and the butler entered the room. His mood had not improved.

"Now, Wilkins," said Holmes. "Can you give us your version of events?"

"Where would you like me to start, sir?" said Wilkins.

"From wherever you think best," replied Holmes, placing his hands together under his chin in his favourite judicial pose.

Wilkins placed his hands behind his back. "Well, I am sure the mistress has told you what happened, sir. There was very little I saw that the rest of the household did not. On the night Mr. Walker was brought home I went out into the street to see if I could see his umbrella. I knew it had belonged to his father and was of sentimental value. I do not mind telling you, sir, that I got almost as wet as he had in my search for it, but I could not find it. Lord knows where he left it.

"Jones took him up to his room and he later asked for Lucy to prepare the fire. I went to the kitchen to dry off. Miss Walker was in the parlour with Evans."

"You do not care for Evans, do you?" said Holmes.

"No sir, I do not. He does not know his place. When Miss Walker's young man persuaded her not to dismiss him, I was put out."

"Am I to take it that you had argued for his removal?"

"I would not be so bold, sir. I did complain that he was treading on my toes but she told me not to be concerned. I tried to endure it, sir, but I feel like I am being pushed out. I would rather go on my own terms."

Holmes's face showed his lack of interest in the butler's plight. "I understand that, following the arrival of these letters, Mr. Walker would come in here and have you fetch him a pot of fresh coffee?"

"That is correct, sir. It did not matter if there was one already in the parlour or dining room, he would ask for a fresh one."

"I also understand that it was not usual for Mr. Walker to have coffee in this room?"

"It was not, sir. Mr. Walker kept all his important papers in this room. Nothing that could cause damage was allowed in here. No coffee, no tea, no wine, nothing."

"And yet," said Holmes, "he was now ordering coffee. What do you make of it?"

"I have no notion," replied Wilkins. "On one occasion he ordered a second pot and he was in an appalling temper when he did. I answered the bell and he just snapped at me to get him another pot. That was not the strangest thing though, sir."

Holmes stared at the butler intently. "What was strange, Wilkins?"

Wilkins took a step closer and bowed slightly to be closer to my friend. "He never drank any of the coffee, sir."

Holmes looked surprised as, indeed, was I. "Never?"

"Not once, sir. Every time I cleared the room the pot was full. Colder, but full."

Wilkins left the room and Holmes leaned back in his chair. His expression was one of frustration. I had seen this before. He had the information but could not identify the key component. I laid a hand on his shoulder to get his attention. "What do we do now, Holmes?"

"I believe we must visit Mr. Walker's bedroom."

We left the study and headed upstairs. Despite not knowing the layout, we quickly found the room – based largely on the valet's earlier description. Again, Holmes searched and he was not surprised when he found nothing. He took a poker and, absent-mindedly, stirred the ashes in the grate.

"There is something that I have been told that is key to this," he said, as he finished stirring and replaced the poker. "I am running it all through my mind but it is eluding me." After a further minute he left the room and headed in the direction of the stairs. I followed him as he descended and crossed the hall.

He marched into the parlour where Miss Walker had remained. "Miss Walker, at which numbers may we find the Brewer and Hartley households?"

"You will find the Brewers at number thirteen and Mrs. Hartley at number nineteen," she replied.

Holmes nodded his thanks and went into the hall in search of Wilkins. Miss Walker asked me when she could expect to hear from us and I was forced to admit that I did not know. Her expression cut me to the quick, and I made a swift exit from the room. I found Holmes being helped into his coat. As the butler began to assist me, Holmes was already advancing to the door.

In the end, I had to chase him into the street. During the time we had been inside it had started to rain. The rain was light but consistent and this probably explained why Holmes headed for the nearer of the two houses, the home of the Brewers. He rang the bell and the maid answered. She admitted us both and took our cards.

"Let us hope that they are informative," said Holmes.

"Good evening, Mr. Holmes, Dr. Watson."

We turned to see a middle-aged man advancing towards us. He was below average height, slightly overweight and cut a rather comical figure in his smoking jacket. I struggled to suppress a smile. He reached us and stretched out his hand. Holmes seized it. "Good evening, Mr. Brewer. Apologies for the unsolicited visit."

"Not at all," said Brewer, as he shook my hand, "my wife and I read regularly of your exploits. It is an honour."

He beckoned us to follow him into his front parlour where we found his wife. Holmes, with his usual courtesy, bowed and we were invited to take seats as Mrs. Brewer rang for tea.

"About Mr. Walker, I take it?" asked Brewer.

"Quite so," replied Holmes. "What can you tell me about the night you came to his aid?"

"It was unsettling," replied Brewer. He looked at the window which was now being audibly battered by the rain. "It was a far wetter night than tonight. I was returning home from a small gathering held at a public house close to my office. My cab dropped me at my front door and I was about to run straight in due to the rain. My key was in the door when I heard this deep, wailing sound. I turned to see Mr. Walker stumbling up the street. He was soaked through and weaving across the pavement like a drunkard. I did not understand him to be a drinker so it struck me as unusual. He was sobbing loudly like a child and fell over. I immediately went to his aid."

"He fell over?"

"Yes. I got to him and helped him to his feet."

"Did he say anything to you?"

"Yes. Something about not getting some news he was desperate for. Whatever he was waiting to hear about, it had not come and it had made him upset."

"Did you have any idea to what he was referring?"

"None at all. By this time, I was as soaked as he and it was not going to be any good for either of us. I got him into his house and made my excuses."

It soon became apparent that Mr. Brewer could add little further. His wife relayed how he had come through the door something of a mess, and she had helped him with his clothes, but that was the end of their account. Holmes bid them good evening just as the maid brought in the tea tray. If the Brewers had entertained the idea of a social evening, they now knew differently.

Holmes was straight onto the street and headed for the Hartley house. We had neglected to bring umbrellas from Baker Street, so we both sprinted to our destination. He rang the bell and a similar looking maid admitted us and showed us into Mrs. Hartley. She was a striking woman, emerald eyes, dressed in black as society demanded, and evidently some considerable years younger than her late husband.

"Do sit down, gentlemen," she said. "Would you care for some tea?"

Before Holmes could answer, I declined for us both. There was no point wasting three pots of tea.

"Mrs. Hartley," said Holmes, "I am sorry for your loss but wondered if you could tell me anything about the night Mr. Walker died."

"Not much I am afraid, Mr. Holmes. George came in that evening to say that he had been intercepted in the street by Mr. Walker who had been in a state."

"What did Mr. Walker say to your husband?"

"George was not clear on that. He said Mr. Walker had been rambling and slurring and, of course, it was filthy weather. He told me that Mr. Walker had asked him something that he did not quite understand but that he had agreed to try and help him."

"What happened next?"

"Mr. Walker was apparently unsatisfied with this response and said he would try asking someone else. George asked him if he was okay to get to his house and got a positive response. George felt a little guilty leaving Mr. Walker but he had poor health himself and feared he would not fare well if he remained in the rain. We learned later that Mr. Brewer found Mr. Walker, only moments afterwards, in an even worse state."

"Can you tell us anything else?"

"Only one thing. The next morning, George and I were having breakfast when George suddenly broke into a huge grin. He said, 'I now know what Walker wanted,' and without a word he left the room and went out of the house. No more than ten minutes later he came back with a different demeanour to let me know that Mr. Walker had died overnight."

Holmes was briefly lost in thought. He looked back up at Mrs. Hartley.

"Have you lived in the area long?"

Mrs. Hartley looked a little surprised, and possibly annoyed, by the question. "Is that relevant, Mr. Holmes?"

"Forgive me," said Holmes. "I was merely trying to ascertain how long you had known the Walkers."

"I would not say we knew them well. I suppose we have watched Miss Walker grow up. My husband already lived in this house when we met and later married. I had returned to England from India after losing my first husband. By the time of our marriage, I think Mr. Walker had just lost his wife and his daughter was around ten years old."

Holmes thanked Mrs. Hartley and soon we were on the street again. We walked briskly to busier streets in search of a cab, finally securing one. In about an hour we were back at Baker Street. We walked into the sitting room and my eyes fell upon the letters and envelopes still upon the carpet. "What are you thinking, Holmes?"

"I am thinking that I am an idiot," said Holmes. "I feel that more than one thing we have been told is key to this mystery. I need to think."

He disappeared into his room and shut the door leaving me standing there.

It was difficult for me to give anything the attention it deserved the following day. Holmes was convinced that we were already in possession of key information. I had heard everything he had, and I could not think what it was that was so important. I could only hope Holmes had made sense of it since I had seen him last.

In the afternoon I headed out to attend to some errands. Once they were dealt with, I wasted no time getting back to Baker Street. I walked into the sitting room to see Holmes perched in the window smoking.

"Good evening, Watson," he said. "I saw the speed with which you vacated your cab. I am afraid to say I have made no progress."

"None?" I asked, disappointed.

He turned and smiled weakly. "It is as frustrating for me as it is for you, dear fellow. I have been churning events over in my mind. I have read and reread the letters without matters falling into place. I am also without a response from the Indian police. I have been thinking for so long that I was forced to send out for extra tobacco."

It was only at that point that I became aware of how intense the atmosphere was in the room. "Can I help?" I asked.

Holmes smiled indulgently. "Be my guest, Watson."

I moved to the dining table, where Holmes had deposited all Miss Walker's letters. He had replaced all the letters in their respective envelopes. At once, I recognised the letter that Miss Walker had singled out. I picked it up.

"I wish we had a clue as to what the arrangement was?"

Holmes snorted. "Yes, my boy. It would facilitate matters greatly."

I turned the envelope over in my hands and removed its enclosure before doing the same with the others. "You noticed that the letter Miss Walker singled out has no holes in it?"

"I did."

I looked up and down at them all. "I do not know, Holmes. As far as I can see, the only consistent thing is that all the letters with holes in came in envelopes with more than one stamp."

I was not prepared for the reaction. "Watson," he said. "You have shone light where shadows earlier resided. I should commit myself to an asylum for being so slow."

He arranged all the letters on the table into chronological order. His eyes darted around. "You have hit upon something, Watson. All the envelopes containing letters with holes have excessive postage paid. In other words, they are carrying more stamps than needed to get them to their destination. In fact, each one is at least twice what it needs to be. But why?"

I thought for a moment. "Did Walker's valet mention something about that?"

"He did, Watson, he did. He must have seen the final letter when it arrived because when he saw it in the evening, he was able to say that it was missing its stamps. That is the word I was reaching for."

He tapped his pipe stem against his forehead with increasing force. As if he were expecting to conjure forth the answer. However, it did not immediately come. He pulled out a chair and sank into it. His face was a blend of excitement and frustration. I removed myself to my chair and lit a cigarette.

Holmes fell silent. I could see his lips moving. It was as if he were replaying the conversations we had had as if he were recalling a play or opera. I poured myself a brandy. I had done my part and for me to interject further would not help. It was a waiting game.

I must have fallen asleep because I was suddenly startled by a door being thrown open. I looked up to see my friend disappearing onto the landing.

"Mrs. Hudson. Coffee at once please."

"What's going on, Holmes?" I asked as I brushed ash off my trousers.

He marched back into the room. "Wait and see, Watson. Wait and see."

A few minutes later, Mrs. Hudson walked into the room with a coffee pot and cups. "You will be up all night if you drink this, Mr. Holmes."

Holmes, in his efficient but kindly manner, waited for our esteemed landlady to place the tray on the table before ushering her out.

As the door closed behind her, Holmes spun round, rubbing his hands together. "We must strike while the coffee pot is hot."

He took a seat back at the dining table and selected an envelope. He held it over the spout of the coffee pot. "Miss Walker's domestic staff knew a lot between them. It needed us to put it all together."

"Whatever do you mean?"

"Mr. Walker received a lot of letters before his death but he only ordered coffee upon receipt of one with holes in it. Yet we also know he did not drink any of it."

"I am not following."

"As you observed, the letters we have here, with holes in, also had excess postage paid in the form of multiple stamps. We may reasonably assume this also applied to the ones he received before his death. In fact, we know this already from Jones."

"I am still not with you, Holmes."

Holmes did not answer but focused on holding the envelope over the spout. After about ten minutes he smiled. "There we are."

He put the envelope on the table. With his fingers, he carefully picked at the edge of the stamps before lifting them from the envelope. He took extreme care as the stamps were stubbornly adhered in parts. "Take a look at this, Watson."

I looked over his shoulder. Where the stamps had been, there was some writing in dark pencil. It ran thus:

TILN15BR

"What does it mean, Holmes?"

"I do not know, Watson," he replied. "It does however explain the choice of envelopes and notepaper."

"It does?"

"Yes. Our correspondent chose thicker paper to reduce the risk of this message being seen by the expedient of holding it up to a light source. This was a message for one person only."

"So, what do you deduce from that?"

"Clearly, Mr. Walker knew that messages would be under the stamps. He asked for an, admittedly slow, method of loosening them that would not arouse suspicion in his daughter or servants. We now know that one envelope proved difficult so he had to order a second pot to complete the task. He was eager to read the message, hence he was decidedly prickly with his butler.

"This also explains why the observant Jones did not mention any writing on that final letter. It had presumably been destroyed by the rain the envelope had been exposed to. Walker's tears may have been triggered by the loss of the message."

"A message," I said, "that only he knew how to read."

"And the sender," replied Holmes. "Now we have made progress, perhaps some of the other events we know of will become clear. In the morning I will need to send another wire to India."

Following a late supper, I left Holmes to his deliberations and went to my room. To me, it felt as if we had learned a lot but, at the same time, I felt as far removed from the answer as ever. A man's life was very likely in the balance and every day that passed brought him closer to his doom. I could not bear the thought of the lovely Miss Walker losing a second man so close to her in the space of less than two years.

I slept poorly and it was the afternoon when I rose the next day. I could hear noises below so knew Holmes was in. After getting shaved and dressed, I descended to the sitting room. Holmes was in his chair looking quite contented.

"You have learned something," I said.

He chuckled. "Once again, the faculty of observation is

contagious. I have indeed." He held up a piece of paper. "First thing this morning I headed out the door to send another telegram to India. I nearly knocked over the messenger boy. A few extra coins easily compensated him for the encounter and it turned out he was carrying my answer."

"Is that it?"

"Yes. It is from the Superintendent of Police. I knew him before he transferred out there, and I had even helped him solve a few cases here in London. Thus, he was more than amenable to returning the favour by poring through records."

"So, what have you learned?"

"I asked him for details of any significant crimes where the perpetrators had left the country. He identified two from the right period. Only one of those involved more than one person."

"Tell me."

"In the area known as Kashmir a bank was robbed. The bank did not normally hold much money so when it was robbed on a day that it was holding more than customary it was immediately suspected to be the work of someone inside. A bank employee was killed in the robbery.

"Suspicion fell upon one George Hamilton, an employee of some five years, who was one of the few people who knew about the increase in holdings. A surprisingly competent local investigation was able to determine that he had been coerced into assisting by a local gang who had discovered he was having an illicit liaison with a prominent local politician's wife. The investigation managed to keep this affair secret, and out of the press, at the request of the politician concerned. Despite this, he and his wife divorced about a year later and she left the country.

"In return for identifying the gang members, Hamilton was spared jail but deported. The remaining members were sentenced to twenty years apiece except for one who was hanged for the murder."

"So, these are the people who pursued Mr. Walker?"

Holmes nodded. "And now his daughter. It is not too difficult to read events. They get out of jail determined to seek vengeance for, what they see as, his betrayal. They presumably knew of Hamilton's deportation and quickly ascertained that he returned to England. They followed and lost the trail.

"Because he had become Mr. Walker?"

"Precisely. He had developed his Indian banking experience and carved out an honourable career. Alas, they did not see it that way. This gang refuses to accept that they were responsible for their own fate. What I do not yet know is how they managed to locate him."

"But, Holmes," I said, "you said yourself that they have acquired new members."

"Yes. The younger man with a fondness for knives has found his way in. Perhaps a family member of the original gang. This sort of group is not likely to bring in a stranger. Perhaps this is the son of one of the original gang members who feels aggrieved for the incarceration of his father."

"What is the next step?"

Holmes waved the paper again. "I have the names of the gang and descriptions. The value of this may be limited as they are likely to have, like Walker, adopted new identities. I took the liberty of conveying this information into the hands of our friends at Scotland Yard. If we are fortunate, this gang will not have sat idle in this country. Let us hope that they have occupied themselves with activities other than the pursuit of the Walkers."

I turned to look at the table. "Did you remove the stamps from the other envelopes?"

"Yes. I have written it all down." He handed me a piece of paper. It was two columns. On the left, the date of the postmark. On the right, the message. I focused on the right-hand column.

TG10TR
TILN12BR
TS2TR
TILN17BL
TS20TR

I scratched my head. "Well, it baffles me, Holmes."

He smiled and lit a cigarette. "For the moment, I find myself in the same state." He stared into the fireplace and said no more.

The remainder of the afternoon was spent in silence. I read the paper and Holmes alternated between pipes and cigarettes. As the afternoon gave way to evening, Mrs. Hudson popped her head round the door to tell me that a steak and kidney pudding was in the oven. Holmes, as usual, expressed no interest in filling his stomach whilst on a case. Feeling the opposite, I immediately offered my gratitude.

The bell rang. "Are you expecting anyone?" I asked.

"No."

There were heavy feet upon the stairs and the door opened to reveal Inspector Bradstreet. "Good evening, gentlemen."

"Good evening, Inspector," said Holmes. "To what do we owe the pleasure?"

"I have been looking into the information you supplied this morning. It turns out that there have been several crimes with a gang conforming to your description. We had not made the link before."

"What have they been responsible for?"

Bradstreet looked surprised. "I thought you were on top of these things, Mr. Holmes. There were quite lengthy reports on this gang in *The Times*, *Telegraph*, and *The Graphic*."

"Oh, yes," I said, as I reached into Holmes's rack of

newspapers. I soon found the copy of *The Times*. I flicked through the pages. "Here it is. Gang Robs Post Office in Barnet."

Bradstreet nodded. "That is the one, Doctor. Thanks to Mr. Holmes, and eyewitness statements, we have been able to determine that this same gang has been responsible for a number of commercial and domestic robberies over the last eighteen months."

I turned to Holmes, "This must be the same gang."

Holmes did not respond. He sat motionless, his expression one of barely suppressed excitement.

"What is it?" I asked.

"A sliver of light, my boy." He scribbled some notes and handed the paper to Bradstreet.

"Scotland Yard is not at your beck and call," said the inspector, after he had finished reading.

"If you would be so good, Bradstreet," was Holmes's concise response.

Time passed slowly the next morning. The post was delivered but contained nothing that Holmes wished to read. Envelope after envelope was opened and thrown down with disdain. Holmes was always at his most intolerable when events did not go his way. I eventually left for a walk, to escape his grumbling and pacing. I spent two hours walking the local streets and collected some of his favourite tobacco on my way in the hope it would improve his mood.

The room I eventually returned to was one of organised chaos. Newspapers were scattered everywhere and Holmes was seated in their midst. The sparkle in his eyes surely meant progress. "What have you found?" I asked.

Holmes grinned. "Bradstreet, despite his irritation, carried out my request. He got some poor soul to go the offices of certain newspapers and secure back issues for me."

"Why?"

"It was something Bradstreet said. He referred to a copy of *The Graphic* when discussing the gang."

"Yes. And?"

Holmes handed me the list he had shown me earlier. "Look at the top entry again."

I did so.

TG10TR

He continued. "Now, imagine, just for a moment, that the TG stands for *The Graphic*. Assuming that is correct, what do you suppose the rest is?"

"I guess the number could refer to a page?"

"Bravo. And the remainder?"

"I have no idea, Holmes."

He looked disappointed. "We will come back to that. It occurred to me at once that if one refers to a newspaper, so do the others. TS naturally suggests *The Sketch* and TILN becomes *The Illustrated London News*."

"That is brilliant, Holmes."

"It is a theory, of course, but newspapers have been a theme in this case. Mr. Walker was buying one after the arrival of every letter. It is not a huge leap to assume that they were copies of these newspapers."

"I follow."

"Now, I draw your attention to the latter. Think of Mr. Walker's last night alive. We have more than one witness who stated that Mr. Walker repeatedly said that there were none left. He asked his neighbours if they had heard the news?"

"Please continue," I said, eager to hear the rest.

"Let us suppose that they misheard. He was delirious after all.

What if he had been trying to ask them if they had a copy of *The Illustrated London News*. He had been out to get one and had not been able to because?"

"There were none left," I said.

Holmes smiled. "I recalled some of the later commentary on the matter. The publishers of that excellent periodical produced a special Jubilee edition which came out on the 19th of June. However, they grossly underestimated the level of interest. Many people, who were not regular readers of the paper, sought a copy as a memento. Although a second print run was later made it was not in time for poor Mr. Walker.

"Now the arrival the next morning of Mr. Hartley makes sense. He visited Miss Walker carrying a newspaper. His widow told us that he had suddenly worked out what Mr. Walker wanted. He realised Walker wanted the most recent issue of *The Illustrated London News*."

"Amazing, Holmes."

"So, we now have the method of communication. It occurred to me that the last two letters in each message refer to a position. TL means top-left etc."

He grabbed one of the letters and one of the many newspapers. He pointed to the top-left of one of the pages. "What do you see there?"

I bent to read. It was an advertisement for a gentlemen's outfitters. "Well, Holmes," I said. "It refers to a store called Jefferson's at 2 Oldfield Road. It says that a popular brand of boot is on sale, that they have one hundred pairs left and the sale ends tomorrow."

Holmes placed the letter he was holding over the advertisement. "Now, what do you see?"

It took me a moment. "Holmes, it is a demand for money."

"Yes. If you look at the words visible through the holes it says 'two hundred tomorrow.' Clearly this amount of money is expected to be placed into an account or left at a location. The latter is more likely to make tracing the money difficult. We can theorise that the location concerned was detailed in the first letter Walker received."

"But, Holmes. Miss Walker does not know what to do and her fiancé is in danger."

He raised a hand. "Calm yourself, Watson. I have already set the wheels in motion."

"What have you done?"

"Fortunately, all three of those newspapers are published weekly and have issues coming out in two days. I am hoping the members of our gang are regular readers of them. I have placed a simple advert to get their attention."

"What did you say?"

"I wrote 'Walker ignorant. 221B ready to assist.'"

"Will they understand that?"

Holmes looked affronted. "My dear Watson. I do not think I am flattering myself when I say that 221B is well-understood in criminal circles."

My friend's boast was well-founded. Shortly after the latest issues of the newspapers were published, he received a letter. It provided an address in Crystal Palace and asked us to come alone. We were assured that lookouts would ensure that was the case before the gang would show up.

"An interesting letter, Watson," said Holmes. "The phrasing is enough to tell us what to do but it is vague enough to mean many things to someone who read it without context. That is clever. This gang conveys information that does not expose them to action."

He sat at his desk and scribbled a note. Mrs. Hudson was summoned. Holmes handed her the note and whispered something to her. She left with a scowl.

"They must be desperate if they are prepared to come into the open," I said.

"Well," he said, "we must play by their rules for now. That is not the only reason why the letter is interesting."

"What is the other reason?"

"Different handwriting, Watson."

I looked again. It was so obvious that I felt stupid. "Yes, Holmes, the writing is a lot less..."

"Elegant?"

"Yes."

"Well, it certainly settles the matter. We are dealing with at least two people. The question is why is this second person the spokesman now?"

We were at the address in Crystal Palace on time. It was a modest house at the end of a terrace. It was a quiet street with only a few scruffy children playing by a house two doors down. We knocked and were admitted. The house was in darkness and a lamp was shone in our faces. We were ordered into the rear parlour and took the two seats we could see there. Our escort, kept the lamp fixed upon us and told us we would be met presently.

"Well," said Holmes. "The house is rather sparsely furnished."

It was true. Apart from the two basic chairs on which we sat, the only other furniture in the room was another chair.

We did not have long to wait. The door opened and a man walked into the room. The lamp was kept in our faces to obscure his identity. We heard the man take the remaining seat.

"Mr. Holmes," said the new voice. "We are aware of who you are. Please tell us why we should not simply kill you and do the criminal world a favour?"

Holmes was unruffled. "You need me to help you with Miss

Walker."

"I do not see why."

"Because she does not know how to do what you want her to do."

The man laughed. "We have it on good authority that she knows precisely what we want."

"Then we are at an impasse," said Holmes.

"Not at all. You can convey a message to Miss Walker. Her fiancé has another week to live if she does not do as instructed."

"I am pleased that you raised the matter," said Holmes. "I am sorry that we have failed to convince you regarding Miss Walker's knowledge of this affair. If we are to make any headway, we will need to be able to assure her that her fiancé is alive and well. Surely, you understand that?"

There was a grunt in response. Our host left the room. He was gone for about fifteen minutes during which the lamp was kept trained upon us. We heard several pairs of feet in the hallway. The door was suddenly thrown open and a man was hurled onto the floor at our feet. It was hard to see him fully in the light available but I could see that he was a man of around twenty-five years of age. He was clearly in a bad way. He had cuts to his face that were bleeding, and signs that he had been recently struck with a stick or something similar. Holmes knelt at his side and raised him so he was resting on his knees. Holmes rolled up the man's sleeves before rolling them down again. "Why have you treated this man so harshly?"

"Frustration, Mr. Holmes. The boys must take it out on something." The man chuckled at his own joke. I clenched my fist; Holmes placed a hand on my arm.

"It also demonstrates that we are serious, Mr. Holmes."

"May I ask one more question?"

"Certainly, Mr. Holmes, but I cannot promise to answer it."

"How did you hit upon your elaborate method of communication?"

The man laughed. "You will appreciate the poetic justice. I am sure you know that we persuaded Walker to help us in India by using his affair against him?"

"Yes," said Holmes.

"It was the same method the lady used to write to him to arrange their meetings. It has the advantage that it can be explained away. An innocent letter on a harmless subject is used to convey a far from innocent message. Also, using it showed Walker we were serious. Something you may not know, is that she died not long after Walker left India."

Holmes clearly did not know this. "Tell me how?"

Our antagonist's confidence was clearly high. High enough that he did not seem to fear answering Holmes's questions. "Her husband kept up appearances for a few months but eventually threw her out. He set her up in a remote part of Kashmir with a house and a modest allowance. She was told it would be cut off if she spoke a word against him or about the affair. A few months later she hanged herself."

"Come now," said Holmes. "A story like that would have found its way into the newspapers."

"Mr. Holmes. I am surprised that you are so innocent in these matters. The powerful can hide whatever they want to hide."

Holmes rose from the floor and resumed his seat. "I feel there is nothing more to be said. Miss Walker really does not know what to do but we will endeavour to help her."

"You do that, Mr. Holmes," came the response. "By the way, please do not trouble to come back to this address. The lady who owns it will be rather surprised as she does not know we are making use of it. We will not meet again."

We were escorted onto the street and the door was shut behind us. Holmes walked a couple of streets in silence. "I think we are far enough away now, Watson."

"What are we going to do, Holmes?"

"We have a week, Watson," he replied. "I think that is more than enough time."

"Are you going to bring Miss Walker into this?" I asked.

"Heavens no," he replied. "That would do more harm than good. I have high hopes that our new found friends are as unintelligent as they appear."

"Why do you say that?"

"Because, despite their best efforts to hide details from us, they actually confirmed a good deal."

"Really? What?"

"You can often infer age from posture, voice, and gait, Watson. The man who kept the lamp in our face was middle-aged going by his voice and his walk. The odds are good that he is one of the original gang members from India. The man we spoke to was younger, going by his speed and ill-placed arrogance. He was almost certainly responsible for the wounds delivered to the young man thrown at our feet. You noticed, I assume, that they were all quite recent wounds?"

"Yes, Holmes. The cuts were still bleeding. They were quite small and would normally stop bleeding within a few minutes. So, they were almost certainly inflicted moments before he was thrown into the room."

We resumed walking. "Precisely. The same goes for the areas where he was struck. They were inflamed but not yet bruised. So, they were almost certainly also delivered just before he was introduced to us.

"You will recall me examining his arms. They showed no evidence of prior ill-treatment. His face also showed no evidence of older wounds. So, we can infer that the wounds we saw today were the first he has received."

"I imagine they delivered them all to his face so that we could see them."

"That's one interpretation, Watson," said Holmes. "There is also another."

He stopped walking and listened intently. As I stopped beside him, I could dimly hear a whistle.

"Excellent," said Holmes, as he marched off in search of a cab.

As usual, it was all too obvious that Holmes was keeping me in the dark. The showman in him had to have something to reveal to his audience.

When I descended the next morning, I found Holmes at the dining table. He had clearly had, by his standards, a late breakfast and was stubbing a smouldering cigarette into the remains of a boiled egg.

"Good morning, Watson," he said. "Coffee?"

"Yes please, Holmes," I replied. "It is rather unlike you to eat on a case."

"Even I have to put fuel on the fire occasionally, Watson," he replied with a smirk.

I pulled out the chair opposite him as he poured coffee into the second cup. "So, what has happened since yesterday?"

"To use the vocabulary of the turf that you know so well, we are in the final furlong, Watson. Part of the reason for my late breakfast is that I was up all night going over all that we have heard and seen. My current theory meets the facts but I am missing a crucial piece of evidence which I hope to secure this evening.

"I dispatched three telegrams this morning. One to India, to gather some further details, and another to Bradstreet. Regrettably, I expect the answer to the former to take a few days."

"That takes us rather close to the date set by the gang, Holmes," I said.

He stood and went to the fireplace. He selected a fresh cigarette from the box. "I really do not think we need worry about that date, Watson. Amusingly, it is a date that will motivate our opponents more than us."

"Whatever do you mean, Holmes? I wish you would not be so cryptic."

There was a ring at the bell. A few moments later, we were joined by Bradstreet. "Good morning, Mr. Holmes, Dr. Watson."

"How are they faring, Bradstreet?" asked Holmes.

"They are a little terse, Mr. Holmes," replied Bradstreet with a wry smile. "We won't be able to keep this from the press for long."

"There is no need after tonight."

"Holmes," I said. "You mentioned three telegrams."

Holmes smiled. "Oh yes. I had an answer to the third already, Watson. We are expected at seven o'clock tonight. Another coffee?"

I spent the intervening time in a state of irritation. This was not lost on my friend who opened his mouth to speak on more than one occasion but always thought better of it. The hours passed slowly. So slowly that I even attempted to read the volume on India that Holmes had drawn my attention to a few days earlier.

Mercifully, a little before six, Holmes asked me to get my coat. We headed onto the street and into a waiting cab.

"Where are we going, Holmes?"

"We are heading for Knightsbridge," he replied before lapsing into silence.

Before long, we pulled up outside an impressive townhouse. Holmes alighted and headed for the door, while I paid the cabby. I joined him just as it was opened. A surly butler took our cards and invited us in. We stepped inside and he closed the door. He asked us to wait.

No sooner had he vanished from sight, Holmes charged into an open room off the hallway. He was gone no more than twenty seconds and returned just before the butler.

"What did you just do?" I asked.

"Not now, Watson."

The butler led us to what turned out to be the rear parlour. There, sitting upon a settee, was a stout, bespectacled, and stately woman of about forty-five to fifty. Evidently a good-looking woman in her youth, the passage of time had not been unkind. "Good evening, Mr. Holmes," she said.

"Good evening, Mrs. Markham," replied Holmes, bowing.

The lady waved us towards two chairs. "I was surprised to receive your telegram, Mr. Holmes. I cannot see how I can assist you with my poor goddaughter's plight but I am willing to do so."

"I doubt that, Mrs. Markham," said Holmes.

Her face went dark. "I beg your pardon, Mr. Holmes."

"I am sorry," replied Holmes. "I do not doubt your willingness to help. I doubt your surprise at the receipt of my telegram."

"I am afraid I do not follow," replied the formidable lady.

Holmes sighed and reached into his pocket. He withdrew, and placed on the arm of the chair, the exotic dagger. The lady's eyes were immediately drawn to it.

"Let me enlighten you. You are, or were, Lady Sarah Montague, former wife of Sir Henry Montague."

The lady rose to her feet. "I grow tired of this, Mr. Holmes." She moved towards the bell rope.

"If you do that, Lady Montague," said Holmes, "your son is lost."

She paused. "What do you know of my son?"

"I know him to presently be in the hands of a ruthless gang who plan on injuring him or worse in a matter of days."

The lady returned to her seat. She looked both beaten and relieved. "How much do you know?"

"I fancy I know all of it," said Holmes. "While in India you came to know one George Hamilton, and you began an illicit relationship with him. Your relationship became known to a gang who used it to force Hamilton to facilitate a robbery that resulted in murder. He later helped to turn in the gang and was deported rather than jailed."

Lady Montague held up her hand. "I can only assume you have made enquiries in India. How did you confirm my identity?"

"Up until to a few moments ago I merely suspected it. I confirmed it when I saw this." Holmes produced two letters from his pocket. He unfolded one revealing an elaborate crest and the name Montague. "I procured this letter from the study and compared it against this one sent to Miss Walker. The handwriting matches. It was decidedly careless of you to retain this correspondence."

The lady sighed. "Very well, Mr. Holmes. It appears in my interests to be open with you."

"I am pleased that you recognise that," said Holmes.

"What you say is true. George was deported soon after the trial. My husband, for the sake of appearances, was prepared to overlook my affair. As a politician, appearances were everything to him. I was just a means to an end, a wife on his arm lending him respectability. A month later I discovered I was with child. This was something he could not stomach and he wanted nothing more than to be rid of me. That said, he still needed to keep the details from wider society and the press for as long as he could. I was quietly dispatched to a remote house some twenty miles away and paid an allowance to keep silent while he began discreet divorce proceedings.

"My natural hope was to return to England, marry George and raise our child together. During our affair, George and I had one confidant, whom I will not name. She brought me a letter from George almost a year after his deportation. When I read it, I was distraught. He casually informed me that he had changed his name and was starting a new life. Furthermore, he was engaged to be married.

"You can imagine how I felt, Mr. Holmes. He showed no interest in how I had fared. I was clearly nothing to him. I was as disposable as yesterday's newspaper. Little did he know that I had given birth to his child."

"So, what did you do?"

"I was bitter, Mr. Holmes. I think even you will understand that. What was I to do now? I had given birth to a child that my husband would not acknowledge and George had abandoned me." She looked towards the ceiling. "I yearned for justice and prayed to God for an answer." She lowered her head and looked directly at Holmes. "When none came, I decided to turn to the Devil.

"I am not an unintelligent woman, Mr. Holmes. I am sure you have ascertained that. It occurred to me at once that I shared an injury with the now incarcerated gang. Using my few remaining contacts in society, I engineered a meeting with the gang in prison. I spoke to their leader and explained my proposition. To my relief, he was more than ready to fall in with my plans. So much so that he revealed that one of my own servants had given away the details of the affair that they had later used. Of course, I hated this gang for destroying my life but, for now, we had a common goal."

"So," said Holmes, "you returned to England, as soon as you had saved enough money from your husband's allowance, and set yourself up under your new identity."

"Yes. I initially resided in Crystal Palace where I raised my son. I adopted the name of Markham, my late mother's name, and avoided questions by saying my husband had died in the army. To alter my appearance, I put on weight, wore spectacles and a wig. After a few years devoted to my son's upbringing, I decided to commence the plan. The first objective was to locate George. His final letter to me had carried a postmark and I engaged private agents to make enquiries. I almost considered approaching you, Mr. Holmes, but decided against it given my aims."

Holmes smiled. "That was wise of you, Lady Montague."

She smiled back. "In the end, it was surprisingly easy to locate George. I know not what underhand methods my agents used and I do not care to know. Once I had his address, it was no great hardship to slowly insert myself into his life. I began by befriending his wife through her charity work. She later introduced me to the man now known as Edgar Walker. My modest disguise worked as he had no reason to look for someone he believed to be on the other side of the world.

"When their daughter was born, I was asked to be godmother. This was hard to endure, but it was necessary in order for me to further entrench myself into their lives. But I could not neglect my son, of whom they were ignorant.

"I explained to them that I was a regular traveller abroad. This way I could return to my son for weeks or months at a time without arousing suspicion. When I was absent, he was left in the capable hands of his nanny.

"When Adelia was eleven her mother died. Edgar was bereft and I almost felt sorry for him. The pain he went through was almost enough for me as it was clearly equal to that which I had experienced at his hands. However, I had made a commitment and had to see it through. Edgar began to depend on me for emotional support, and I gladly gave it."

"And this went on until the gang was released?" asked Holmes.

"Yes. By this time, I had been playing the part for so long it was second-nature. I had moved to this house by this time. My former husband's generosity knew no bounds when it came to protecting his career. Because of this, I had been able to retain my former house in Crystal Palace. I placed this at the gang's disposal. As my son had grown up, I told him a version of our story, and he was as determined to wound Edgar as I."

"I am assuming that he does not know that Walker was his father?" asked Holmes.

"No. I told him that his father was someone I met later and who died just before we came to England."

"I am glad to hear you say that under the circumstances," said Holmes.

As I sat there listening to the two of them talk, the importance of what Holmes said became clear. I felt unwell. I looked at Holmes who flashed me a glance.

Lady Montague continued. "For me, the motive in all this was to wound Edgar. For the gang it was all about getting the money they had been cheated of. Edgar was now a wealthy man and they wanted to bleed him of every last shilling.

"As you have surmised, I wrote all the letters that they later used to send to Edgar. I also placed the relevant advertisements in the newspapers. This helped to hide the gang. When he ignored the first letter, they immediately came to me. I arranged for one of their younger members to be on hand to scare Adelia. This brought Edgar into line and the first instalments of money were paid to the gang. Then it all stopped."

"Because Mr. Walker had died," said Holmes.

"Yes," said Lady Montague. "For me, it was over. Edgar was dead. For the gang, it was not over. They had not yet received all the money, and they wanted the rest. They demanded I find a way."

Holmes took on a look of disgust. "I cannot say I approve of your method."

Even Lady Montague looked ashamed. "I know, Mr. Holmes, but they threatened my son if I reneged on the deal. I asked Arthur to court Adelia. He was against it as he had his eye on another. I eventually persuaded him to fall in with the plan saying that we would find a way to annul the marriage so he could return to his true love. I reminded him of the hurt I had suffered. I engineered a meeting at a ball and events took their course."

"So, the plan was to get access to the Walker money through marriage?" I asked.

"Yes, Watson," said Holmes. "Then a curious turn of events."

Lady Montague almost managed a smile. "Of course, I felt terrible about what I was asking my son to do – especially as he was ignorant of the true relationship. We arranged him lodgings so Adelia had an address for him. We installed a housekeeper and Adelia would call for him there. After one of their evenings together Arthur came home happy. I asked him what it was."

Holmes interrupted, "He told you there was no need to go through with the marriage. He informed you that Miss Walker knew the method of communication and it was his idea to pretend that he was kidnapped."

"Yes," said Lady Montague. "We did not say that explicitly in the letter we sent her as it was vital the letters contained nothing incriminating. I knew Adelia was an intelligent girl."

"Unfortunately, Lady Montague," said Holmes. "Your son misunderstood Miss Walker. He was so keen to get out of the marriage plan that he read something into what she said that simply was not there."

Lady Montague hung her head. "That makes sense now. The gang rapidly lost patience with the delay. They demanded a meeting with Arthur and I foolishly let him go."

"With the poetic result," said Holmes, "that they actually

kidnapped him."

Lady Montague's eyes moistened. "They plan to use him to force Adelia's hand. If she does not act soon, I dread what they will do to him."

"You can rest easy on that score, Lady Montague," said Holmes. "Your son and the gang have been in custody since yesterday evening."

Lady Montague rose to her feet. "How?"

"Dr. Watson and I met with them and demanded to see your son. As soon as I saw his face, I suspected that he was related to Miss Walker. The gang clearly knew this hence their ill treatment of him. It was a poor, and rather late, attempt at concealing that familial connection."

"What happens now, Mr. Holmes?" asked Lady Montague.

"That lies in your hands," said Holmes. "This is your doing. If you need guidance, I suggest you do your best for the gang. They will go to jail for the other robberies they foolishly committed but you can no doubt pay them the money they feel they are owed for when they are released. That should placate them and prevent them from revealing the truth to your son. Having that on your conscience is your punishment, Lady Montague. Your other task is to extricate your son from his commitment to Miss Walker. The cost of not doing so will be high as well you know."

We left Lady Montague to her thoughts and returned to Baker Street. Once in our usual chairs, Holmes was ready to rid me of my ignorance.

"The more I thought about it the more I returned to the godmother. It was too convenient that our knife-wielding friend was on hand for when Miss Walker was dropped off after the theatre. If he had been pacing the area for some time the neighbours, in such a relatively close community, would have likely noticed him and alerted the authorities. Equally he could have been challenged by the local bobby. No, he had to know when to be there and who else could tell him that information?

"Then there was the fact our attentive godmother was supposedly abroad often yet never brought her goddaughter presents from the countries she visited, or wrote to her. Of course, she could not give presents from countries she had not actually been to. It was however quite easy to spin a yarn to an innocent young girl about exotic places."

"But why did she not write?" I asked.

"Two reasons. The most obvious is that they would clearly not be from abroad. A Crystal Palace or Knightsbridge postmark is hardly a foreign country. Secondly, it was important that the Walkers did not see her handwriting as it was going to be on the letters they would later receive and would give our Mrs. Markham away. It must have been quite the challenge to achieve."

"Surely," I said. "Walker would have recognised the handwriting from his time in India?"

"Not so," said Holmes. "Remember, they had a confidant. I suspect that lady, for it is almost certainly a lady, wrote the letters that were sent. Lady Montague could not risk evidence of her affair that would be hard to deny if exposed.

"When I communicated with my contact in India, I learned of the affair that the gang had used to manipulate Hamilton. The details of the lady concerned indicated that she was of the right sort of age and the fact that she was no longer in India meant that she could be in England. As her country of birth, it was a likely destination. I did briefly consider Mrs. Hartley and tested that theory. It hardly matters now but she could either be totally innocent in all this or she could be the close confidante to whom Lady Montague alluded. As I said, it does not matter and is not worth following up.

"The letters the Walkers received were undated because they had all been written in advance to be used as and when needed. Our Lady Montague ensured the newspapers carried the desired adverts to convey the messages. Each time she did so, the gang had to obtain the relevant newspaper, cut the required holes into the chosen letter, and write the code onto the envelope in pencil which they later covered with stamps. This is why those short codes were in rough pencil. A different hand and one we later saw on the letter which summoned us to Crystal Palace. It is also why they used weekly newspapers rather than daily ones. They needed time to produce the appropriate letter and send it. Also, being a weekly paper meant that sellers would hold copies for longer than a daily."

"But why did they write that letter to us?"

"Greed and impatience, I would surmise they were unhappy with the slow pace under Lady Montague's direction. I think our young gang member lacked the caution of his elders and tried to accelerate matters. All it actually accelerated was their capture."

"I was going to ask about that."

"Easy enough. Once we had the address, I got Wiggins to dispatch a few of the lesser-known Irregulars to the area. Perhaps you saw them? As soon as we were inside, and the gang's guard was down, they ran to fetch Bradstreet and his men. As soon as we were far enough away, they swooped in and arrested them."

I had to raise the subject. "Do you think Lady Montague would really have let her son marry his half-sister?"

"I do not know, Watson. It is unsavoury to say the least. I must admit to feeling sorry for Miss Adelia Walker."

We made contact with Miss Walker to say that her fiancé had been freed, but that we did not know his present whereabouts. We later learned from her that he had broken the engagement. Miss Walker informed us that her understanding godmother had helped her get over the loss and had managed to introduce her to some other potential suitors.

We received a separate letter from Mrs. Markham to inform us that she was going abroad with her son for some time. "Probably for the best," was all Holmes would say.

The Problem of Hazlewood Grange

(Mid-1894)

T was a wet Friday evening in London. I was closing my practice for the day, having seen my last patient some half an hour earlier. I was, I had to admit, deliberately delaying my departure as I had been giving a lot of thought recently to my late wife, and the prospect of my empty home held little attraction.

I was tidying away my instruments and writing up the last patient notes when it occurred to me that I could avoid my lonely evening by paying a visit to my friend. Holmes had returned to my life a few weeks earlier during the events I later chronicled as "The Adventure of the Empty House." He had been sensitive to my loss and had begun quietly suggesting that I should consider a permanent return to Baker Street as an alternative to my lonely existence. I had spent time thinking about it and had begun making enquiries about selling my practice.

I seized my umbrella and headed out into the wet streets of London. Thanks to the inhospitable weather, I struggled to find a cab and was forced to walk much of the way to Baker Street. As I walked the streets, upon whose wet paving stones puddles had formed, reflecting the lights of the buildings they adjoined, I passed many a shop where the frustrated proprietor found himself an unwilling host to people who were doing their best to avoid the rain rather than dip into their pockets. The lack of umbrellas I could see demonstrated that many people had been caught out by the downpour. In a city as regularly wet as London, I had to admire the optimism of people who did not consider an umbrella a mandatory accessory. I was thankful that I kept one at both my home and practice for these very eventualities.

Fortunately, I was still in possession of my old key and this saved me from having to wait on the wet doorstep. I let myself in, hung up my coat and stowed my sopping umbrella. As I ascended the stairs, I was sure I could hear my friend pacing in the sitting room. I was but two stairs from the first-floor landing when I heard him speak. "Come in, Watson."

I finished my climb and opened the door. He was, as I had heard, pacing up and down, with a piece of paper in his hand. "Your arrival could not be better timed, old fellow."

"How is that, Holmes?" I asked.

He waved the paper at me. "I have a letter here from a person hitherto unknown to me. It is from one Inspector Henry Wilkins of the Surrey Constabulary." He waved me into a seat, passed me his cigar box, and crossed the room to pour me a brandy.

"So, what is the problem?" I asked, as he handed me a glass. The warmth of the initial sips immediately acting as a counter to the cold rain.

Holmes thrust the letter into his pocket and reached for his pipe. "Wilkins has a murder on his hands, believes he has the offender in custody, but has some major hurdles to overcome in proving his guilt."

"How does my arrival assist you?"

"Because, my friend, I need to prevail upon you to go in my place."

Needless to say, I was startled. "Me?"

He smiled. "Yes, you, Watson. The news of my return has travelled fast with the result that I am already tied up in town with a few cases which I am confident you arrived unannounced to enquire about. The fact that you came here in such weather suggests that you are experiencing one of your melancholy episodes."

"Correct, as usual, Holmes."

He patted me on the shoulder. "You never were all that comfortable with solitude. This little trip offers you more distractions than you could possibly hope for. If you would be so good, kindly head down there, determine the facts, write to me daily, and I will assist from here."

The presumption of my help irked a little and this was obviously writ large across my face. "You have commitments, Watson?" he asked.

"Nothing I cannot delegate, Holmes," I said, with a degree of resignation.

"Excellent. I shall wire Inspector Wilkins in the morning to expect you. In the meantime, how about that supper you also came for?"

The next day I was on a train out of Waterloo heading for the town of Godalming in Surrey. Holmes and I had spent the evening looking at maps of the locality so even though it was not a place I had been to, I did feel that I had a grasp of the geography. Thankfully, the rain of the previous evening had given way to glorious sunshine, and I was able to enjoy the fields and trees of that charming county as the train rattled southwards. Holmes had requested that Inspector Wilkins meet me at the station. When I pulled into the platform, he was easy to spot. He was around forty years of age, approximately six feet, and was possessed of a fine moustache. You did not need Holmes's skills of observation to see that he was unhappy that it was me he was greeting.

"Good morning, Dr. Watson," he said as he shook my hand and led me out to a waiting cab. "I am grateful for your interest but I feel we really need Mr. Holmes."

I tried not to take offence. "I understand that, Inspector. Mr. Holmes simply cannot leave London at present but I will be in regular contact with him."

We climbed into the carriage and left the station. Wilkins looked absent-mindedly ahead and I realised that if we were to speak further it was down to me to lead the conversation.

"Holmes gave me your letter, Inspector, but it does not offer much detail."

He snorted. "That is because I expected to be telling him the details in person, Doctor." He resumed his silence for a minute or two before turning to face me. "I am sorry, Dr. Watson. This is not your fault. I am under pressure from the Chief Constable."

I warmed to him at once. "Please tell me what you can."

Wilkins took a deep breath. "To begin with, we are heading to Hazlewood Grange. It is a grand house on the outskirts of the town. It is home to the Hazlewood family. The head of the house is Mr. Jonathan Hazlewood. He is sixty-six years old, a member of minor aristocracy, and a former banker. He has a daughter Alice, aged twenty-five, and a son Simon, aged twenty-two. Mrs. Hazlewood died a few years ago. Simon Hazlewood is a lieutenant in the Royal Navy and presently in Portsmouth on service. Hazlewood senior and his daughter were, aside from the staff, the only residents.

"Mr. Hazlewood is on cordial terms with the Chief Constable and managed to arrange for his house to be on the beat of the local bobby. Two nights ago, this was Constable Jack Bull. Bull approached the gates of the house at around nine in the evening. The house is set back from the road and its drive is lined with gas lamps that are operated from the house. Mr. Hazlewood is, shall we say, careful with his funds, and only lights the lamps if someone is expected. On this occasion they were not lit. As Bull approached the gates he heard a piercing, loud scream followed by a slightly quieter and deeper one. He began to run up the drive, taking care as he had only his lamp to light the way.

"As he approached the front door, it was thrown open and Mrs. Patrick, the housekeeper, ran out. She saw Bull and immediately pulled him inside. He was taken through the hall to the rear parlour. The scene he found was chaotic."

I was drawn in by the inspector's tale but was endeavouring to discern the key facts for my later report to Holmes.

The inspector continued. "Prone, in the middle of the room, clad in her evening dress, was the body of Alice Hazlewood. She had been stabbed just below the base of the neck. Right next to her body was the whining family dog, a Labrador named Sam. Pinned to the floor by two valets and the butler, was one Henry Johnson. He was the young lady's former fiancé and a friend of Simon Hazlewood. He was a man possessed and shouted at Constable Bull to get after the killer whom he insisted had fled through the open window that faced onto the house's rear garden.

"At this moment, Mr. Hazlewood entered the room. He pulled Bull to one side and made clear that he was convinced that Johnson was to blame. Bull was out of his depth and requested that one of the servants be sent to fetch me. I arrived some little time later, with other constables and the police surgeon, and took charge. Mr. Hazlewood informed me that, in addition to his daughter's murder, a valuable piece of jewellery known as the Hazlewood Necklace was missing. He believed Johnson to have killed his daughter for it. With the assistance of the staff, we searched the still raving Johnson for it but could not locate it. Johnson confirmed that Miss Alice had been wearing it but claimed that the killer had taken it.

"I thought it wise to remove Johnson from the scene. I placed him under arrest, which only stoked his anger further. He had to be dragged to the Mariah and cursed us repeatedly for letting the killer get away."

"Was there no sign of the murder weapon?" I asked.

The inspector frowned. "No, Doctor. That is one of the two reasons for my letter to Mr. Holmes. We could find nothing that could have delivered the wound. No sign of the weapon and no sign of the necklace. No one had a chance to leave the room."

"How do you know that?" I asked.

"Apologies, Doctor. I am missing out some parts of the story. I asked Mr. Hazlewood why he was so sure of Johnson's guilt in the matter. He explained that Johnson had come to know the family through his son, Simon, some years previously. They had been at naval college together, and Henry Johnson had met Alice when Simon brought him to the house one weekend. Not long after they met, Mrs. Hazlewood became ill. It turned out that she had cancer that had gone unnoticed until it was too late.

"Johnson and Alice had become closer in the aftermath of Mrs. Hazlewood's death. Mr. Hazlewood was convinced that Johnson took advantage of the family's grief to get close to Alice. He was understood to be a gambler and constantly in need of funds. Only a few months later he was dishonourably discharged from the navy for his gambling. Surprisingly, this did not affect Miss Alice's commitment to him.

"It seems this young man did everything he could to cement himself into her affections. Against her father's wishes, he bought her a dog, which she called Sam, and two cats. Mr. Hazlewood is no admirer of domestic animals but reluctantly gave way due to his daughter's extreme grief at the loss of her mother.

"That dog is quite the beast, Dr. Watson. You will recall me mentioning that it was lying next to the body? It was in the room with them both when the crime took place yet no one recalled it making a sound. Despite being a very average-sized Labrador, it had a sturdy collar that almost seemed excessive until I saw how much strength was needed to remove it from the scene. One of the valets really had to drag it out with all his might."

"So, why were they alone to begin with?" I asked.

Wilkins continued. "In the aftermath of Johnson's discharge from the navy, his gambling increased as it became his sole method of funding his lifestyle. He began to borrow money from almost anyone, including Miss Alice. As time passed, and her grief began to fade, Miss Alice started to see Johnson for what he was and called off the engagement. She made up a reason for doing so in order not to cause Johnson any embarrassment. It was more consideration than he deserved according to her father.

"He went away to lick his wounds for a few months and the family heard nothing from him. Miss Alice went on to get engaged to a promising local Q.C. named James Cooper, who resides in Guildford. News of this engagement came to Johnson's attention via the local press, and he took it badly. It seems he had hoped for a reconciliation. He began to write a series of increasingly menacing letters demanding Miss Alice return to him. She refused police involvement according to Mr. Hazlewood.

"This continued sporadically until the other day. Johnson wrote to Miss Alice requesting an evening interview promising to not bother her again if she granted it. The letter arrived on a day her new fiancé was visiting and both he and Mr. Hazlewood requested that she reject the interview. Miss Alice was headstrong and said she was determined that it would go ahead. She sent Mr. Cooper away, who had demanded to stay, and resolved to be ready. The results of this decision you now know. Ah, here we are."

I turned from the inspector to look ahead. We had turned onto a gravel drive and I could see the house in the distance. It was impressive, as befitted a minor aristocrat, but it looked as if its upkeep had fallen behind. As I had been told, the drive was lined with half a dozen lamps on each side. A constable was posted near the front door and the inspector informed me that others were to the rear as well as inside.

We alighted and entered the house. The inspector took me to the dining room which, he informed me, he had been given permission to use as a base. Sure enough, the dining table was covered with papers that appeared, from the quick glance I took, to be witness statements. We deposited our coats and hats before he led me to the rear parlour.

The constable at the door nodded and let us in. It was an impressive room, south facing, and the sun was already starting to stream through. There were a number of impressive ornaments and luxurious pieces of furniture.

"Aside from the removal of the body, nothing has been touched," said Wilkins. "Let me know what you think."

I will confess that my heart started to beat faster. I could feel the full weight of the inspector's hope. It gave me an insight into how Holmes felt at times like this. But I was not Holmes. I endeavoured to concentrate and remember what Holmes would do. I turned to look back at the door. There was evidently recent damage to it. "What happened here?"

"It seems that Johnson arrived sometime after dark," said Wilkins. "The lamps had been lit for his arrival."

"I thought you said Constable Bull had been forced to use his lamp to guide him up the drive?"

"Quite so," said Wilkins. "The staff insisted the lamps were lit and no one noticed that they were no longer so until the housekeeper opened the front door following the crime."

"Where are the valves that control the gas flow?"

"There is a discreet cupboard in the hall in which the valve is concealed. The butler, Williams, admitted Johnson, took his coat, and asked him to wait while he informed Miss Alice. Williams entered this room, where Miss Alice was waiting, and informed her. She asked for Johnson to be admitted. As an aside, Mr. Hazlewood, being an elderly man, informed me that he had cancelled all staff time off in order that they would be on hand in case Johnson had to be evicted by force.

"Williams returned to the hall and Johnson followed him to this room. He admitted Johnson and closed the door. He almost immediately heard a click. I later learned that the key was kept in the lock.

"Following his orders, Williams summoned one of the valets, named Richards, who stood guard at the door. Williams returned to his other duties. During the next thirty minutes it seems that there was no one in the house who was alone for any time at all. Mr. Hazlewood was served dinner in the dining room by Williams and all the other staff were in the kitchen below stairs."

"Well, Inspector. We do not know that Richards did not leave his post," I said.

"Well spotted, Doctor. Actually, he did. He walked the short distance to the stairs and called down. One of the maids, called Jane, came up to talk to him. They are sweethearts by all accounts. So, it does seem that everyone was in sight of someone. Then it all went wrong."

"Go on."

"Well, Doctor, there was a piercing scream, which is the one that got Constable Bull's attention. It was followed by a lower pitched yell and, according to Richards, the smashing of crockery. He tried the handle which did not work so he put his shoulder to the door. The door was tough but he was soon joined by the butler and the other valet. Between them they got it open."

The inspector pointed to an area of the floor. I walked over to it. It was close to a settee, in front of which was a particularly dark patch of carpet that was out of step with the rest. I pointed downwards. "Here?"

"No, Doctor," said Wilkins. "Just beyond that settee. Alice was face down dead there. A few feet away, lying on the floor and holding his head was Johnson. Mr. Hazlewood had reached the room by this time and ordered his staff to restrain the supine man. This enraged Johnson who insisted the killer was getting away. He even claimed he had tried to capture the killer who had thrown a China vase at him. You can see the shattered remnants of a vase just there and he had scars on his face consistent with being hit by such an object. Mr. Hazlewood sent his housekeeper to fetch the police and that is when she bumped into Constable Bull. So, what do you think, Doctor?"

My head was in a whirl. "I must say, Inspector, that Johnson's account has a lot to commend it. He has been injured, the window over there is open, and he had neither the necklace nor weapon on him when he was searched." At this point I ran out of words.

"You see the problem, Doctor," said Wilkins. "Matters get worse. The wound in Miss Alice's body was deep and there would have been blood when the knife was pulled out."

"Most definitely," I said.

The inspector pointed back to the carpet. "Yet, you can see none and there was none on Johnson."

"And yet he is guilty," came a booming voice from behind us.

I turned to see an imposing, yet elderly and balding, man in the doorway. I guessed at once that it was Mr. Jonathan Hazlewood.

He remained at the threshold. "I will extend you every courtesy, Dr. Watson. I do not approve of amateurs but my friend, the chief constable, has endorsed this approach to Mr. Holmes. Needless to say, I am unimpressed at his failure to attend in person."

"I apologise on his behalf, sir." This appeared to please Hazlewood who clearly interpreted it as a form of deference. Deference to which he clearly felt entitled. I immediately felt dislike for the man. Perhaps a little boldly, I said, "There seems to be more evidence in Johnson's favour than against him."

Jonathan Hazlewood frowned. "I realise that, sir. Nevertheless, he is guilty. You and Wilkins here need to prove it."

"Holmes would not approve of such an approach," I said. "We must be led by the facts. We cannot be led by a pre-determined conclusion clouded by bias."

"Then let me give you some facts," said Hazlewood, sternly. "Johnson was up to his eyes in debt. Even my son despaired of his habit. He was familiar with this household and knew of the necklace and its value. I believe obtaining the necklace was his sole motivation for coming to this house. The fact we possessed it was not a secret but nor was it common knowledge. He is the only person with a motive for taking it."

"And yet he does not have it," I said.

"You seem determined to be on his side, Doctor," said Hazlewood.

"Not at all. I am, however, a strong supporter of the notion of innocent until proven guilty."

Hazlewood sneered. "Get on and prove it, gentlemen." He turned and walked away. His very pace suggestive of his anger.

I turned to Wilkins. "Is it just me, Inspector, or does he seem more bothered by the loss of his necklace than his daughter?"

Wilkins sighed. "It is not just you, Doctor. Godalming is a small place and Mr. Hazlewood is not popular. Your observation is shared by many in the town and there is an increasing body of people

76

who believe not only that Johnson is innocent but that Hazlewood may be guilty."

I was shocked. "Guilty of killing his own daughter? How?"

"I do not believe it, Doctor," said Wilkins. "Not in the face of the facts as we know them. But folk will invent facts when they do not have them. He has already made enquiries to his insurance agent regarding the loss of the necklace. He will clear six figures if the policy pays out. You have seen the house. You have surely seen the wear and tear?"

Wilkins led me out of the house and round to the rear garden. At his request, I followed immediately behind him, stepping exactly where he stepped. We approached the open window to the rear parlour.

"As you can see, Doctor," said Wilkins. "There is evidence that a person seized the window frame and pulled themselves up. Also, you can make out footprints in the grass."

I followed his gaze. There were two sets of tracks. One coming to the window and one going away. Under the inspector's guidance, I followed them. Both sets seemed to terminate at the drive. "So, Inspector," I said. "It looks as though the incoming prints take quite a direct route to the rear window and the outgoing prints take a longer winding route."

"Yes, I saw that," said Wilkins. "You will also notice that just over there is a large impression in the ground. I do not know what to make of that. What would you like to do next?"

I thought for a moment. "If possible, I would like to see the body. Then I would like to visit Johnson. Following that, I will need to write a report to Holmes and seek instructions."

"I have secured you rooms at the King's Arms Hotel in the town centre," said Wilkins. "Bear in mind that Godalming is a town where news travels fast. You will become part of the story now, Doctor.

Be wary of to whom you speak and what you say."

We got into the same cab that had brought us and headed into town. We arrived at the police station and Wilkins led me to the nearby mortuary. The cool air inside was welcome. I was led to the relevant slab and Wilkins pulled back the sheet.

Alice Hazlewood had been a beautiful woman. She looked peaceful, almost asleep rather than dead. Her golden hair rested upon her shoulders and she had a porcelain-like complexion. I could easily see how any man could fast become enamoured of her. Wilkins summoned the police surgeon who helped to turn the body over. The wound was deep and had clearly severed the spinal cord and, along with it, the carotid arteries.

The police surgeon handed me the post-mortem report. As I took it, I saw the sad look on his face. "Did you know Miss Hazlewood?"

"The whole town did, Dr. Watson," he replied. "She was a lovely young lady and was admired by us all."

I rested a hand on his shoulder before directing my attention to the report. As I studied it something leapt out. "You mention traces of material in the wound."

"Yes," said the surgeon. "They were tiny but they were there."

"From her dress?"

"That was my first thought," he said. "When I re-examined the dress, I noted that, aside from some blood staining, the dress was intact. The knife clearly entered above the dress's neckline."

"Interesting," I said. "Thank you, Doctor. I do not think there is anything else of note here. Inspector, may we visit Johnson now?"

Wilkins led me out of the mortuary and into the main police station. As he did so, a sergeant came up to him. "Inspector Wilkins, one of your problems is solved, sir."

Wilkins looked perplexed and the sergeant saw it. "You were

saying, sir, that you feared we'd have to let Johnson go if evidence against him didn't start to turn up."

"Yes," said Wilkins.

"Well, we have the next best thing," said the sergeant, rubbing his hands.

"Explain."

"After you left to pick up Dr. Watson this morning, one of the constables went to the cells to give Johnson something to eat. Something he said provoked Johnson who punched him to the ground. The constable managed to get out of the cell and call for help. Johnson tried to escape but they forced him back in. So that is good, isn't it?"

"Good, how?" I asked.

Wilkins smiled. "I think, Doctor, that Sergeant Boyle here is telling me that we can hold Johnson on the charge of assaulting a constable even if we cannot hold him for murder."

We made our way down to the cells, passing a constable with a disturbingly large black eye. Only one of the half-dozen cells was occupied. Wilkins slid back the shutter. "Johnson, we have a distinguished visitor for you. Do not be stupid now, and stay seated."

He had a constable unlock the cell door and we went inside.

The man on the cell bed was imposing. Even seated, you could see that he was tall and muscular and you could understand how it took three men to subdue him. In contrast to the picture that had been painted of him, he now seemed rather docile. The only hint as to his aggressive nature was the bruised knuckles from his earlier encounter.

"I am sorry about your constable," he said. "He made a smart remark that could not go unanswered."

"Well, your answer is going to get you in trouble," said Wilkins.

Johnson snorted. "I am already in trouble unless you have come to your senses and realized that there is no evidence against me."

"I cannot comment on that," said Wilkins. "Now, kindly answer the questions from this gentleman."

Johnson stared at me, stood, and held out his hand. Without thinking I took it. "How do you do, sir?" said Johnson.

"My name is Dr. John Watson," I said. His face suggested that he had not heard of me. He resumed his seat. "I've spoken to so many people one more won't hurt."

"I am told that you saw the killer. Can you describe him?"

"A little shorter than me. About five foot ten I would say."

"Anything else?"

"Apart from the fact it was a man, not much," said Johnson. "He wore a hooded cape."

"You saw nothing else?"

"Look here," said Johnson with evident frustration. "Alice and I were talking. I was trying to convince her that I had changed and that she should discard this Cooper fellow. Nothing against him you understand but Alice was mine.

"There was a noise and we both looked up to see this hooded figure jump through the window into the room. Without a pause he grabbed at the Hazlewood necklace. He spun Alice round, I think to get at the necklace's clasp, ripped it from her and plunged a knife into her back. It was so fast and I could not get to her because Sam was in the way trying to defend her. Alice dropped to the ground and he made for the open window. I advanced towards him, he seized an old vase from a pedestal and hurled it at me. It struck me in the face and sent me to the ground. I lost vision for a moment but could hear him escape. Shortly after, the Hazlewood staff broke into the room and restrained me on Hazlewood's orders."

"He clearly does not like you," I said.

"He is a possessive old man. He lost his wife to cancer and his son to the navy. He was determined not to lose control of his daughter.

She could not see it but I could. I bought her Sam and the cats as I knew it would please her and annoy him in equal measure. He is a cold man. Even in here I have heard that he is putting in an insurance claim for the necklace."

"Are you aware," I said, "of the rumours that he is responsible for her death?"

Johnson rubbed his chin. "Not in person. I would not put it past him to engage someone to do it for him though."

"Well thank you, Mr. Johnson," I said. "I will return if I have any other questions."

Johnson turned to Wilkins. "So, when do I get out of here?"

Wilkins laughed. "If nothing had changed you might have got out of here in a couple of days. Now that you have assaulted a constable, you're in here until a judge determines bail."

Johnson flushed red and I feared an assault. Wilkins could see it too and we backed out of the cell quickly. Wilkins nodded to the constable who turned the key.

"Inspector," shouted Johnson through the door. "I would like to ask a small kindness. I will need someone to defend me in court. Please ask that Cooper fellow to do it. He is the only barrister I know of."

Wilkins said he would comply. As we walked away, he said, "Rather optimistic of him to ask the fiancé of the victim to act on his behalf."

"Optimistic is certainly one word," I said.

It was now early evening and I was in need of food. Wilkins escorted me to the hotel where my room was booked. He took his leave and said he would collect me in the morning for the drive to Guildford to see Mr. Cooper. After depositing my belongings in my room, I adjourned to the bar for supper. I took a discreet table and ate under the watchful gaze of the locals but no one approached me other than the serving staff. The décor created a cosy and comfortable atmosphere, and I noted that it was just the kind of place that Mary would have enjoyed. Back in my room, I wrote my report to Holmes all ready to post in the morning.

The next day I was collected by Wilkins and we drove to Guildford. I dropped my letter at the local post office, just in time for collection it turned out, before we arrived at the offices of Mr. James Cooper. The man himself soon joined us and we all shook hands. Wilkins explained the purpose of the visit and Cooper was suitably appalled.

"He can find someone else," he said. "The nerve. He took my fiancée from me. If I see him in court, it will be to prosecute not defend."

"You are certain of his guilt?" I asked.

"Based on what Mr. Hazlewood has told me and what Alice herself told me, yes."

"You are aware that there is little direct evidence?" said Wilkins.

"Yes. I am aware that he stands a good chance of getting away with it."

I was suddenly struck with a thought. "How tall are you, sir?"

"Five foot ten, why?"

"Just a routine question," I replied. Cooper did not look convinced but said nothing.

After a few pleasantries, Wilkins and I left to return to Godalming. "Do we know that Cooper did indeed leave Godalming when Miss Alice asked him to?"

Wilkins pondered the matter. "Good question, Doctor. I will make some enquiries."

Upon our arrival back in Godalming, Wilkins learned that the

Chief Constable wished to see him. This annoyed Wilkins because it meant an immediate return to Guildford. Before he set off, I was introduced to Constable Bull, and he suggested I accompany him on his beat while we talked. On this occasion his beat was through the centre of the town. As we walked, the young constable talked me through every shop, who owned it, and everything about them that he knew.

"That there is the jeweller," he said. "It was there that Mr. Hazlewood recently got his necklace revalued."

"Really?" I said. "I should like to speak with the proprietor."

We both entered, the bell ringing as we did so. It was a modest size shop with cabinets displaying a surprisingly large range of items. In fact, there were so many cabinets that Constable Bull and I took up most of the remaining available space. The owner was fortunate that Surrey did not have the crime rate of London. I had barely finished the thought when a man emerged from the back. "Good morning, Constable Bull," he said.

"Morning, Mr. Metcalfe," said Bull. "This gentleman is interested in hearing about the Hazlewood Necklace. He is working with us so you can speak freely."

Metcalfe nodded by way of acknowledgement. "It was about four weeks ago. Mr. Hazlewood came in and just produced the necklace. I had heard about it of course but had never seen it."

"Odd for him to be carrying something so valuable, so casually," I remarked.

"Quite so. I do a lot of valuations for insurance purposes so I gave it a look over. I informed Mr. Hazlewood that it was not worth less than one hundred thousand pounds. He seemed happy with that and left."

"Thank you," I said and turned to leave.

"Did you know that Mr. Johnson came in here only recently?"

said Metcalfe.

Both Bull and I halted. "You never mentioned that," said Bull.

"Apologies. It has just come back to me. He explained he was here to ask about engagement rings."

"What did he want one for?"

Metcalfe grinned. "He was direct about it. He said it was for Miss Alice. Bearing that in mind I was not impressed with the ring he ultimately selected. It was very much at the lower end of the scale. I gently warned him, but he said it was all he could afford now and Miss Alice would understand."

We thanked him again and left the shop. The next shop we passed was a chemist. "We have got different problems here," said Bull.

"Such as?" I asked.

"Missing poison," said Bull. "The owner, Mr. Holder, did a stock take and discovered he was short of a few grains of arsenic. The amounts listed in the poison book did not account for it. Under pressure, his young assistant said he had given some to Johnson who had asked for it not to be recorded. Johnson handed over quite a lot of money to persuade him."

"Has Johnson been challenged about this?"

"Yes. He said that it was not true. He said that the young assistant was well known to be sweet on Alice Hazlewood and had probably wanted to help the case against him."

"Well," I observed, "having met Johnson I can see that he would not need poison to kill someone. It is more a woman's weapon in my experience."

We next approached a butcher. "This is Lufton's," said Bull. "What he does not know is not worth knowing. My wife has asked me to pick up some chops for dinner. Do you mind?"

We entered the shop. The smell of raw meat was strong. The ringing of the bell brought the owner out from the back, wiping his bloody hands on a cloth as he did so. "Hello, Constable," he said. "Hello, Dr. Watson."

I was a little taken aback. "You know me, sir?"

"I certainly hope to, sir," he replied. "Word gets around in Godalming, sir."

"I have noticed."

"My daughter, Lucy, pointed you out to me first thing when you were collected by the inspector. She does all the deliveries so she sees most of what goes on round here. If I have a reputation for knowing everything, it is only because Lucy tells me."

"How is Lucy?" asked Constable Bull.

"Still upset," said Lufton. "She'll get over it in due course."

Bull purchased his chops and we left the shop, leaving Mr. Lufton to return to his cleaver. "What will Miss Lufton get over?" I asked.

A smile crossed Bull's face. "She is a funny one, Lucy. Just turned sixteen. A real romantic, always with her head in those magazines. I sometimes think it was a shame she was taught to read."

The remark lowered my opinion of Constable Bull but I kept it to myself. "She was taught at school presumably?"

"Yes, but it never sank in I am told. It was Alice Hazlewood who eventually got her to read. Lucy idolised her and that is why she is so upset. Alice was not the cold fish her father is. By the by, Lufton here and Metcalfe share something in common it seems. Both had Johnson in as a customer over the last few weeks."

"What did he want in the butchers?" I asked.

"We do not know. Lufton himself was not serving. He allows Lucy to serve on certain mornings while he prepares meat out the back. Lucy was asked but said that he had just asked for some directions but she could not remember where to. That was entirely in character for her. Head in the clouds. I understand that only yesterday her father had a complaint that she had not delivered a ham to one of his customers."

"What did she say?"

"That she had delivered it but there was no answer to her ring so she had left it round the back by the kitchen door. Poor Lufton had to supply another at his own expense. She probably took it to the wrong house and would not admit it."

Bull and I continued our walk along the High Street. I was wondering what purpose this was serving and whether there was something else I could be doing that would advance things, but Holmes had always prized local gossip and had never failed to find it useful. I resolved to continue with Constable Bull a while longer.

A middle-aged lady waved at us. Bull clearly recognised her and headed over with me right behind. "Hello, Mrs. White," he said.

"Hello, Constable; hello, Dr. Watson," she said. I could only assume she had spoken to Mr. Lufton. "Have you heard the awful news?"

"What's that?" asked Bull.

"That frightful Mr. Hazlewood is getting rid of Miss Alice's pets. She's not even in her grave yet, and he cannot wait to be rid of them. The cats have already gone to the local schoolmaster."

"How do you know this, madam?" I asked.

"Lucy told me. She made a delivery to the Grange and the maid told her. Apparently, his son, Simon, is coming home on compassionate leave from navy. The Hazlewood solicitor, Mr. Armitage, is meeting him at the station and escorting him to the house. Mr. Hazlewood will give Armitage charge of the dog. Lord knows what will happen to the poor thing. Miss Alice adored him. It's not right."

"When is this supposed to happen?" I asked.

"In about an hour, sir. Young Simon is due into Godalming at two-fifteen, I understand."

We thanked Mrs. White and went on our way. I turned to Bull. "I think I should like to be there for that exchange."

"Very good, sir," said Bull and we parted company.

I walked the route as I needed to think. The more I thought, the more I became convinced of Johnson's innocence or at least the absence of anything really pointing to his guilt. My mind turned again and again to Cooper. He was the right height and could have easily been in the area. But what was the motive? He was about to marry into an influential family that would no doubt advance his career. None of it made sense.

I reached the gates of Hazlewood Grange. The constable on duty recognised my name and waved me through. I took the opportunity to again study the footprints in the garden. They were considerably fainter now but, in a moment of clarity, I used my stick to measure the distance between the prints. It was not a large stride. Another peculiarity for the next report to Holmes.

I heard the crunch of gravel and turned to see a cab enter the grounds. This must be the son and the solicitor, I thought. I watched from my position as the carriage passed me. It stopped near the door and two men alighted. The young blonde man looked impressive, vibrant even, but was not wearing a uniform. The older man followed him, his slow progress suggesting that his health was not at its best. As I watched, the front door was opened and Mr. Hazlewood emerged dragging the dog. His face was a disturbing shade of red showing that he was summoning all the strength he could muster. The dog was resisting and doing so effectively.

I moved closer so I was in earshot.

"Ah, Armitage," gasped Hazlewood. "You are late. Take the damned beast." He strained to hold out the end of the leash. Armitage looked hesitant. Clearly wondering if his own strength was up to it.

As he held out his hand the dog stopped dead and sniffed the air. It suddenly took off with such speed that it almost pulled Hazlewood over. He had the good sense to let go and both his son and Armitage tried to intercept the dog. It was to no avail and the animal careered off down the drive and out of sight.

"Good riddance," said Hazlewood, his face beginning to return to a more normal colour. "Perhaps it will just starve out there. If you can find it, Armitage, all well and good, but do not exert yourself." With that he ushered his son inside and his butler closed the door on the ruffled solicitor. He turned, saw me, and without a word of acknowledgement or greeting, got back into the cab, and headed away.

I felt I had learned a lot and decided to head back to write a fresh report to Holmes. I joined the main road and began turning the events over in my mind as I walked. So absorbed in the process was I that I nearly failed to hear my name being called. It was Inspector Wilkins calling to me from a carriage. He got the driver to stop and I got in. As we moved off, I told him all I had learned and seen.

"Fascinating," he said, rubbing his chin. "I have news too. The Chief Constable says we can hold Johnson for a few more days. He will be charged, and no doubt sentenced, for his assault on the constable but he will have to be given the opportunity for bail. There is not enough to hold him on the murder charge. Also, there's news on Cooper. He was seen by the local newsagent the morning after the murder. He was later seen at the station buying a ticket to Guildford."

"So, he did not go home after seeing Alice," I said.

"No, he did not."

The route we followed back to town took us past some buildings that appeared industrial in nature. Wilkins informed me that there were two properties. A small holding and a large builder's yard. Given the time of day, the latter seemed rather deserted. I mentioned this to Wilkins.

"Nothing odd about that, Doctor," he replied. "That is the

business of Reg Hurst. He employs a lot of people hereabouts. He shut the yard down about a week ago so he could spend some time with his elderly ill mother in Reigate. He is due back in a couple of weeks or so."

Wilkins dropped me back at the hotel and said he would make arrangements to question Cooper. I went to my room and began work on my next report. A couple of hours later, courtesy of the pageboy, it was on its way to the post office.

Once again, I took a table in the bar for something to eat. The locals decided not to keep their distance this time. Almost all of them approached me to either question me on what I knew or to tell me what they thought they knew. Many asked when Holmes would visit. I gave the vaguest answers that I could and even bought a few drinks to placate some of the dissatisfied patrons.

Wilkins popped into the bar a couple of hours later. Cooper had been embarrassed to be confronted about his deceit. His explanation was that he had been jealous at the prospect of Alice and Johnson spending any time together. He had resolved to take some rest in a field before returning to the house in the evening to be on hand. He had duly fallen asleep and woken up too late to reach the house in time. He said he had felt so foolish and ashamed of his lack of trust in his fiancée that he had remained camped in the field until the early morning. According to Wilkins, Cooper had not sought a hotel as he did not want his presence in Godalming to be common knowledge. Looking rather unkempt, he had made his way to the newsagent for a newspaper before boarding an early train to Guildford. He later learned of the murder courtesy of a telegram from Mr. Hazlewood.

Wilkins was not entirely happy with this explanation, but recognised that there was even less evidence against Cooper than there was against Johnson. He had told Cooper not to leave Guildford for the time being. "I do not think he did it, Doctor, and there is no motive for him to do so. He may be a little stupid and jealous but that is all."

Wilkins was now off-duty so he agreed to join me in a drink. We had been talking for about an hour when a disturbed looking man stood up from several tables away before heading over to us, his gait rather unsteady. "Mr. Wilkins, sir. I need a word."

Wilkins turned to me. "Dr. Watson, may I introduce Thomas Franklin, the local postie."

The man bowed and, without a word, pulled out a chair and sat down. "You know I have told you before about the spirits here in Godalming?"

"Yes," said Wilkins with a sigh. "Let me see. Firstly, it was groaning near the haberdashery. About a week ago it was disembodied voices near the chemist. Last, but not least, it was singing in the churchyard."

Franklin, was not put off by Wilkins' scepticism. "You mock, Inspector, but now there are noises at Hurst's yard."

"What took you out there? You know he is away."

"Yes," said Franklin, sounding a little frustrated. "But if he gets a letter, I still have to deliver it. He had a letter in the afternoon post. So, I took it round. Pretty much my last stop before heading home. I went to the gate where he has a letter box. As I was popping it through, I heard this strange scratching noise in the distance."

I looked at Wilkins whose face showed a loss of patience. "Franklin, there is an animal smallholding that backs onto Hurst's yard as well you know. There are pigs and geese there. Now kindly stop wasting my time."

The young postman stood up unsteadily. A ripple of laughter could be heard around the bar. "Spirits, I'm telling you," he said as he walked out, bumping into a few unoccupied chairs as he did so.

"Good man but he drinks," said Wilkins. "Hammond. I asked

you not to serve him."

The landlord came out from behind the bar. "I did not. He arrived like that. I suggest you speak to the people at The Star."

"I will," said Wilkins. He drained his glass. "I had better go, Doctor."

I read the evening paper for an hour and retired.

The next morning, I rose early and breakfasted. I took a stroll around the town and endeavoured to think. It still did not make sense. The case against Johnson did not stand up despite him having a strong financial motive to take the necklace. Cooper had withheld information about his movements but lacked a motive. Then there was the missing poison. Had Johnson really bought it despite his denials? Where was the necklace? Where was the murder weapon?

I went into the local post office and dashed off a lengthy telegram to Holmes to add the extra information from the previous night. I hesitated to tell him anything supernatural as I knew what his reaction would be. However, I eventually elected not to omit anything. The post mistress handed me a letter. The postmark clearly showed it was from London and that could only mean Holmes. I thanked her.

I found a bench nearby and sat down. In his letter Holmes complimented me on my initial report and the details contained therein. He shared my concerns about the evidence against Johnson but also agreed that he was the only one with motive. He instructed me to gather the word in the town on all parties. I smiled as I had already done this to my satisfaction. I looked forward to his response to my second letter and my telegram.

As Holmes's letter contained no instructions that I had not already followed, I chose, in the absence of anything more constructive, to take a look at the locations mentioned by Franklin in his tirade about spirits. I had already seen the chemist so I made my way to the haberdashery and the churchyard. I was not surprised to find them quite ordinary and decided to omit visiting any of the other locations. I was convinced by this time that the only spirits Franklin knew came out of a bottle.

I bought a newspaper and found a small tea room, close to The Star public house, where I could sit and read undisturbed. I spent a few hours reading of matters less sinister and will confess to allowing my eyes to linger over the sporting pages.

Suddenly there was a knocking at the window. I looked up, startled. It was Franklin. He opened the door and came in.

"Sorry about yesterday," he said, now very much sober. "We do have spirits round here, but I should not have bothered you with it. Old Mrs. Thackery is regularly in contact with them. However, that is not why I am disturbing you. I was walking past, on my way to the hotel, when I saw you." He reached into his bag and took out some papers. "I have just come from the post office. You have two telegrams. Mr. Holmes, I guess." He grinned, declined the shilling I offered him, touched his hat, and went on his way.

It was clear that two telegrams had been necessary thanks to the sheer amount Holmes had to say. They had been sent one directly after the other. The first telegram was mainly concerned with the contents of my second letter. Again, Holmes was complimentary about my report and said he had formed some working theories. The second telegram was far shorter and notably concluded with the instruction, "Release Johnson this evening and follow him."

The sense of urgency ensured that I paid my bill and was at the police station in a matter of minutes. Wilkins read the telegrams and looked suitably surprised. "We were not planning on releasing him for another day or so."

"Well, Inspector," I said. "From the outset you wanted

Holmes's opinion. I suggest you follow it now that you have it."

Within the hour it had all been arranged. Johnson was informed that he would be released a little after seven in the evening. He was predictably pleased and said it should have happened far sooner. I spent the intervening time with Wilkins in his office. Wilkins had decided that when Johnson was released, he and I would follow him, along with Constable Bull. As soon as Johnson's destination became clear, Bull would be sent back to the station for reinforcements.

The time passed slowly and I found myself wishing that Holmes had been transparent about what he expected to occur. Sergeant Boyle eventually knocked on the door to say that Johnson was in the process of being released. Wilkins and I left his office and made our way to the station entrance.

"Come to see me off, gentlemen?" said Johnson with no attempt to conceal his happiness.

"Show some respect, Mr. Johnson," said Wilkins. "Your former fiancée is still dead with her killer at large."

The smile did not fade from Johnson's face. "True, Inspector, but I rather think I am entitled to be pleased to regain my freedom." He was handed back his possessions by Sergeant Boyle and, with an ostentatious wave, he left the building.

Wilkins and I followed. We could see Johnson moving at quite a pace. "We had better move or we will lose him," said Wilkins. With Constable Bull in tow, we followed, maintaining the largest distance that we dared.

Johnson moved with a purpose but remained on foot. It was clear he was heading out of the town centre. Was he heading for the station? Why not hail a cab? It was a little perplexing.

Wilkins tugged my sleeve. "There are a number of places he could be heading, but I'm damned if I know which."

"As long as he doesn't see us, we will soon find out," I replied.

For another ten minutes we walked and we soon saw a familiar sight ahead.

"How odd," said Wilkins. "He seems to be heading for Hurst's yard."

As Johnson reached the yard, he slowed down and began to look around. Wilkins, Bull, and I had to duck out of sight. As we watched, Johnson scaled the fence and dropped down on the other side. Wilkins sent Bull back to the station to bring all available constables. The two of us approached the yard. We could hear Johnson walking away from the fence.

Wilkins leant towards my ear, "At the rear of the yard there are some buildings that Hurst uses for storing the more expensive materials and his papers. It sounds like that is where Johnson is heading."

Wilkins gave me a leg up and I was able to observe Johnson enter the buildings to which the inspector had referred. Once he was inside, I climbed the fence myself. Wilkins followed and we advanced slowly towards the same building, taking care not to be where we could be easily seen. There was a small window on one side of the building and a light suddenly appeared as Johnson presumably lit a candle or lamp. We approached, eventually on our hands and knees, to avoid detection. Slowly, we raised our heads to look inside.

Johnson was kneeling in the middle of the room and was stroking a black Labrador that was chained to one of the walls. "That's Sam," I said.

"So it is," whispered Wilkins. As we watched, Johnson stood up. His expression was one of annoyance which contrasted with Sam who seemed pleased to see him, tail wagging furiously. Johnson turned his back to us and approached some shelving on the opposite side of the room. He seemed to know where he was going. A few seconds later he swore an oath. I could only assume something was not where he had expected to find it. He immediately began to search the entire shelf. He was impatient and hasty and consequently knocked a few items to the floor. At one point he spun round to retrieve a tin that was rolling away from him. If Wilkins and I had been any slower, he would have seen us.

After about a minute he came upon a small envelope. He relaxed immediately. He opened it and peered inside. Satisfied, he advanced towards a bowl on the floor that contained water the dog had clearly been drinking. As we watched, he tipped the envelope and some powder fell into the bowl. I realised at once. "That's the arsenic," I said. Without thinking, I charged into the building. Johnson was briefly frozen in shock at the sight of me, and I took advantage to kick over the bowl. The next moment he was advancing on me. He would have overpowered me quickly if it had not been for Wilkins who produced his revolver and ordered Johnson to halt. Johnson was red with rage and Sam had begun to bark. The dog, blissfully unaware of what Johnson had planned for it, was now endeavouring to attack Wilkins, only the chain preventing it.

Johnson noticed this and edged towards the dog clearly with the intention to release the chain. In his effort to prevent this, Wilkins got too close to Johnson. When the gap had closed enough and Wilkins allowed himself to look at the dog, Johnson knocked the gun from his hand. Although outnumbered, Johnson had strength on his side. Quickly, he reached for a nearby roll of material and produced a knife from inside it. He waved the bloody blade at us and gestured for us to move away from the door. He was speaking but it was hard to hear him over the sound of the dog barking. Wilkins and I had to keep our distance or risk being bitten. Slowly, Johnson reached the door and fled. A few seconds later he returned, hands in the air. Behind him we saw a hand holding a revolver. Over the barking a distinctive voice rang out.

"Good evening, Inspector; good evening, Watson. I apologise for my tardiness."

Sherlock Holmes stood in the doorway.

With Holmes's aid, Wilkins handcuffed Johnson and we waited for reinforcements from the station. Johnson was returned to his cell and the dog was put into the adjacent one. At Holmes's request, Mr. Hazlewood was sent for. We adjourned to Wilkins' office to wait for his arrival.

"How long had you been there, Holmes?" I asked.

"I arrived at the yard about one hour before you, old fellow," he replied. "Having read your excellent reports, I realised it was a place of significance. I located the dog but decided not to disturb anything."

"But the poor dog, Holmes," I said. "He could have killed it."

"I knew you would not permit that to happen. Besides, had I moved anything it might have roused Johnson's suspicions and it was vital that he not only be seen with the dog but that he also attempt to poison it in front of witnesses. Let us keep the remainder of the explanation for when Mr. Hazlewood arrives."

Mr. Hazlewood arrived within an hour and was introduced to Holmes. After some strained pleasantries, we all took seats.

"I do wish I had been able to be on the ground in person, Inspector," said Holmes. "However, all's well that ends well and Watson here has acted for me effectively."

I felt myself glow with pride at the compliment.

"I must also congratulate you, Inspector. Your skills are somewhat in excess of your metropolitan colleagues. Your initial investigations furnished me with many important clues."

Mr. Hazlewood, who had remained quiet since the initial greetings, chose this moment to speak. "If you do not mind, Mr. Holmes. Could you get to the point? I still have a daughter to bury and a missing necklace for which I need reimbursement."

Holmes looked at Hazlewood with a mixture of pity and disgust. "Very well. Based on the details I have been furnished with, the events seem straightforward.

"On the night of the murder, Johnson arrived at the Grange after dark. That was telling when he could have visited at any time of day. As a gambler with no conventional occupation, he had no other obvious calls upon his time that would have prevented a more sociable hour. Darkness was therefore important to his plans.

"He arrived at the house on foot and walked up the drive. He was admitted and was asked to wait in the hall. It was after dark so all the curtains in the house were closed. As soon as he was alone, he moved to the gas valve and cut the supply to the lamps. They went out and no one could see it had happened.

"He soon entered the parlour to meet Alice Hazlewood and locked the door from the inside. If the windows in the parlour were closed, I have no doubt he asked for them to be opened. Perhaps he claimed to be too warm. Alice Hazlewood was likely to be in the mood to be accommodating bearing in mind the promise that this would be the last time the two of them would meet. Johnson meant this sincerely but not in the way that Alice Hazlewood assumed.

"What they talked about is largely irrelevant. Johnson was buying time. His accomplice, under cover of near total darkness, made his way round the house and approached the window to the parlour.

"The window frame was seized from the outside. Alice spun round to see and Johnson took a knife from his pocket, seized a throw rug from in front of the settee and plunged the knife through it into her neck. His height accounted for the position of the wound. The purpose of the rug was to prevent blood splashing onto him which would ruin the story he would later tell.

"His accomplice screamed because the murder was not

something they had discussed. It was unexpected because Johnson had not shared his plans in full. This told me that the accomplice would not have been willing to play a part if the full details had been known.

"But now the accomplice saw that the plan had to be seen through. Johnson rolled the knife up in the rug and handed it over. The accomplice headed back, taking a longer route in order to minimise the risk of being seen. Constable Bull was advancing up the drive at this point so the accomplice sat down on the ground, accounting for the large impression you noticed, Inspector, and waited for Bull to pass before making an escape."

"But the necklace, Holmes," I said.

Holmes gestured for us all to follow him. We went down to the cells where we could hear Johnson furiously pacing. We opened the cell containing the dog. Holmes had earlier requested it be overfed with meat from the nearby hotel. Consequently, it was more docile. Holmes gently approached and removed its collar.

"The comment was made that this collar seemed unnecessarily sturdy for the dog." He turned it over and pulled at a seam. The seam came apart and Holmes reached inside. Slowly he pulled out the most beautiful necklace I had ever seen.

"Good Lord," said Hazlewood loudly. "That's my necklace." As he said it, we heard a cry from next door and thumping against the wall. "Let us return upstairs," said Holmes.

Once back in the inspector's office, Holmes continued. "Johnson had the necklace and it was time to act swiftly. All this had happened in seconds. He made a scream of his own and inserted the necklace into this special compartment. He, proceeded, with considerable dexterity, to smash a nearby vase and injured himself with one of the pieces. He lay on the floor and began to play the part of the man who tried to save his fiancée and who got injured in the attempt. He told his story and it seemed not only possible but probable."

"How did you deduce about the rug?" asked Wilkins.

"It fitted the facts. Assuming Johnson was the culprit he had to shield himself from the blood that would come from the wound when the knife was withdrawn. The port-mortem report spoke of fabric in the wound and there was the dark patch on the carpet that indicated something had been there protecting that part of the carpet from the fading which the sun had caused elsewhere."

"Brilliant," said Wilkins.

"Not as brilliant as Johnson," said Holmes. "Despite the horrific nature of the crime, this man planned everything exactly." He turned towards Hazlewood. "He expected to be accused by you, sir, as he was well aware of your hatred of him. He also expected that your influence would lead to him being placed in the cells but he also knew he would be released when the absence of evidence became clear. No blood on him, no weapon, no necklace, and a story of an intruder that would be backed up by the footprints to and from the house's rear garden."

I looked at Hazlewood. His expression was that of controlled anger. He said nothing.

Holmes continued. "Johnson read you all too well, Mr. Hazlewood. He knew the routine of this house; he knew the layout. This had been so long in the planning I suspect he began as soon as he first met your daughter and heard of the necklace. He learned of her desire for a pet. He knew of your strong aversion to the idea. His keen mind saw an approach. He supplied a dog and cats, the latter of which were a distraction. He guessed, under the circumstances of your late wife's death, that you would tolerate the animals for your daughter's sake. He trained the dog and it knew him well which accounted for the lack of noise from the animal during the crime. It was therefore easy for him to conceal the necklace on the dog.

"You will forgive me, Mr. Hazlewood, but you are a cold-hearted man. Johnson knew you would waste no time disposing of the animals after the crime. When that time came, his accomplice was on hand to attract the dog and intercept it."

Hazlewood now had a face like thunder. Clearly, he was not accustomed to being criticised to his face. "Who was this accomplice?" he demanded.

Holmes's face softened. "I will tell you but must insist on amnesty in that direction. Pursuing the accomplice will achieve nothing. She was duped."

"She?" we all said in unison.

"A number of things pointed to that conclusion," said Holmes.

"Firstly, the initial high-pitched scream. It could conceivably have been made by a man but it was more likely to be a woman. Then there was the engagement ring."

"What of it?" said Wilkins.

"Your Mr. Metcalfe commented on its poor quality. If there is one occasion where a gentleman goes beyond his means to impress it is when purchasing an engagement ring. We know that Johnson, as a gambler, regularly went overboard so it was obviously for some other reason that he bought a ring of such poor quality. It was because it was destined for a lady who would be impressed by it. In short, a lady of much humbler origins."

We all stared at him in silence.

"Dear oh dear," said Holmes. "Think, Watson. Think of the day Sam ran away. What did he do before doing so?"

I thought back. "He sniffed the air."

"Precisely. What do you think he smelled?"

"Food?" suggested Wilkins.

"Yes. And?"

We all paused.

"Come now, gentlemen. What lady knew all the comings and goings in the town, had ready access to food appealing to a dog, and was humble enough to be impressed by a cheap ring?"

It dawned on us all. "Lucy Lufton," I exclaimed. "But, Holmes, she is a child."

"Yes, Watson. A child with a romantic disposition. Her head in the clouds according to Constable Bull. A child who reads romances in magazines. Someone easy to sweep up with talk of a future marriage by an attractive man. For all his bad characteristics, we must grant Johnson that he is charismatic."

Wilkins had clearly begun to understand. "So, Lucy gets hold of Sam and leads him, presumably with the missing ham, to Hurst's yard. It was widely known that he was away. The dog could be hidden there and if it made noises, it would be easy to suggest that they came from the neighbouring smallholding."

"Yes, Inspector," said Holmes. "That said, Johnson did not want too much noise. He procured the arsenic from the chemist as the corrupt assistant asserted. It was probably the late-night transaction that your inebriated postman took to be spirits. Johnson stored the envelope containing the powder in the yard buildings days before the crime. Lucy was under instructions to take Sam there and poison him. When he, Johnson, was released, which he expected to be soon, he could go to the yard and simply retrieve the necklace and disappear.

Amusingly, he impeded his own plans when he foolishly attacked your constable. I realised that every day that passed would make him more impatient so I knew, if released, he could not stop himself from heading straight to claim his prize. I sent Watson instructions and immediately boarded a train. When I reached the yard, I discovered that the dog was alive. It seems that, after everything she had done, Lucy drew the line at killing an animal. Especially one that had belonged to a woman she had idolised and about whose death she felt partly responsible. She entered the building with the intention of carrying out her instructions and retrieved the envelope from where she had been told to look. Once she decided against it, she left the building placing the envelope back on the shelf but in a different location. This caused Johnson's frantic search of the building when he discovered its absence."

"Surely, if Johnson had claimed the necklace and vanished, Lucy could have exposed him," said Wilkins.

"Lucy may be young," said Holmes, "but even she would have seen that to do that would expose her. She would have had to keep silent to protect herself. Please bear in mind, gentlemen, that she was, effectively, seduced and placed in a state of internal conflict through witnessing Miss Alice's death. Convinced that she loved and was loved by Johnson, she gave her loyalty to him. If taken to court, a clever counsel will make her out, with considerable justification, to be another victim of Johnson. I think, under the circumstances, a jury would be loath to condemn a sixteen-year-old girl to jail or worse."

"But there is no keeping her out of matters now," said Wilkins. "Her evidence will be needed as she was the only witness to the crime."

"That is true," said Holmes. "She will need the advice of an outstanding Q.C. I believe there may be one in Guildford who could offer advice. I am confident he will be very amenable to the idea."

A month later, Holmes received a copy of the local Surrey newspaper from Wilkins. In it was coverage of the trial. Johnson was found guilty of murder and theft and sentenced to death. Lucy Lufton was praised for her evidence and was seen as Johnson's second victim. In an accompanying letter, Wilkins informed us that Mr. Hazlewood had sold the necklace to fund repairs to Hazlewood Grange.

"One is tempted to wonder," said Holmes, "that if he had sold the necklace earlier his daughter might still be alive."

The Adventure of the Naval Architect

(Early-1896)

HE routine and habits of Sherlock Holmes could never be taken for granted. His mood was often dictated by his workload, as was his timekeeping. During the years that we shared rooms in Baker Street, it was not uncommon for me to rise only to find he had breakfasted and gone out hours earlier. On this spring day, I woke to find I had overslept and it was mid-morning.

I put on my dressing-gown and descended to the sitting room. My friend was at the dining table drinking coffee and doing his utmost to ignore the food, lovingly prepared by Mrs. Hudson, that, even to my untrained eye, had long since gone cold. He bid me good morning and pulled out a chair for me. As I took my seat, he breezed past me onto the landing and shouted down to our landlady that another mouth was ready to be fed.

He returned, picked up the coffee pot, and poured what remained into my cup. I could see at once that something was on his mind as he had clearly lost track of the amount of coffee in the pot. As I watched, my cup was barely filled to half-way and the liquid was joined by the dregs. He snarled and added a fresh pot of coffee to Mrs.

Hudson's list.

"Well, Holmes," I said. "What is it that is distracting you this morning?"

He smiled indulgently at my attempt at deduction, sat down and slid a piece of paper across to me and tapped with his fingertips. My eyes went straight to the bottom and I saw the familiar name.

"Mycroft?"

He grimaced. "Yes, Watson. My dear brother has elected to communicate with me. He has chosen to be both frustratingly cryptic and concise." He slid the paper back, before I could finish it, crumpled it petulantly, and thrust it into his pocket. "He simply states that someone official will be calling upon us soon and it is vital to Her Majesty's government that we go with that person."

"We?"

"If you would be so good, Watson," he said with a smile.

With some relief, I left the unpalatable cup in front of me and went to get dressed. When I returned, Holmes was pacing up and down. I noticed the fresh coffee pot had arrived and poured myself a cup. As I lifted the cup to my lips and tasted the rejuvenating liquid, the bell rang.

At once, Holmes was excited. "At last," he said.

Heavy feet upon the stairs spoke of haste. Soon, the familiar face of Inspector Bradstreet appeared in the doorway.

"Good morning, gentlemen," he said. "I believe you are coming with me?"

"Am I to conclude," said Holmes, "that you do not know why you are here?"

The inspector looked frustrated. "I was rather hoping that you'd have some answers, sir." He removed his hat and scratched his temple. "All I know is that our destination is Waterloo station."

"Well, that is something at least," said Holmes. "Shall we?"

I sighed and put the barely touched, yet much needed, coffee cup back onto its saucer.

Outside was a four-wheeler into which we all climbed. No sooner was the door closed than we were on our way.

"So, Bradstreet," said Holmes, as we turned onto Marylebone Road, "what can you tell us?"

The inspector frowned. "Not very much, sir. I was called in by the superintendent about an hour ago. I was told that someone senior in government wanted a police presence at Waterloo station. I was ordered to collect you on the way. When we arrive, the stationmaster will escort us to whatever it is we need to see."

"Well," said Holmes, "so enigmatic a start to proceedings strongly suggests the more covert elements of state are playing a part. With Mycroft, I would expect nothing less."

"Wonderful," said Bradstreet, without conviction.

I would like to say that there was a welcome party at the entrance to the great terminus but the group gathered for that purpose would have looked more at home at a funeral. As we alighted from the carriage, the senior man stepped forward to greet us. He announced himself as the stationmaster and briefly indicated that his companions were his immediate subordinates.

Hasty introductions over, we followed them into the building and onto the concourse. Our destination was platform one. We passed through the gate and it dawned on me that the area was almost entirely free of the general public. We followed the stationmaster and his colleagues along the length of the platform and onto the track. As we began to traverse the rougher ground, and cleared the station buildings, we were buffeted by a strong breeze that was of sufficient force that I needed to hold onto my hat. After a few more yards, the stationmaster began to speak for the first time since we had arrived.

"I was told I should prepare you for the scene, gentlemen. The nine forty-eight train from Portsmouth arrived on time today. The guard always walks the length of the train to make sure all passengers have disembarked but was unable to rouse the occupant of one of the reserved first-class compartments. After several failed attempts to elicit a response, he entered the compartment only to discover a body."

"The identity of this body?" asked Holmes.

"Sir James Underwood," said the stationmaster.

Holmes whistled. "That explains Mycroft's interest."

"It does?" said Bradstreet.

"Forgive me, Inspector. Sir James Underwood is the chief naval architect based in Portsmouth. This explains the interest of the government and the Naval Intelligence Department."

We soon approached the sidings. There sat the nine forty-eight train. The ground by now was very rough which had given us all the gait of unsteady infants. The stationmaster walked us to the rear of the train and indicated that we should follow. We all climbed up and into the last carriage. We paused once we were all aboard.

"Gentlemen," said the stationmaster, "the body is here in the first compartment."

We could see nothing as the door was blocked by a constable and the adjacent blinds were down. Further down the corridor we could see an agitated member of staff. The stationmaster excused himself and indicated that the nervous man, who was the train's guard, would answer any questions. We thanked him and the constable stood to one side at Bradstreet's request. Bradstreet gently opened the compartment door. As he did so he was struck in the face by an airborne sheet of newspaper. Despite the seriousness of the situation, I struggled to suppress a smile. The inspector stepped inside and we followed.

Looking over Holmes's shoulder, I surveyed the cramped scene. Sir James was seated in the direction of travel on the side furthest from the corridor. A little remained of his newspaper by his side, the rest being spread about the carriage. His bag and cane were above him in the rack. His hat could not be seen initially but was later found behind the door.

Sir James was a large man who, at the time of his death, had been around fifty years of age. While not portly, he was tall. I estimated him to be at least the height of my friend if not an inch or two taller. Consequently, even from a seated position, he took up the greater part of the compartment. He was impeccably dressed, his clothes freshly laundered, largely uncreased, and his overcoat had been carefully folded and laid on the seat opposite him. His hair was in some disarray.

Initially, the cause of Sir James's death was not apparent but, as we manoeuvred around the carriage, we could see the reason. Partly hidden by his frock coat was a neat stab wound which I could see lined up with his heart. Holmes took all this in at speed and summoned the guard. The man appeared in the doorway.

"Good morning," said Holmes, "your name please?"

"Edward Fisher," said the man.

"Mr. Fisher," said Holmes, "were the blinds down in the compartment when you found the body?"

"Yes, sir," replied Fisher, "always."

"I beg your pardon?" said Holmes.

Fisher paused, presumably to gather himself. "Sorry, sir. Sir James was a creature of habit, sir. Always one of the first three compartments, blinds always down."

"Do you happen to know why?"

"Privacy, sir," said Fisher. "He always boarded the same train because he preferred to travel the fast route to Waterloo via Guildford. He would seek out the guard on the platform at Portsmouth and display his ticket before entering his chosen compartment. It was an arrangement we had with him as he preferred not to be disturbed for the entire journey to London. My understanding was that he worked for a lot of the journey sir and was not to be interrupted on account of the sensitivity of his work."

"Ah," said Holmes, "the blinds were down for secrecy as well as privacy."

"Yes, sir. He often booked the first three first-class compartments."

"Three?"

"Yes, sir. He said he wanted no one adjacent to him who might conceivably interrupt or overhear him. I believe he tended to, what is the expression, think out loud. On this occasion he had booked only one compartment."

"Were any of the other first-class compartments booked on this occasion?"

"Yes, sir, but only one of them, about two compartments up. An elderly couple, Mr. and Mrs. Finlay. We spoke briefly when I checked their tickets. They were heading into town for some sightseeing, I believe."

Holmes thanked and dismissed Fisher having also elicited from him that it was not Sir James's habit to obstruct his compartment door on the grounds that he did not feel he needed to. The compartment was marked as reserved and the staff knew not to enter or permit others to do so. A man as imposing as Sir James was not someone you were likely to trifle with.

"It is all clear to me," said Bradstreet, who had been bent over the body but was now straightening up, an expression of satisfaction on his face.

Both Holmes and I turned. "Please enlighten us, Bradstreet," said Holmes.

"Sir James was a creature of habit. You just heard that. It seems likely to me that almost anyone who wished him harm would know when and where to find him. If they had studied him, they would have known that he would be easy to reach. The staff on the train have duties that take them away from first class. There would have been many times a person could have got in here unseen."

"Go on," said Holmes, who was not looking unimpressed.

Bradstreet was more than willing to continue. "His assailant enters the compartment and, after a short interview and struggle, stabs Sir James. Moreover, he was left-handed."

At this, Holmes really did take an interest and smiled. "Capital, Bradstreet," he said. "Pray, how did you arrive at that conclusion?"

Bradstreet beamed, evidently pleased with himself. "It is all a question of angles, Mr. Holmes. A right-handed man, in my opinion, could not have dealt that wound in a face-to-face confrontation. It is not a straight thrust. It seems to come in from the left."

"Well done, Bradstreet," said Holmes. "It all hangs together.

That said, you do have a pressing problem."

"I do?"

"Yes, indeed. The body was discovered after all the other passengers had disembarked. Only then was it relocated to the siding. While a percentage of passengers will have booked; many will have bought tickets just before boarding. How do you plan to locate them all?"

Bradstreet flushed red. "Where is that stationmaster?"

A few minutes later, Holmes and I were back on the platform. As we left the train, Bradstreet had beckoned to two constables who were standing by with a stretcher. With some difficulty, they had managed to remove the body of Sir James. As they passed us with their burden, we both bowed and removed our hats.

"Bradstreet seems to have it all worked out," I said.

Holmes lit a cigarette. "It is good as far as it goes. That is, until you start picking at it."

"What do you mean?"

"What is the motive to kill Sir James? We are told that he often carried out secret work on the journey, but he did not always do so. If he were carrying out such work, where is it? His bag contained nothing of that nature and he had nothing else with him apart from his clothes, cane, and newspaper. Was there another bag which has been taken or did his murderer take papers from the bag we have seen before leaving the carriage?"

"I see."

"Then there is the lack of any sound. Someone steps into his carriage, attacks him and he says nothing. He makes no discernible attempt to defend himself and does not call for help."

"Perhaps the guard was at the other end of the train?" I suggested.

"Perhaps. But he had neighbours only two carriages up, Watson. Did they not hear anything? I would also add that it is possible for a right-handed person to deliver that wound but only if they were at an angle to Sir James. Currently, the evidence points to his killer being someone he knew and did not expect violence from."

"Such as who?" I asked.

"The evidence at the scene does rather point towards the guard or someone masquerading as the guard."

"So, you believe that is what happened?"

"No, Watson, I do not. At least, not yet. I am simply drawing your attention to the fact that there are other explanations. We need more data before we can start to fit a theory to our facts. We need to get to Portsmouth to find out more. We shall return to the concourse. Kindly secure two first-class tickets to Portsmouth Harbour. I shall locate Bradstreet and ask that he wire details of the post-mortem as soon as possible. I will also send my brother a wire. His influence is going to be necessary."

About twenty minutes later we were seated on a train bound for Portsmouth. Several trains were due to leave for that city but Holmes insisted on waiting for one that went via Guildford. It was important, he said, to travel the same route as Sir James – albeit in reverse. Our journey was to take just short of three hours.

Holmes was quiet until the urban scenes gave way to those more rural in nature. Due to the time of day, it had been possible to secure a first-class compartment at short notice. As we sat across from each other, I could see that if either of us had been of Sir James's stature, we would have started to intrude upon each other's space.

"Have you been able to come up with any theories?" I asked.

"Some people complain, Watson," he said," that the social conventions of our time are too stiff, too restrictive. On this occasion, I believe they will prove an ally."

"Whatever do you mean?"

"I examined Sir James before we left the carriage. His clothes were in an impeccable state. You could clearly see that they had been donned not long before he boarded the train. There was no evidence of the kind of creases that active use would have left upon them. It is hardly scientific but the evidence suggests that he pretty much rose that morning, got dressed and headed for the train. It would account for the negligible impact on his clothing."

"Anything else?" I asked.

"It also clearly precludes any form of violent confrontation. His clothes showed no sign of the disarray that would be caused by that level of physical exertion. It is my strong belief that once he sat down, he barely moved before he was killed."

"I see."

"So, we now come to the notion of a visitor. Someone who could enter and remove whatever Sir James was working on."

"Is this where our conventions come in?"

"Indeed, old fellow. We have those rules drilled into us. Those rules are also dependent on, and directed by, one thing above all others."

"And that is?"

"Manners, my friend. Manners."

Holmes often made me feel slow and it clearly showed on my face. He took pity on me. "My dear Watson. Your every move is dictated by manners. Well, manners and money. Let us say you were in our sitting room and a lady was admitted. What would you do?"

"I'm not sure I follow."

"Of course, you do. If you were sitting in your chair and a lady was shown in, you would stand."

"That's only proper, Holmes."

"Yes. A habit drilled into you. If you were at your club and the waiter came in with your drink, would you stand?"

"Of course not."

"Precisely. You would stand for your equals and superiors but not servants."

"So, what are you inferring from that?"

"I am suggesting that if someone did enter that compartment, Sir James very likely did not feel the need to stand. This suggests that he considered that visitor not to be an equal."

"It's a bit farfetched, Holmes."

"On its own, perhaps. But there is also the overcoat."

"The overcoat?"

"Yes. It was on the seat opposite him. Clearly placed there by him soon after he entered the carriage and before he sat down. Had he been visited by someone he considered an equal, manners would have demanded that he offer them a seat. I contend that he would have moved his coat to accommodate them."

"They could have sat beside him," I said, "or diagonally across from him. In fact, his size might have made that necessary."

"But from such a position, Watson, how are they to launch an attack that would kill Sir James with him barely moving and deny him any chance to defend himself? There were no signs of defensive wounds. To achieve that level of surprise, and that particular wound, you would need to be close. Your diagonal theory does not work and the side-by-side theory does not facilitate the kind of wound Sir James received."

"Perhaps the murderer placed the coat there after the deed?"

"To what purpose, Watson? It is not going to hide the fact that there was a murder. What does placing the coat there achieve?"

"So, we are back to the right-handed murderer at right angles or the left-handed murderer face on," I said.

"At the moment," said Holmes, "it would seem so." He became

more subdued and looked out of the window onto the countryside.

The next major stop on our journey was Guildford. When we arrived, we learned that there was to be a delay while another train was permitted to pass us. It was clear that the impact caused by withdrawing the other train from service was going to be felt by passengers on this route for some time. We sat there and watched as all the trains came into the sizeable station and paused alongside each other like horses at the races waiting for the starting pistol. I instinctively touched my pocketbook and decided I would permit myself a modest wager when this case was over.

Suddenly, Holmes got up and intercepted the guard who was on his way to the front of the train. As they exchanged words, I looked in the opposite direction. I came face to face with a small child sitting in the train alongside. The young girl smiled, stuck her tongue out at me, and giggled before being caught and disciplined by a lady I took to be her nanny. I struggled to suppress a smile and the stern lady looked at me with almost the same level of disapproval that she had shown towards her charge.

I turned to the left just as Holmes popped his head into the compartment and informed me that he was going to step onto the platform.

"The train might leave," I said.

"No, no," he said. "The guard has told me it will be another few minutes, and he will blow his whistle before departure."

He returned to the corridor, opened the carriage door, and stepped out. Once on the platform he lit a cigarette. As I joined him, he offered me one.

"It is good to stretch the legs, Watson. This is quite the interchange, second only to Clapham Junction, and perhaps Woking on this line. Look at everyone scurrying between trains to make their connections. Sir James's killer could have used a stop such as this to make his escape and reach a wide variety of destinations." A strange look crossed his face. "Give me a moment, dear fellow," and he disappeared into the crowd.

I felt confident he would not miss the departure so I finished my cigarette and reboarded the train. Shortly after doing so, I heard a whistle. Its volume indicated either our train or one immediately nearby was going to depart. Still there was no Holmes. A judder made it all too clear that our train was the one to be moving on. It began to inch forward, gathering pace. I could not see out to the right due to the neighbouring trains and the view to the left onto the platform revealed little. I was starting to worry when Holmes leapt onto the train and into our compartment.

"Apologies, Watson," he said, evidently a little short of breath. "I decided to purchase a Bradshaw." He dropped the timetable onto the seat as he straightened out his attire. "We left Baker Street so quickly that I neglected to bring a copy."

"We are not making any connections, Holmes," I said. "Is that to work out the return journey times?"

"That too," he said.

As we rattled our way through Surrey it occurred to me that, had we been on the other line, we would have gone through Aldershot. My mind briefly wandered back to my army life, and yet here we were heading into our country's naval sphere. We passed stations with names such as Milford and Witley before stopping for some five minutes in Haslemere, thus permitting passengers from a train already there to join ours. After that, we made our way into Hampshire.

"Not too long now," said Holmes. "I asked Bradstreet to arrange a Hampshire Constabulary welcome. It is always good to have local knowledge. Let us hope they are a little more able than their Metropolitan colleagues."

As we pulled into Portsmouth Harbour station it was nice to

see the sea and hear the gulls. The sounds and smells reminded me of when I embarked on my passage out of England en route to India and, eventually, Afghanistan. It produced mixed emotions and I endeavoured to push the subject from my mind.

"That," said Holmes as we came to a halt, "looks like our police escort. The sergeant looks excited and the inspector looks annoyed."

"How can you tell? He has his back to the train."

"Precisely, Watson."

We alighted and walked towards the two men. The younger one said something and the older man turned to face us dropping and stepping on a cigarette as he did so.

"Welcome to Portsmouth, Mr. Holmes," he said. "My name is Inspector Wreyford and this is Sergeant Oakley."

"A pleasure, gentlemen," said Holmes. He introduced me and we all shook hands. We emerged from the station and the inspector stopped.

"I realise you find our presence here inconvenient," said Holmes.

Wreyford smiled. "Because I had my back to your train? No offence I am sure, Mr. Holmes. Whenever the Yard or its experts come down from town, the local force tends to be treated like junior partners."

"You will not find that with us, Inspector," said Holmes. "If our murderer is here, I will be more than happy for you to take both the lead and credit."

Wreyford smiled. "That is decent of you, Mr. Holmes." The mood lightened at once.

"Where was Sir James based?"

"At the dockyard itself or offices nearby," said Wreyford. "By all accounts, he was often directly involved in the manufacture of his designs. He was not a man to spend all his time in an office. He designed a gun that bears his name which will soon be installed on many of Her Majesty's ships. The only blemish he seems to have suffered was when he permitted a traitor to operate under him."

"What can you tell me about that?" asked Holmes.

Wreyford gestured to his sergeant. "A little before I transferred here. Oakley knows more."

The sergeant was quick to speak up. "Horrible business, Mr. Holmes. It was Sir James's protégé, Mr. Stephen Miles. A gifted engineer and heir apparent to Sir James by all accounts. It seems he needed money to fund his forthcoming wedding to one Miss Julia Morris. The word was that she had, shall we say, expensive expectations so Miles decided to sell naval papers. Evidence to that effect emerged, and Sir James quietly passed word to the authorities. However, it seems even that could not be kept secret and young Miles committed suicide before he could be formally accused. He hung himself from a beam in his attic the night before we planned to arrest him."

So sad, I thought. The lengths some men will go to for love.

The inspector spoke once more. "That is the only reason the likes of us know anything about the Underwood gun. That was one of the secrets that was sold to the Germans, I believe. It is still a formidable weapon but no longer unique to us. There were calls for Sir James to resign for such poor judgment but someone high up saved him. His skills as a naval architect were clearly too good to lose."

We had been walking towards the dockyard for the entire duration of this conversation. As we approached the entrance, a man came towards us with a decidedly unfriendly demeanour. He was a little under six feet, around thirty years old, with slicked back, thinning brown hair, and plain, metal-framed spectacles.

Under his breath, Wreyford spoke. "Be cautious, Mr. Holmes.

This is Samuel Miles, Stephen's brother. He works here too, believes in his brother's innocence, and does not like us much."

Holmes nodded.

"Back again, Inspector?" said the bespectacled man. "Back to harass more innocent people?"

"Before my time, Mr. Miles, as well you know. I would like to introduce you to Mr. Sherlock Holmes."

If he was in any way moved at my friend's name, Miles did not show it. "Yes, I know. We had a high-level telegram from Whitehall. It is the only reason I am out here rather than attending to my duties."

Holmes bowed ever so slightly. "Mr. Miles, I am here on the commission of Her Majesty's government to learn what I can about anything that may have contributed to the death of Sir James Underwood."

The young man snorted. "Now that he is dead, I feel safe to say that his egotism probably had a lot do with it."

"Excuse me," I said.

"Dr. Watson, I presume?" said Miles. "He was a tyrant who believed his own press. Every headline about his genius fuelled his self-image. Even the scandal did little to dent his opinion of himself."

"The scandal caused by your brother," said Wreyford.

Miles flushed. "I do not accept that Inspector and never will. My brother was no traitor, and I care not a jot for your evidence to the contrary. As I have said to you before, when I find who really betrayed our country they will suffer at my hands."

Holmes leaned into the inspector and lowered his voice almost to a whisper. "My dear Inspector, I strongly believe I will get more from Mr. Miles if you are absent. I stand by my earlier commitment. I will not do anything to undermine you and will share any information that I am permitted to."

Wreyford's face showed that he trusted Holmes. "Very well,

Mr. Holmes. You can find us at the station. He touched his brim and led Sergeant Oakley away. "Behave yourself, Miles. Leave the law to the professionals," he shouted over his shoulder as he lit a fresh cigarette.

Holmes turned back to Miles. "Now that we have dispensed with the official police, I can speak frankly. I have an open mind, Mr. Miles, and I have no agenda. I am focused on the death of Sir James. If, along the way, we find evidence connected to your late brother, I will pursue it, wherever it may lead and to whatever conclusion. I trust you will accept that as fair and reasonable."

Miles was calmer now that the police had gone. "I will never believe in my brother's guilt, but I am content to know that you start from a neutral position. How can I assist you?"

"Well, we can begin by going somewhere warmer," said Holmes.

Miles took us into one of the many buildings where rows of draftsmen could be seen working on papers. "These are sensitive documents, Mr. Holmes, but I understand you both to be trusted with such matters."

Not for the first time, I noted that Mycroft Holmes's reach was long.

Miles led us to a room at the far end. "This is my office."

We took the seats that we were indicated to take. Miles took his behind his somewhat battered desk. In his own domain, Miles was confident, bordering on arrogant.

Holmes began. "Can you think of any reason why someone would want Sir James dead other than in connection with his naval work?"

Miles pondered the question. Something in his face told me that he was tempted towards a smart remark but decided against it. "In all honesty, no, Mr. Holmes, although it pains me to say it. He was happily married and lived for his work. He remained in Portsmouth during the week, occasionally travelling into town to see people from the government. He would also head into town on weekends."

"To see his wife?" I asked.

"No. Lady Underwood lives at their house in nearby Southsea. She was born and raised in these parts and does not care too much for his world. He was a great lover of theatre and opera, Doctor. He would often travel up to stay at his club, the Reform Club if I am not much mistaken, and return on the Monday morning."

"You seem to know his habits," observed Holmes.

"Not long after my brother's death, Sir James started to bring me closer and involve me more. I think he had me in mind to succeed to my brother's position. Absurd, isn't it?"

"How so?" I asked.

"It speaks to his egotism that he thought he could appoint me to a sensitive position when my brother is tainted as a traitor and his judgment was under scrutiny. Nevertheless, here I am."

"Did he speak out in your brother's defence?" asked Holmes.

"Only after his suicide," said Miles. "To be fair to him, there was not much time between the rumour emerging and Stephen's death."

"What was the evidence?"

"Certain papers went missing to which only my brother, Sir James, and one or two other senior people had access. All of them had unshakable alibies apart from Stephen. I believe, had it gone to trial, it would have been dismissed as unsound. It was not so much that there was evidence against Stephen. It was that there was no evidence against anyone else."

"You found him, I understand?"

"Yes. I went to his house early in the morning. I did not live too far from him, and one of our neighbours told me that there had been a light on at my brother's house for most of the night as if he were up late working on something.

"I had a key to his house so decided to let myself in when there was no answer to the bell. I made my way through the house until I got all the way up to his attic. There I found him and that vision will stay with me. I was with his body for less than fifteen minutes before the police arrived."

"What did his suicide note say?"

"There was no note."

"Odd," said Holmes. "Were there any other clues?"

"I confess that I did not look around," said Miles. "I had so little time before the police arrived. As soon as they did, I was asked to leave."

"If we may return to Sir James," said Holmes. "We have heard from more than one source that he was a creature of habit. Same trains into and out of town; same carriage and so on. What do you know of this?"

Miles stroked his chin. "We all knew about the regular train. I cannot say I was aware of him always sitting in a particular carriage. That said, it is, or was, in character. Everything had to be just so."

Holmes stood up. "Thank you, Mr. Miles, I cannot promise you what you seek but you can rest assured that I do not presume your late brother's guilt. In the meantime, we will need to visit your late brother's fiancée. Can you write down the address for me as my memory is not what it once was?"

Miles complied and we bade him farewell. As we left the dockyard, we saw the familiar figure of Sergeant Oakley coming towards us. As we approached each other he held out an envelope. "Telegram, for you, Mr. Holmes. It arrived at the station about fifteen minutes ago."

Holmes tore open the envelope. "Fascinating," he said. "Please tell Inspector Wreyford that we are going to pay a call on Miss Morris."

Oakley nodded and returned the way he had come. Holmes hailed a cab and, when one stopped, Holmes handed the cabby the piece of paper from Miles.

As it happened, like the Underwoods, Miss Morris was a resident of nearby Southsea. As we made our way there, Holmes re-read the telegram. "It is the summary of the post-mortem, Watson. I asked Bradstreet to let me know of anything he thought of interest. He is quite pleased with himself about the angle of entry. It does lend weight to his left-handed theory. The curious part is the depth of the wound. It was about eight inches deep. That is quite a sizeable blade to wield inside a train carriage."

About ten minutes later we drew up outside a typical, red-brick, terraced house. I must admit that I struggled to imagine that so modest a home would house a woman with the kind of taste that would drive a man to treason. I voiced this to Holmes who nodded but added that many a person is driven by modest means to seek grander ones – his distrust of women coming to the fore once more.

We rang the bell and a maid answered. We sent in our cards and were summoned in. As we followed the maid, we had to negotiate our way past a host of sporting equipment. The house was clearly home to a cricket lover. Upon our arrival in the parlour, we found a lady of middle-age dressed in black. Upon the mantelpiece were various family pictures. The room, despite the clutter, felt empty.

"Mrs. Morris," said Holmes, bowing, "we are hoping to have some words with your daughter."

"The lady looked somewhat blank but smiled and nodded."

"My mother is deaf, sir."

We turned to see a small young woman in the hall. She indicated that we should follow her. We both bowed to the elder lady, who nodded her head in response, and took our leave. We were led into the modest dining room where the young lady took a seat and motioned to us to do the same. We introduced ourselves as we sat.

As we sat, she spoke. "I am Julia Morris. I can only assume that you are here in connection with my late fiancé, Stephen."

"Yes and no, Miss," replied Holmes. "We are here in connection with the death of Sir James Underwood."

A peculiar expression crossed the face of Miss Morris. She rapidly got to her feet, swayed, and would have fallen to the floor had I not caught her and lowered her back into her seat.

A few moments later, and thanks to the brandy I had located in the house, Miss Morris was composed once more.

"You tell me Sir James is dead?"

"Yes, Miss Morris," I replied.

"I wonder what will happen to Samuel."

"Why do you wonder that, Miss Morris?" asked Holmes.

"He maintains he only has his position due to Sir James. He fears his family link with Stephen will lead to his demotion or dismissal without Sir James's support."

"That's as may be," said Holmes. "Can you tell us anything that might have a bearing on either the death of your fiancé or the death of Sir James?"

"Only that the rumours about me are false."

Holmes and I said nothing but our faces clearly did.

"Oh, I know all too well what has been said. That somehow my expensive taste drove Stephen to treason. It is a mercy my poor mother cannot hear what is said. Our closest friends do not believe it and, if your skills are what people say, you will find it is not so."

"I am prepared to believe you, Miss Morris," said Holmes. "However, money appears to have been a motive. Can you think of any other reason your fiancé would need that kind of money?"

"None at all," she replied.

"How did you hear the news of Mr. Miles' death?"

"I knew about it early on. That was only proper for me as his fiancée. There was a mercifully short time when only Samuel, the police and myself knew. Then it all came out, and the bad opinion of me began to circulate."

Holmes stood. "If you have nothing to add, we will be on our way. Advise the local police if anything occurs to you and they will communicate it to me."

After leaving the house we made our way to busier streets in order to locate a cab.

"Holmes, should we not visit Lady Underwood? We cannot be too far from her residence."

"Not at present, Watson," he replied. "I have a theory I want to test. Let us make our way back to the police station. I believe the good inspector will be able to furnish us with some hot coffee and a little space to work."

Inspector Wreyford was indeed accommodating and permitted us access to a desk normally used by a constable who was on holiday. With nothing to do, I looked out of the window onto the hustle and bustle outside. I tried to divine the occupations of passers-by as I had so often seen Holmes do. Holmes sat down at the desk and proceeded to start flicking through his Bradshaw. Occasionally he paused to jot something down on a sheet of foolscap. After an hour he stopped.

"A train back to town leaves in twenty minutes. I believe Mrs. Hudson was planning to serve a steak and kidney pudding this evening. Not on a par with Simpson's but good nonetheless. I would hate for you to miss it, Watson."

I checked my watch and it was a little after five. We could easily be back at Baker Street in time for Mrs Hudson's cooking which was better than Holmes gave her credit for. I had to admit that it was an attractive prospect.

Inspector Wreyford was surprised at our departure but was reassured by Holmes that he was pursuing a line of enquiry. Upon our arrival at the station, we found the train ready and reached our compartment. Moments later, we were on our way.

For about an hour Holmes said little but continued to look at his Bradshaw and the notes he had taken in Portsmouth. He looked at his watch and appeared to be excited. As we pulled into Haslemere he turned to me.

"Sorry, dear fellow, but I need to get out here. You carry on and enjoy that excellent pudding. I shall find accommodation here and test a theory."

"Shall I not come too?"

"No, no. For you to stay will not help us. I will wire Mycroft from here. I will direct his answer to come to Baker Street. I will be with you as soon as possible in the morning. Good evening."

He jumped out onto the platform and headed for the bridge that would take him towards the station's exit. As the train moved on, I was at a loss what to think. I resolved it was probably best not to do so and to do as directed. Mrs. Hudson's pudding was awfully good.

I reached Baker Street by a little after eight. Mrs. Hudson was irritated, but not remotely surprised, when she learned that she had cooked for but one diner. I ate well and attempted to distract myself with the evening papers. By ten I was weary so I retired.

The next morning, I woke to noises from below. I looked at my watch, it was a little after half past ten. Hastily donning my dressing gown, I made my way downstairs.

"Ah, dear fellow," said Holmes. "I am only just in myself." I could see he was holding a piece of paper. I gestured towards it. "Mycroft?"

"Yes, indeed. It arrived about five minutes ago. I asked my

brother which of the many foreign agents currently circulating in London would be most in the market for our naval secrets. The answer, of course, was all of them but my brother singled out one whose recent movements made him of special interest."

"And he is?"

"His name is Walther Müeller. Ostensibly, an embassy official, but one of the top German agents. He is suspected to be the agent who obtained the plans for the Underwood gun, for which the late Stephen Miles is the current suspect."

"How is that connected to your actions yesterday?"

He smiled. "I did not stray far from the station, Watson. Whatever delights Haslemere may hold, I remain in ignorance of most of them. I spent an informative hour with the local stationmaster and, later, with the patrons of the hotel across from the station, where I was able to secure a room. I do believe I have been able to put it all together based on this Bradshaw, Miss Julia's mother, my conversation with the Haslemere stationmaster, the nine forty-eight train, and Stephen Miles's final late night. I need to dash off a telegram to our friend Wreyford, another to Bradstreet, and I think that will do.

Holmes disappeared to send his telegrams and returned to eat a hearty breakfast. It was refreshing to see him do so given how often he would leave a full plate. He then distracted himself with the newspapers. A few hours later he received an answer to his Portsmouth telegram. He smiled the smile that indicated he had been proved right, but said nothing. A short while later, Bradstreet appeared. He looked perplexed.

"I do not know where you get your ideas from, Mr. Holmes, but you were correct. The seven fifty-five train out of Waterloo to Portsmouth on the day of Sir James's death had the first three of its first-class compartments booked out to one man – a Walther Müeller."

A little over an hour later, the three of us were on a train bound for Portsmouth.

"I do not understand, Holmes, why a German agent would book train compartments in his own name."

"Officially, Watson, he is a diplomat, so why would he use a false name? It is not a crime to book multiple train compartments. The conclusion I have reached is that Sir James was a traitor."

Bradstreet and I were stunned. "Sir James..." I said.

"I am afraid so. The available facts fit that theory. It all started with why Sir James had his carriage window open on such a cold and windy day."

We clearly looked confused. Holmes continued. "Come now, gentlemen. It is clear as day. He was killed by someone outside of the carriage."

"Now, Mr. Holmes," said Bradstreet. "You have come out with some theories in your time but this is too far."

"Not at all, Bradstreet," said Holmes. "Let us go back a little. We heard from the guard on the train that sometimes Sir James booked three of the first-class compartments. However, not on the day he died.

"Now it all comes down to where the carriages are. Commonly, on that route, when trains leave London, the first-class carriages are near to the engine which pulls the train down to Portsmouth. On the return journey, as the carriages are not turned round, the first-class compartments are at the rear.

"So, if a southbound train and a northbound train met at any point the first-class carriages would very much line up - with a small margin for error.

"I therefore studied my Bradshaw, using Sir James's train as the reference point. I determined that at Guildford and Haslemere Sir James's train would rest at the platform alongside trains heading south.

I ruled Guildford out due to the short length of time the two trains would be there, the number of platforms, and the busyness of the station. That left Haslemere, where the station is quieter and the delay longer."

"I am not following, Holmes," I said.

"Think back to Guildford, Watson. I did not miss your brief interaction with that little girl. If you had opened your carriage window, and she had done the same, you could have had a conversation with minimal difficulty."

"So?"

"Imagine that you were Sir James and the girl was Müeller. Now what could you do with that time?"

"Exchange naval secrets?" said Bradstreet.

"Bravo," said Holmes.

"That is amazing," I said. "But they could not guarantee to line up."

"Hence the booking of three compartments. We were told this was, in Sir James's case, to give him privacy from eavesdroppers and that was, to an extent, true, but it was also to permit a way to deal with that margin of error. If the compartment Sir James was in did not line up, it was possible that better communication might be achieved from one of the others."

"So, that is why the agent did the same?"

"Yes. It seems clear to me that Sir James and Müeller had a long-standing arrangement to exchange secrets in this way. Sir James very likely gave away the secret of his own gun in this fashion."

"Hang on a moment, Mr. Holmes," said Bradstreet. "Sir James only booked one compartment on the day of his death."

"Indeed," said Holmes. "Our friend Müeller booked three. That tells us that they were both set up. The agent set out clearly with the understanding that some form of interview or exchange was to take place. Sir James had no such plan. Which is why he did not need three carriages on that occasion.

"It must have been quite a shock to him at Haslemere when he saw Müeller staring at him from the adjacent train. What must have gone through his mind? He probably suspected some kind of emergency. I suggest that he leant forward to lower the window in order that they could speak. At some point soon after, Müeller stood and stabbed Sir James through the open windows with his swordstick – hence the depth of wound and the angle. Sorry Bradstreet, no left-handed murderer."

Far from downcast, Bradstreet was clearly fascinated. "Surely, you did not get all this from a Bradshaw?"

Holmes smiled. "Certainly not. I spent yesterday afternoon and evening in Haslemere. The stationmaster there was a helpful fellow. He has been there a few years and, over that time, he has learned the names and faces of the regular passengers. He told me that the station is popular with railway enthusiasts who like to watch the comings and goings of the various trains from both the platforms and the overbridge at the station. The fact that trains are frequently held there facilitates this pastime."

"That seems a rather dull way to spend your time," I observed.

"Well, Watson, be that as it may, it proved useful. I was introduced to some of these gentlemen. Their knowledge of the route was impressive. They told me that for a period of a few weeks their group had been occasionally joined by a young, slightly dishevelled, man, in ill-fitting clothes who had asked them questions about train times and who had spent a great deal of time observing the first two platforms where trains were frequently held alongside each other at the required proximity."

"Samuel Miles," I cried.

"That was my initial thought too. I asked Wreyford to

investigate Miles's movements and it seems that, for at least some of the time, he cannot be accounted for. That said, my instincts are against it."

"Why so?"

"All in good time, Watson."

For the remainder of the journey, Holmes would not be drawn further on his theory. Much to my surprise, we got out a station early at Southsea. We climbed into a carriage and were on our way.

"Are we finally going to see Lady Underwood?" I asked.

"No, Watson," said Holmes. "We are going to see Miss Morris."

When we arrived at that modest home. I could see that a constable was at the door. We went straight inside, past the parlour where Mrs. Morris sat looking upset. We headed into the dining room where we found Inspector Wreyford and an evidently angry Julia Morris."

"I understand that all this is at your insistence, Mr. Holmes," she spat.

"My apologies, Miss," said Holmes. "I asked that you be encouraged to remain here so I could ask you one specific question."

"And what is that?"

"May I have the letter?"

Miss Morris's face paled. All hostility appeared to drain from her. Without a word, she left the room and went upstairs. Holmes took advantage of her brief absence to introduce Bradstreet to Wreyford. Moments later she was back with a thick envelope which she held out to Holmes.

As he took it, Wreyford spoke up. "I have read about your theatrics, Mr. Holmes. You know how to build tension."

Holmes smiled. "Thank you, Inspector. This, gentlemen, is Stephen Miles's suicide note."

"Samuel Miles said there wasn't one," I reminded him.

"Quite so," said Holmes. "You may recall that I thought this odd at the time. Why, on his last night alive, when he knew the police were coming for him, did Stephen Miles stay up late rather than make an escape. I hypothesised that he was writing a letter." He held up the envelope. "Rather a long one."

"I had been worried about him for some time," said Miss Morris. "He kept reassuring me that he was fine but I was not convinced. I called upon him every day to satisfy myself that he was well. The day before he died, he appeared even more agitated."

"That was because he had learned of the accusations against him and that the police would be coming for him," said Holmes.

"I realise that now," she said. "Because of his agitation I resolved to visit him earlier than usual the following day. I knew where he kept a spare key so I let myself in. Eventually I found him. As you have seen, I am not given to emotion so, after my initial shock, I noticed the envelope beneath his feet. I realised what it must be and took it. I knew he would be missed, and people would arrive, so I left the house in order to be able to study the letter."

I was unnerved at the cool nature of Miss Morris. Holmes seemed impressed.

"When I got back here, I went straight to my room and opened the envelope. What I read was painful."

"You learned that your fiancé was a traitor."

"Yes."

Bradstreet spoke up. "Both Sir James and Miles were traitors?"

"Yes," said Miss Morris, "and it pains me to say it. It is all in the letter. My Stephen, without letting on to me, was a gambler. I do not know how I failed to see it."

I frowned. "Some men are very adept at hiding their addictions."

"He had gotten himself into terrible debt and was worried how he was going to fund our wedding or explain himself to me. He decided to confide in Sir James whom he regarded as a father figure. Sir James, seeing his weakness, offered him a way out."

"To join him in selling secrets."

"It is shameful," she said. "Sir James offered to pay Stephen to help him and told him all about the arrangement with a man from the German Embassy. In his letter, Stephen explained that Sir James had asked him to retrieve the Underwood gun papers from where they were kept and to bring them to him."

"You see, gentlemen," said Holmes. "Rumours were already circulating around Sir James. I have that from my brother. Sir James clearly had Miles set up to be his scapegoat. That is why he got him to extract the papers when he could have done so himself. He did it in order to get the papers to sell, leaving Stephen Miles as the only person who could have obtained them on that occasion."

"You are correct," said Miss Morris. "Stephen had worked all this out but too late. He knew he was doomed. No one was going to believe him over Sir James. It was he who had taken the papers. Their journey would be possible to track. He was the only plausible suspect."

"So, you decided to avenge him?"

"My first thought was to speak to Samuel. I quickly reconsidered. He worshipped his brother and I had no wish to shatter his faith. Also, if you have met him, you will know that he is headstrong. There is no way he could have helped without potentially giving the whole plan away. I had to act alone.

"All the details about the way Sir James exchanged messages with Müeller were in the letter. It immediately occurred to me to get this German to do the work for me. There was no way I could get to Sir James and I needed to remain free of suspicion in order to look after my mother."

"So," said Holmes, "you decided to test the information in your fiancé's letter. You dressed in your late father's clothes and made several trips to Haslemere station to see how the northbound and southbound trains lined up. You even consulted with regulars at the station."

"I feared, as a woman, I would stand out more if any enquiries were made subsequently."

"Clever, indeed," said Holmes. "May I suggest that, using the information from your fiancé, you wired Müeller, pretending to be Sir James and, using whatever coded language was necessary to make the pretence convincing, stated that you planned to turn yourself in out of remorse at the death Stephen Miles."

"You have it precisely," said Miss Morris. "My understanding of this Müeller was that he would try to prevent this. In the telegram, I gave Müeller the time of travel with the pretext that telling Müeller would give him sufficient time to flee the country. I felt confident that Müeller would rather eliminate the threat than be exposed."

"And you supposed that he would attempt this at Haslemere rather than after Sir James arrived in London."

"Well, yes," said Miss Morris. "It seemed more probable to me that he would try to intercept Sir James somewhere quiet, where they had conversed before, rather than try to do so in town where it would be far harder to avoid witnesses."

"And if Müeller had not acted?"

"There was a risk of course, but Stephen's letter made me think it unlikely that Müeller would sit passively by and be exposed as the agent he was. As a last resort, I always knew I could send Stephen's letter to the authorities. Sir James's death or imprisonment would have been enough for me."

"Well," said Holmes. "You read all the men very well. Your steel and intellect impress me even if I find the results appalling."

A short while later we were all standing outside the house. Miss Morris had been taken away by Wreyford. Bradstreet, Holmes, and I remained.

"How did you know she had impersonated a man?" I asked.

"When we first entered her home, her mother was clearly in mourning. Miss Morris was, however, not wearing black. Convention dictates a year of official mourning in such cases so it seemed clear to me that Mrs. Morris, rather like Her Majesty, has prolonged her mourning. The strength of her loss was partly indicated by the fact that the late Mr. Morris' cricket equipment was still in the hallway. Mrs. Morris cannot face disposing of it. Keeping it all where it was left allows her to feel he is still alive. If she is of that frame of mind, it seemed very likely that she would also have retained his clothes.

"Miss Morris could not go out and buy gentlemen's clothing without attracting some attention so she made use of what was at her disposal. This is why the railway enthusiasts at Haslemere described the inquisitive young man as dishevelled. It was because the clothes were not an especially good fit."

Bradstreet was wearing a quizzical look. "Mr. Holmes. What do you imagine was said when the two men met?"

"That is hard to say. Müeller may not have said anything at all. He might have simply acted as soon as Sir James opened the carriage window. From Mueller's perspective, Sir James was a threat to his liberty."

"I wonder where Müeller is now?" I said.

"I think we can assume he is in Germany," said Holmes. "It is suggested by the direction each man took. In the past, as soon as Müeller obtained secrets from Sir James, he would carry on to Portsmouth and board the first available passage to the Continent. I shall encourage my brother to look into that in order to determine what other secrets Müeller may have been responsible for stealing.

"Mycroft can also see to it that he receives a suitable welcome when he dares to set foot on our shores again."

He looked at his watch. "I think it is high time we exchanged this sea air for the air of the capital. I believe Mrs. Hudson has lamb chops on the menu this evening and I would hate to disappoint her a second time."

The Adventure of the Drury Lane Pawnbroker

(Mid-1897)

HROUGH my long acquaintance with Sherlock Holmes, I have met and observed the actions of many Scotland Yard detectives. Holmes once described himself as the last and highest court of appeal when the professionals found themselves at a loss. Going by the number of occasions he was called upon; it was clear the professionals often found themselves in that unenviable state.

On this particular August evening, young Stanley Hopkins found himself upon the settee seeking Holmes's counsel. Of the many Scotland Yarders, Hopkins was the one who resented the need for Holmes's help the least. His willingness to admit to falling short, and his equal willingness to put justice before his own reputation, had endeared him to my friend who exerted himself more for Hopkins than he would for any of his colleagues.

"I do not know what to make of it, sir. I really do not," said Hopkins as he sipped the brandy he had been given upon his arrival.

"Calm yourself, Hopkins," said Holmes. "I am sure that, if you lay it all before us, we will be able to steer you in the right direction."

He rose and disappeared into his room forcing the detective to turn in his seat and shout after him.

"I certainly hope so, sir," said Hopkins, trying to make himself heard over the sound of drawers being rapidly opened and closed. "It all began about three weeks ago. I received word that a pawnbroker's shop close to Oxford Street had been broken into overnight and ransacked. The owner, one Mr. Hooper, reported that several items, with a total value of some twenty-five shillings, had been taken. The most surprising aspect was that items of greater value were left untouched. A few days later, a report came in of a further break-in at a pawnbroker off the Strand. In both cases, a similar pattern."

"This is all sounding rather mundane, my dear Hopkins," said Holmes as he returned, clad in his familiar dressing gown, and reached for some tobacco. "Pawnbrokers are a necessary evil to many people in the metropolis and they are not amongst society's most revered. They are regularly targeted by those forced to use them. That said, your current state of agitation suggests that something far from mundane has occurred."

"Correct, sir," said Hopkins. "Two nights ago, events took a darker turn. You no doubt are aware of a pawnbroker just off Drury Lane?"

"Yes," said Holmes. "The proprietor is one Mr. Lawrence."

"Was, Mr. Holmes. He was found murdered."

"Continue," said Holmes as he lit his pipe.

Hopkins took another sip from his glass before flicking to a page of his notebook. "The body was found the next day by the assistant, one Richard Barrett. His suspicions were aroused when he could not access the shop. Mr. Lawrence always opened promptly so to find the shop locked up was unusual. Barrett looked through the window and everything appeared normal. Items for sale in the front window were as they should be. Barrett went round to the rear of the shop, via its yard, and found the back door forced. He entered and found his employer dead and the body surrounded by all manner of items that had been pledged."

"What was the cause of death?" asked Holmes.

"Mr. Lawrence had been struck hard on the head with a cricket bat which we understand to have been one of the items from the shop," said Hopkins.

"Interesting," said Holmes. "That suggests a lack of premeditation. Was anything taken?"

"According to Barrett," replied Hopkins, "everything in the ledgers was accounted for in the shop although a lot of it was damaged."

"Was there any evidence that the intruder entered the front part of the shop?"

"No, Mr. Holmes," said Hopkins.

"Suggestive," replied Holmes.

Hopkins' confused expression was one I no doubt shared. Holmes did not elaborate.

"Any thoughts, sir?" asked Hopkins, his eyes wide with expectation.

Holmes removed his pipe from his mouth, closed his eyes, and gently tapped his forehead with the stem. "Not yet, Hopkins, not yet. I will need to conduct some enquiries of my own." He opened his eyes and pointed at the detective with his pipe. "To facilitate matters, please contact the affected pawnbrokers and ask them to expect a visit from me and to answer my questions frankly."

Hopkins knew the interview was over. He stood and drained his glass. "Very well, sir."

As he walked to the door Holmes spoke again. "Fear not, Hopkins. I feel confident we will get to the bottom of this. Be so good as to give me details of the affected establishments. I would also advise you to do your best to notify all pawnbrokers as yet unaffected to be on their guard."

Hopkins paled. "There are hundreds of pawnbrokers in London, Mr. Holmes."

"I appreciate that, Hopkins," said Holmes, as he resumed smoking, "but I fear this will not be the last incident. Start with those closest to the already affected and work outwards."

Hopkins scribbled down in his notebook the addresses Holmes had asked for before tearing out the page and handing it over. Holmes briefly glanced at it before placing it in his top pocket.

A few moments later we heard the outer door close and, from the window, I observed Hopkins hail a cab. "Poor fellow," I said. "He looks worried."

"As he should," replied Holmes. "He has quite the task on his hands if he is to prevent further loss of life or property. However, as we cannot reliably predict the future, we must focus our attention on the recent past. It is too late to act now. We shall start promptly in the morning."

The next morning, following breakfast, we engaged a cab. Our destination was not, as I expected, the scene of the murder. I queried this.

"Thanks to Hopkins, I already know a great deal about what we will find in Drury Lane," said Holmes. "It is the others about which we know comparatively little. We are going to start with the pawnbroker off Oxford Street."

Traffic was busy so it was some forty minutes before we reached the scene of the first incident. From the outside nothing seemed untoward. The shop front consisted of a black central door flanked by large windows in which items for sale were on display. Neither the door nor windows showed any evidence of damage or tampering. Holmes opened the door causing the bell to ring.

Upon entering, we could see that the shop was devoid of customers. I closed the door just as, in response to the bell, a young man in shirtsleeves and waistcoat emerged from the back room rubbing his hands with, what I believed to be, a sense of expectation. He bid us an exuberant good morning. We asked for Mr. Hooper and were informed that he was not serving at present. Holmes explained that we were not customers and gave some limited details as to why we were there. The young man, unsure of how to proceed, headed into the back. There followed some muffled discussion. The young assistant emerged carrying his jacket and promptly left the shop, turning the sign on the door from open to closed as he did so. An older man, whom we took to be Hooper, appeared, and beckoned us over to the end of his counter furthest from the door. He was dressed similarly to his assistant but there was something of the rat about him, and he did not so much walk as scurry. He was cautious from the first and it was clear that he had sent his assistant out on purpose.

"You won't tell anyone I spoke to you, Mr. Holmes?" he said, looking around as if he might be overheard even in an empty shop. "My customers appreciate my discretion. I'll be finished if word gets out that I spoke to the police."

Holmes smiled indulgently. "I make no promises, Mr. Hooper. Anything you tell me that is pertinent will have to be shared with the authorities. Anything otherwise will not be breathed to another soul."

"I guess I'll have to make do with that," replied Hooper, with a shrug. He lent forward in a conspiratorial manner that I found unsettling. "What do you want to know?"

Holmes also leant forward. "Any details you have about recent events and anything unusual that happened in the lead up to the break-in."

Hooper paused for a moment before speaking. "The man

forced his way in through the back. Made a right mess of my door. Several items were taken, Mr. Holmes."

"Yes," said Holmes. "I believe you have lost a set of six glasses, a modest wooden box, and a small metal container. All from the window and they were likely in poor condition."

Hooper looked astonished. "It's true, sir. Glasses, as you say; a box of chessmen; and a cheap vesta case. How did you know?"

Holmes smiled. "Mr. Hooper. Your shop is in a position where it receives a good deal of sunlight. You cover your shelves in red velvet. Over many years, the material has been bleached of colour by the sun except where items stood. The level of discolouration where the objects had stood was much less thus demonstrating that they had been there for some time. The shapes indicated the type of object. The fact that they had been there so long suggested they were unattractive to buyers. As window items, they were not likely to be expensive, so their condition was likely against them."

Hooper was impressed. "Items were taken from the back too. I lost a modest watch and a strange vase."

"Strange how?" I asked.

"Well, sir," he replied, "I'd not seen anything like it before. It had been brought in almost exactly a year earlier by an old gentleman. It was a peculiar transaction which is why it stuck in my mind."

"How did the transaction proceed?" asked Holmes.

"Well. He was quite imposing despite being nervous and over sixty. He was well dressed in a dark grey suit. I especially remember his watch because he toyed with the chain throughout. I hoped he wanted to pawn it. He struck me as some kind of banker. He asked for the proprietor and I confirmed I was he."

"And then?" asked Holmes.

"I directed him to this very box so we could have a little privacy. The old gent produced the vase from a bag he had been carrying. It was of a modest size, six or seven inches tall, and, despite being an unusual style, it did not strike me as desirable. I offered nine shillings for it."

"And how was your offer received?" asked Holmes.

"Not well, Mr. Holmes, not well," replied Hooper as he scratched his nose in a way that managed to make him seem even more rat-like. "It was all he could do to keep his voice down. He informed me that it was worth at least twenty. I declined to pay that much. He said he would settle for eleven. As this was not too much over my initial valuation, and I could charge more interest on the debt, I agreed to pay. I wrote out and gave him his ticket and money. He left and I never saw him again."

"Go on," said Holmes.

Hooper stroked his chin. "The day before the break-in, this strange fellow comes in. He was young, I'd say around twenty-five, has an old suit on, glasses, and a moustache. He presents a ticket to my assistant and announces he wants to redeem it. My assistant looks it up in the ledger and comes to me because he has orders to do so for anything pledged for more than ten shillings. The ticket was for the vase.

"I have a good memory for faces and I saw at once that this was not the man who had made the pledge a year ago. I asked him to come to one of the boxes for privacy and I told him as much. He came out with a story that he had been given the ticket in lieu of a debt. Now I've been caught out before with people who have stolen tickets so I said he would need to come back with the old gent to vouch for him."

"How did this man react?" asked Holmes.

"He was immediately agitated, sir. He blurted out that it was not possible as the man was dead. Funny thing was that he seemed to regret saying it as soon as it came out of his mouth. I said to bring someone in authority who could vouch for that and perhaps I'd listen.

I also warned him not to take too much time about it as the vase was going to go to auction in a few days."

"What did the man do?" asked Holmes.

"He placed the ticket into an envelope, that he had taken out of his pocket, and walked out, telling me that I would regret my treatment of him. I think the only reason he did not get violent was due to the presence of my assistant and other customers in the shop."

"And you were broken into soon after?" I asked.

"Yes."

"Can you tell me anything about this envelope?" asked Holmes.

The question seemed to baffle Hooper. "The envelope? Well, I couldn't tell you if there was an address on it but it seemed to contain quite a few pieces of paper and some notes."

"Notes?" I asked.

"Money, guvnor," said Hooper. "This fellow was not short of a bob or two. It seemed to me that he could have walked into Regent Street and had his pick of vases."

"Thank you, Mr. Hooper," said Holmes. "You have referred to your memory more than once. Do you think it possible that you could produce a drawing of this vase?"

"I'm no artist," said Hooper.

"If you would be so good," said Holmes.

Hooper retrieved a piece of foolscap and a pencil from under the counter and set to work. He scribbled away for about five minutes. When I saw the result, I barely suppressed a smile. Hooper really was no artist.

Holmes hid any disappointment well. "Thank you, Mr. Hooper," he said as he folded the paper and placed it into his inside pocket. He turned to leave.

"Mind what I said about discretion," said Hooper, tapping his nose.

"Rest assured," said Holmes, "that your reputation will remain intact."

"Would you care to explain all that?" I asked as we strolled down Oxford Street and onto Charing Cross Road.

"Watson. I am forced to conclude that your experience with pawnbrokers is still limited to those marks on your late brother's watch."

I winced. That had been a hurtful moment in our association where I had learned the painful lesson to not doubt Holmes's deductions.

Holmes turned and saw my face. His fell a little. "Apologies, Watson, tactless of me. If you pledge an item at a London pawnbroker you have a year to redeem that pledge. It can vary a little from place to place but it is never less than a year. Each day that goes by you accrue interest on the pledge which you must also pay to secure your property. Therefore, people tend to redeem their pledges in the shortest possible time."

"I still do not see."

"Very likely not," he said, indulgently. "If that period elapses the pawnbroker becomes the owner of the item and can sell it but only if it is worth ten shillings or less. If it is worth more, the item does not become his property but must go to public auction. There the pawnbroker hopes to redeem the amount paid, plus interest."

"So, what conclusions are you drawing?"

"None yet. Just file those facts away for the moment. Right now, it is the envelope that interests me."

"Why?"

"Two reasons. Firstly, that our unknown gentleman placed the pawn ticket into it which suggests a need to protect it. Secondly, for someone in a shabby suit, he clearly had the means to dress much better."

Our next visit was to the pawnbroker off the Strand. There we heard a similar story. The proprietor said that he had received a visit, this time from an elderly man, who had presented a ticket which matched up to a porcelain dish that had been valued at fifteen shillings. Again, the proprietor had sought proof of the man's right to redeem. In response, the gentleman had offered a considerable sum to secure the piece. The owner of the shop had sent him on his way but admitted to telling the man that the dish was due to go to auction in a few days.

"Did you notice whether the gentlemen possessed an envelope?" Holmes had asked.

"Yes, sir," replied the proprietor. "He took the ticket out of it when we spoke and placed it back as he left."

"Can you tell me anything else about it?"

"No, sir. I didn't pay it much attention."

To this, Holmes had tutted and left the shop. I knew better than to ask. Our next destination was the scene of the murder. As it was only a modest distance away, Holmes suggested again that we walk. Our chosen route took us past the Lyceum Theatre and I stole a glance at the third pillar from the left. If Holmes noticed my reverie, he remained tactfully silent.

The pawnbroker on Drury Lane had featured in one of Holmes's other cases, which I may put before the public in future. Due to its location, it was popular with struggling members of the acting profession and contained a good many theatrical items from costumes to stage weapons. As with many pawnbrokers, access to it was via a side street so the financially embarrassed could save face by not being seen to enter it. The side street for this shop was particularly seedy.

The constable at the entrance saluted Holmes and directed us round the back. Another constable admitted us to the shop. Aside from the removal of the body, we were assured all was untouched. Holmes was unimpressed.

"The usual heard of buffalo have been through here, Watson. Hopkins surprises me. I really thought I had him better trained."

"Do not be too hard on him," I suggested.

"No doubt you are right," Holmes turned back to the constable. "What is your name, constable?"

"Peel, sir," came the response.

Holmes struggled to suppress a smile. "Is that so?"

The constable frowned. "Yes, sir. I get teased a lot. I'd appreciate it, sir, if you didn't join in."

"Of course. Where is the assistant?"

"He was banned from entering in case he moved anything."

"In case *he* moved anything," said Holmes under his breath.

"He has lodgings two streets away." Peel scribbled the address down and handed it to Holmes.

"Exactly where was the body?"

"At the foot of the stairs. Mr. Lawrence lived above the shop. I'm guessing his killer didn't know that."

Holmes's face showed surprise. "How do you draw that conclusion, Constable Peel?"

The constable straightened up. Clearly, he was pleased to have secured Holmes's interest. "I know it's not my place, sir, but when the body was removed there were items under it. I took it that his killer was searching for something and the noise roused Mr. Lawrence. They fought and the body was left on top of the items. I thought that if the killer knew Mr. Lawrence lived upstairs he would have made less noise or lured him down to dispose of him before turning the place over. If he had done that, we would not likely have found any items under his body."

"You impress me, Peel," said Holmes. "I cannot fault your logic. I will commend you to Inspector Hopkins."

Peel's chest swelled with pride. "Thank you, Mr. Holmes. The rooms upstairs were also gone over before our killer left. Cupboards and drawers turned out."

Holmes motioned for me to wait and went upstairs. He was up there for around ten minutes before returning. His expression suggested frustration. He walked through to the front of the shop. "Yes. It is clear that this change in pattern was caused by the confrontation. Items of all values were taken the previous two times and always something from the front of the shop. Here we are given to understand that the killer fled empty-handed. That does not seem credible."

"What is the next step?" I asked

"We must talk to young Mr. Barrett."

As it was not far, we walked. Before long, we found ourselves at the address. Holmes knocked. After a few moments, the door was opened by a stern lady. Tall, thin, and dressed in a dark blue dress, she cut quite the imposing figure – somewhat akin to a strict governess.

"May I help you, gentlemen?" she said, looking down her nose and over her glasses.

"Good afternoon, madam," said Holmes. "We are hoping to speak with Mr. Barrett."

The lady looked at Holmes with suspicion. "He is in a terrible state, sir. He does not want to speak to anyone," she moved to shut the door.

Quick as a flash, Holmes thrust his cane into the gap. "Here, what is this?" said the lady.

"I beg your pardon, madam, but please give him my card."

The lady snatched the card that Holmes held out. With a dexterity I would not have given her credit for, she kicked the end of Holmes's cane and managed to shut the door.

"Deft, isn't she?" said Holmes with amusement that rapidly faded as he examined the bottom of his cane.

He did not have long to lament the damage. The door opened. "He will see you but do not upset him. First floor, door on the left."

We ascended the stairs as the lady closed the door behind us. Mr. Barrett's door was already ajar and, as we neared, a shaky voice beckoned us to enter.

Mr. Barrett was lodging in a single room. In one corner was his bed and that was where he had chosen to sit, legs drawn up and resting his head on his knees. He cut a slight figure and was quite clearly wearing second-hand clothes indicated by the less-than-ideal fit. He could not have been much more than nineteen and had light brown hair. Despite being closed, his thin curtains did little to reduce the flow of light into the room. As a result, his agitation was easy to see. "Good afternoon, Mr. Holmes," he said, "I had no idea you were involved in this."

"There is no reason why you should," replied Holmes. "Nevertheless, it is important you speak frankly to me now."

"Very good, sir," replied Barrett.

"I am convinced that someone came to your employer's shop in the last few days to redeem a ticket, and Mr. Lawrence had a confrontation with him. Is that correct?"

Barrett seemed startled. "Yes, Mr. Holmes. How did you guess?"

I waited for Holmes's usual response but it did not come. "Tell me about it," he said.

Barrett took a drink of water from a glass at the side of his bed. "Well, sir, it was the day before. This elderly, unsteady, gentleman wanders in, shows me a ticket, and asks for Mr. Lawrence. I pointed him towards a box and said I would send Mr. Lawrence to him."

"Good. What happened next?"

"Well, the boxes are designed to provide privacy, Mr. Holmes. They do a good job of muffling conversation. But the elderly man clearly lost his temper. He shouted, 'What do you mean that this is not a real ticket?'

"I could not hear what Mr. Lawrence said as he kept his voice down. I think the elderly gentleman realised that he was drawing attention to himself and lowered his voice also."

"What happened next?" asked Holmes.

"I could not hear clearly but the conversation appeared to continue. A minute or so later the elderly man backed out of the box and said, 'No, I will keep it. You will regret this.'"

"What else did you hear or see?"

"As the old man came out, I saw him thrust the ticket into an envelope. He was red with rage and clearly not quite in control of himself. He went to put the envelope into his pocket and missed so it fell to the floor. He did not seem to notice as he was still berating Mr. Lawrence. Trying to be helpful, I made my way round the counter to retrieve it for him. He heard me approach and realised what he had done. As I bent to pick up the envelope, he quickly placed his foot on it to stop me. 'Never you mind that, lad,' he said, 'I can deal with that.' He swiftly bent down and retrieved the envelope from under his foot and placed it into his jacket pocket.

"He directed some further angry comments to Mr. Lawrence before storming out."

Holmes fixed Barrett with a hard stare. "This is important, Mr. Barrett. Can you tell me anything about the envelope or its contents?"

Barrett thought hard. "Not much, Mr. Holmes. I know it contained a ticket because I had seen him place one into it. His foot obscured most of the address."

"So, there was an address?" said Holmes, his excitement evident.

"Well, there was something written on the front of it," said Barrett. "What else would it be? All I could make out was that the address seemed to be only three lines. The first line was mostly obscured. All I could see was an M. The second began with an A, an M, and an E. The third began with a TO and a B."

"Wonderful," said Holmes. "Your observation does you credit. What happened after this elderly man left?"

"Mr. Lawrence emerged from the box chuckling to himself. I naturally asked him what the fuss was about."

"'Silly old gent came in with a ticket not from here demanding an item we do not have,'" he said.

"'It looked like a ticket from here,'" I said.

"'You mind your business,' said Mr. Lawrence. He disappeared into the rear of the shop and I heard him head upstairs. About fifteen minutes later he returned and we carried on as normal."

"You are convinced of the ticket being from Mr. Lawrence's shop?" asked Holmes.

"I'm almost certain," said Barrett. "It had Mr. Lawrence's name on it. I have no idea why someone would fake a pawn ticket."

"Thank you for your time," said Holmes. "I will be in contact if I have further questions."

Barrett nodded and we turned to leave. As we did so we heard someone going down the stairs. We stepped out onto the landing and could see Barrett's formidable landlady waiting for us at the foot of the stairs."

"I hope you gentlemen got what you needed," she said as she opened the front door.

"We did indeed, madam," said Holmes. The door was swiftly shut the moment we were both over the threshold.

"She was listening," I said.

"I know," said Holmes. "She is an unfit woman. I could hear her heavy breathing for some time. It hardly matters."

As usual, Holmes had gleaned information from his investigations that had passed me by. I followed him back to Drury Lane where he left a message with Constable Peel asking for Hopkins to call at Baker Street that evening. Holmes then hailed a cab and asked to be taken to Charing Cross Station. This seemed an odd destination. "Why Charing Cross?" I asked.

"It is a perfectly logical destination if my supposition is correct," said Holmes.

Our cab soon dropped us at the gate of the noted terminus. Holmes and I alighted. "Come, Watson," he said.

"Where are we going, Holmes?" I shouted after him.

"The American Exchange," came the reply.

The building at number sixteen Strand was one I remembered

well as it had briefly featured in our first adventure together. This was destined to be the first occasion I would pay it a visit.

There was a gathering of people outside the small building but Holmes managed to force his way to the front. I was not so fortunate and had to wait for a couple of people to leave before I could join him.

At the somewhat cramped counter I found Holmes talking to a stern looking, balding, middle-aged gentleman. He reminded me of a cross between a bank manager and a bookmaker.

As I approached, I overheard the man say, "I cannot possibly be expected to remember that, sir."

"What's going on, Holmes?" I asked.

Holmes turned to me with a look of frustration. "This gentleman does not believe he can help me with my query. Do you Mr...?"

"Robson," came the sharp response.

"Mr. Robson," said Holmes. "I appreciate that you are especially busy today, and I am asking you to think back, but it is very important."

Even I could see that Mr. Robson was getting frustrated. "Sir, you are asking me to think back several weeks. Do you have any idea how many people come through here in a day let alone a week?"

Holmes's face showed that he had a good idea. His expression softened. "Mr. Robson. We are talking about any time between three and six weeks ago. Someone came here to collect a letter. A letter that had likely been here some considerable time and which you may have been paid handsomely to look after." As he finished the sentence, Holmes slid a few shillings across the counter towards Robson.

Robson's face brightened. "Mr. Holmes, that does recall something to my mind. Bear with me a moment." He swept up the coins before turning his attention to the drawers and pigeon holes behind his counter.

While we waited, I decided to ask. "What led you here?"

Holmes smiled. "It was a bit of a long shot, Watson. Envelopes have one main purpose which is to contain letters. When we spoke to young Barrett, he told us of a possible address being written on the envelope seen in the hands of the mysterious visitor to the late Mr. Lawrence's shop. You will recall that he made no mention of a stamp. A letter without a stamp seldom travels far. Putting together what Barrett told us of what he saw, I arrived at the possibility that what was written on the envelope's second and third lines was 'American Exchange. To be called for.'"

"That seems a leap," I said.

"But a leap worth making given that all the activity has taken place in a modest radius from this very spot. It means that the recipient would have had to come here to get it and that the person who left it did so in person or got someone to bring it for them."

We turned back towards the counter and could see Mr. Robson had produced a ledger.

"Do you have good news, Mr. Robson?" asked Holmes.

"Yes. I believe I do," said Robson as he tapped a page in the ledger. "It was the mention of the payment. We do not normally hold letters for so long." He ran his fingers down the page. "Here it is. A letter was left with us for collection. We were paid ten pounds to look after it and we were warned it could be many months."

"What can you tell me about the person who left it?" asked Holmes.

"Nothing, I'm afraid," replied Robson. "I was not here on the day. All I was told later was that it was an elderly gentleman."

"Were you here for the collection?"

"Yes, I was. It was a little over three weeks ago. A young gentleman came and said that his name was Simmonds and we were holding a letter for him."

"Good," said Holmes. "Continue please."

"Initially I could not find it and I asked him when he believed it had been left here. He got quite impatient and said it would be anything up to a year."

"What did you do?"

"I resumed looking and eventually found it right at the back of a drawer. That was hardly surprising given how long we had had it."

Holmes was excited. "How did Mr. Simmonds react?"

"He was very happy, sir," replied Robson. "He grinned from ear to ear and slapped some coins on the counter before leaving without a further word."

"Did he not open the letter?"

"No, sir. It went straight into his pocket."

"One further question," said Holmes, "as I believe you are omitting an important detail."

"I am?" said Robson, nervously.

"Yes," said Holmes. "How did this man satisfy you that he was Mr. Simmonds?"

Robson smiled. "Oh, that was easy sir. I did ask him of course. Before passing me the coins, he produced a ticket made out in that name for a ship that he said had brought him from South America to Southampton."

"Did he offer any other details about himself? Where he was staying or anything similar?"

"I am afraid not, sir," said Robson.

A few moments later, we were several paces away being buffeted by our fellow Londoners going about their business. We were the recipients of some tutting as Holmes was effectively blocking access to the Exchange as he paused to light a cigarette. I gently tugged at his sleeve and he followed me away from the building. I steered him into nearby Villiers

Street where there were slightly fewer people and it was easier to talk.

"What do you propose to do now, Holmes?" I asked. "It sounds like that lead isn't going anywhere."

"On the contrary," he said. "I have high hopes. Back to Baker Street. I need to consult my index. We also have an appointment this evening with Hopkins."

Holmes spent the rest of the afternoon and early evening smoking and going through his files. Every so often there would be the snort of disappointment or the cry of success. He began to build a small pile of newspaper clippings which I presumed related to his line of enquiry. I knew better than to question him during this process. I tried to occupy myself with that day's newspapers but found I kept falling asleep. It had escaped me how much ground we had covered that day.

At just after seven o'clock, I was woken by the bell and Mrs. Hudson showed up Hopkins. He wore the look of a man whose day had been mixed.

"I hope you have some good news, Mr. Holmes, as I have very little."

"I may well do," replied Holmes, as I poured Hopkins a brandy, "but let us have your less welcome news first."

Hopkins sat down and sipped from the glass. "As per your instructions, I began getting word out to other pawnbrokers in the vicinity of Drury Lane. At an establishment off Tottenham Court Road, one of my constables learned that an elderly gentleman had recently redeemed a small oil painting pledged a year ago. The proprietor remembered because he was so happy it had been claimed. He had no desire to go to auction."

"So, it was valued at over ten shillings?"

"Twenty," said Hopkins.

"Go on."

"I personally visited an establishment towards Piccadilly. There

I heard a different tale. Mr. Gibson, the owner, said that an elderly gentleman had come in with a ticket that matched up to a necklace. Mr. Gibson was forced to tell the gentleman that it had already been dispatched to an auction house in Chiswick. Mr. Gibson was quite nervous about my questions."

"Why was that?" I asked.

"When I pressed him, he was forced to admit that he had sent the necklace before the year was up."

"He had sent it early?" queried Holmes.

"Yes, sir," said Hopkins, "It was only a few days early and he thought it would do no harm. He considered it unlikely it would be redeemed and the auction was to be held after the year was up."

"What was the reaction of the elderly man?"

"The man asked for the address and was given it by Gibson."

Holmes frowned. "Was an attempt made to break into the auction house?"

"Yes. The next night. But it was unsuccessful. They had suffered attempts before so their precautions frustrated the would-be intruder."

Holmes clapped his hands together. "Excellent."

Hopkins and I exchanged glances. "Why so, sir?"

"Because, Hopkins, we now have our best chance to meet our mysterious gentleman. When is the auction to be held?"

Hopkins checked his notes. "Two o'clock tomorrow, Mr. Holmes."

Holmes looked content. "That gives us plenty of time. I feel confident we can be ready by then. Watson, please offer the inspector another drink and see if Mrs. Hudson can rustle up some supper." He held up the newspaper clippings he had set to one side. "I need to make a few calls. Watson, be sure to get a good night's sleep. I cannot have you nodding off tomorrow."

With that remark he was up and out.

Half an hour later Hopkins and I were eating some cold meats that Mrs. Hudson had been able to present at short-notice. We did not really speak as the only questions we had we knew the other could not answer. At nine o'clock Hopkins made his excuses. "I will see you at the auction, Doctor."

I sat in the window and smoked a few cigarettes. Baker Street looked peaceful with only a few intoxicated gentlemen to entertain me. Once or twice, I saw someone I briefly mistook for Holmes. When the clock struck eleven with no sign of him, I headed to bed.

I woke to light streaming under the curtains. I turned to pick up my watch. It was a little after ten. Under where it had been was a piece of paper. It was from Holmes and asked me to be at the Chiswick auctioneers by one-thirty. I headed downstairs for breakfast before getting changed.

Mrs. Hudson informed me that she believed Holmes had returned after midnight going by the noises she had heard around that hour. She had seen him briefly in the morning, when he had ordered coffee, and had been instructed to wake me if I had not appeared by eleven. Holmes had gone out only just before I had woken. Clearly, my presence was pivotal to his plans.

A little after midday, I hailed a cab and headed west. I arrived in Chiswick early and decided to get a little exercise before appearing at the auction house.

Just before one-thirty, I arrived. I could see Holmes standing outside in conversation with an unknown man. The man shook Holmes's hand and went inside as I approached.

"Good afternoon, Watson," said Holmes.

"Afternoon, Holmes."

"The gentleman you just saw is the auctioneer for the sale. I have explained why we are here. You are going to take part in the auction."

"I am?"

"Yes. For the next hour or so your name is Mr. Smith. When the necklace comes up, it is lot twenty-four, you will bid for it. Bid as high as you need to in order to secure it but go in sensible increments so it looks natural."

"I do not have much money, Holmes," I said, before yawning.

"Tired, Watson?"

"Yes. I was awake most of the night trying to make sense of it all."

"And did you?"

"Not really."

Holmes smiled indulgently. "You do not need any money. The auctioneer has been fully informed of the situation. When you win the lot, take possession and leave. If anyone attempts to engage you or hinder you, put them off and leave by this door." Holmes turned and looked up the street. "That alley there is quiet. Head up it. Our man will attempt to take the necklace from you by force. Rest assured we will be waiting." With that remark, he walked off.

I had many questions but no opportunity to ask them. A look at my watch revealed that two o'clock was not all that far away. I headed inside to find a suitable seat.

The auction room was busy but not crowded. The floor was populated by roughly a dozen rows of rather uncomfortable looking wooden seats. About half of these were already populated by members of the public. Towards the front row I spied a corpulent man who was taking up more than one seat. He was engaged in a deep study of the auction catalogue. I wondered if he were my opponent but recalled that I was looking for a younger man and one who was fit enough to commit murder. A few rows behind him a young lady was endeavouring to exert some control over her two small children.

I realised that studying my fellow bidders might draw attention so I took an aisle seat a few rows from the front and, like my competitors, flicked through the catalogue. Most of the items were valued modestly and it seemed clear to me that most, if not all, of the items had come from pawnbrokers. Supporting this notion was the fact that a large number had reserves. I had done some reading following Holmes's explanations and understood that pawnbrokers always set a reserve to minimise the risk of their auction lots going for less than the original pledge.

It was a weary time waiting to get to lot twenty-four. I was somewhat bored and, following the previous late night, started to yawn. Fortunately, I was woken in time by a kick to the back of my chair. I spun round angrily to see a small boy. He laughed, jumped down from his seat, and ran off before I could clip him round the ear.

I turned my attention back to hear the auctioneer describe the lot. It seemed clear that it was worth a bit of money. The bids started to climb. I began to join in. After about five minutes I found most of the bidders had fallen silent. I looked over in the direction of the only voice other than my own. It was a young man of around twenty-five to thirty. He was beginning to sweat. I would have too if I had thought for one moment that I would need to part with the sum we were now at.

"The bid now stands at five hundred pounds," said the auctioneer, whose face showed how unbelievable he found the situation. Many people in the room were staring either at me or my opponent. "Going once, going twice, sold to Mr. Smith."

The hammer came down to the sound of gasps from the other attendees. I rose to claim the necklace. As I made my way forward, I could see my opponent had remained in his seat looking crestfallen. I went to one of the staff and announced myself. After a short delay, I was handed a small box in a bag and I turned to leave.

I was half-way to the door when I heard someone shout my new name. I ignored it, picked up my pace and left the building. Without pausing, I made for the alley that Holmes had directed me to. As I reached the other side of the road, I heard another call for Mr. Smith. I continued to ignore it and, a few seconds later, I was in the alley. I was about ten paces down it when I heard the unmistakable sound of a revolver being cocked.

"Stop right there, Mr. Smith," came the voice. I turned to see my auction opponent. His gun was pointed at my heart.

"If you would be so good as to hand over that box."

"What is the meaning of this?" I stammered. "I saw you. It is hardly my fault if you could not exceed my bid." Without thinking, I swiftly pulled a whistle from my waistcoat pocket. "I can summon the police."

"You have moments to comply, sir," he said. "Place the box on the ground and continue on your way and we will say no more." He had no sooner finished the sentence when another gun was cocked.

"Good afternoon, Mr. Finlay," said Holmes. "It is good to make your acquaintance."

In the moments that followed, Finlay was disarmed by Holmes and handcuffed by Hopkins. Our interesting band made its way to Chiswick Police Station.

The man I now knew as Finlay seemed completely cowed by events. He was handed over to the local officers and taken to a cell. The rest of us gathered in a vacant office placed at our disposal by the local sergeant.

"I am waiting to hear how we got to this point, Holmes," I said.

"I am sure you are," he replied. "It will take a little time to explain. We must begin by going back a year or so. Around that time, an elderly gentleman walks into the American Exchange with an envelope addressed to a Mr. Simmonds. This contains, as we now know, a selection of pawn tickets and some money which we can assume to be a few hundred pounds.

"Almost exactly a year later, our Mr. Simmonds, or Finlay as we now know, walks into the very same American Exchange to claim the envelope and does so with some little difficulty. We can be confident that he knew what was in the envelope because he did not open it despite clearly being desperate to obtain it. Time was short and the contents were sensitive."

"Why sensitive?" asked Hopkins.

"I shall come to that presently. Finlay, as we will call him from now on, goes through the pawn tickets and orders them by date. He begins visiting the various pawnbrokers to claim the objects they relate to. I think we can safely assume that for a few occasions he ran into no issues. The pawnbrokers concerned being more than happy to get the money rather than go to the trouble of an auction."

"But he eventually visits the pawnbroker off Oxford Street?" said Hopkins.

"Precisely. Here he encounters a more thorough pawnbroker. Although he has adopted a modest disguise, he had given no thought to age. It had not been a problem before now. He tries excuses and in so doing makes the mistake of saying the original ticket holder had died."

"Why was that a mistake?" asked Hopkins,

"Because it was true and offered a clue which I later exploited. He leaves and later breaks in to secure what he came for. He takes a few other items to distract casual observers. By the way, Hopkins, did you find any of them?"

The inspector seemed pleased with himself. "Following your advice, we did recover a set of chessmen discarded not too far from Oxford Street."

Holmes smiled. "Finlay's next call is to the pawnbroker off the Strand. Here he corrects his previous error by disguising himself as an older man. Unfortunately, he once again fails to convince the pawnbroker that he is the legitimate owner of the ticket. So, he is forced to break in again and secure what he desires."

I could see Hopkins was getting excited as he knew Drury Lane was next.

"Drury Lane was where things fell apart," said Holmes. "The late Mr. Lawrence was many things. The three most important were that he was highly observant, a crook, and a very knowledgeable man.

"When our very real elderly gentlemen brought an item in a year ago, seeking a modest sum in excess of ten shillings, Lawrence suspected it was worth far more and was suspicious. He saw an opportunity. He could either attempt to extort money in return for keeping the secret or he could sell the item through his criminal contacts and later deny all knowledge knowing the owner could say little without giving away his own deception. He elected to do the latter which is why the item was not in the ledger and we were led to believe nothing had been taken. He hid the item upstairs, where he lived, in order to wait for a safer or, perhaps, more profitable time to sell. Mr. Lawrence was a very patient man.

"Our Mr. Finlay arrives a year later with the ticket and Lawrence denies all knowledge. Finlay entered, as we know from Barrett, in the person of an unsteady elderly man but proceeded to deftly stop Mr. Barrett from taking hold of the envelope when it was accidentally dropped. Lawrence saw this and this removed any doubts he may have had about the mystery surrounding the item he was now hiding. Finlay could not say anything without giving himself away so decided he would repeat a plan that had been successful twice already."

"But this time he was caught" I said.

"Yes," said Holmes. "The previous proprietors did not live

above their shops. Finlay assumed the same would be true in this case and was not careful about the noise he made. Lawrence, already on his guard, confronted him and, in the scuffle, Finlay seized a weapon that came to hand and struck Lawrence down. Although shocked at what he had done, he completed his search of the property, finding what he sought upstairs, and left."

"What brings us to Chiswick?" asked Hopkins.

"That is simple enough. Eventually Finlay ended up in Piccadilly and learned that the item he sought there had already left for auction. He directed his attention to the auction house. He found it was better secured so he hoped he could win the item at auction instead. We had Watson frustrate him and force him to desperate measures. Now he sits downstairs."

"But why?" I asked.

"I found the answer in my files." Holmes took out the newspaper clippings from his inside pocket and waved them at us. "Thanks to the pawn tickets that had already been presented I knew the range of dates to focus on. Thanks to Mr. Finlay's slip of the tongue we also knew that our original pawnshop customer was dead. I made some calls yesterday evening to confirm a point. However, I suggest we let Mr. Finlay finish the story."

We made our way to the cells where the dejected man sat, head in hands. We walked in and surrounded him.

"Gallows, I presume?" he asked.

"I should say so," said Hopkins.

Holmes stepped forward. "You know who I am?"

"Yes, sir."

"I should tell you that I have spoken to your family solicitor."

"Then you know everything?"

"I believe so. It does not hurt to hear the rest from you."

Finlay took a deep breath. "My late father was Herbert Finlay."

The name made sense to me immediately. "The disgraced stockbroker?"

Finlay returned his head to his hands and sighed. "Yes."

We waited a moment for him to gather himself. "My father was successful but not as successful as he wanted to be. He began using his clients' money to benefit himself. He was discovered and it was determined that he had swindled his clients out of tens of thousands of pounds over many years. When he knew the police were closing in, he decided to act. He knew once he was taken into custody his assets would be sold to clear his debts. He selected ten items of value that he wished to hide from the authorities."

"What items?" asked Hopkins.

Holmes pulled a paper from his pocket. "This is the list Hopkins. You will see it includes a dish, necklace, and a vase. They alone are valued at three thousand pounds."

I whistled.

Finlay sat up and continued. "My father had always felt it was his responsibility to leave me looked after financially. He determined to hide items in a way it would be hard to trace. He pawned the ten items at different establishments knowing that they would be looked after for a year."

"Also knowing," said Holmes, "that should a year expire, the items would have to go to auction which would make them easier for you to either acquire or trace."

"Yes. I was abroad at the time. He wrote to me with the details of his plan so I knew where to go to retrieve the tickets. He also informed me that he had left me several hundred pounds with which I was to secure all ten items."

Holmes took over the explanation. "Finlay senior's actions were not discovered until after his suicide. He never had any intention of suffering the indignity of going to prison. The family solicitor arranged the estate auction and only then was it discovered that certain valuable items were missing. Of them, no trace could be found. The money raised at auction fell short leaving several of Finlay's clients out of pocket. Alas, the authorities had no further leads."

"But," I said, "why did it take so long for his son to retrieve the tickets?"

Holmes gestured to young Finlay who seemed eager to unburden himself.

"I am not the most upstanding subject, sir. I admit to sharing my father's fault. Two years prior to his death I had moved to South America. At the time his letter arrived I was in prison for theft. My wife, whom I met out there, told me it had arrived but she could not tell me what it said. She speaks English but cannot read it. It was too dangerous for her to bring it when she visited in case the prison guards confiscated it and we did not dare to take any of our friends into our confidence. I was in an agony of suspense until I was released. You can imagine my panic when I read the letter and saw how little time I had to act. I got the first ship to England, secured lodgings in Soho, and collected the envelope from the American Exchange."

"The rest," said Holmes to Hopkins and me, "you can surmise." He turned to face the young man. "I do not think much of your chances but I am sure your counsel will advise you to plead self-defence when it comes to Mr. Lawrence. It could be argued that you went to Drury Lane without a weapon and with no intention to harm anyone. Only you know how true that line of defence would be. You have a wife waiting for you in South America. You may lose the items you worked so hard to retrieve or you may not. In the event you are not executed, you would do well to offer to compensate the pawnbrokers you stole from and sail to South America never to return."

Holmes motioned for us all to leave the cell. He stopped in the doorway. "Where is it, Mr. Finlay?"

Finlay's face fell. He reached into one of his socks and removed a small item. I saw that it was a brooch. With tears in his eyes, he dropped into Holmes's outstretched hand and said nothing.

We left Finlay and returned to the office. "What was the significance of the name Simmonds?" asked Hopkins.

"Finlay senior's obituary made that clear," said Holmes as he handed over one of the clippings. "It was the maiden name of his wife. The name Finlay stood some chance of arousing suspicion." He held the brooch up to the light. "This belonged to the late Mrs. Finlay and, from a sentimental viewpoint, was the most valuable of all."

Hopkins smiled. "Once again, my thanks, Mr. Holmes."

"Not at all," said Holmes as he took hold of the inspector's hand. "Now, Watson, I do believe that the comforting surroundings of Baker Street would be more appealing than this austere establishment."

As we left the police station I turned to Holmes. "This whole plan of yours nearly went for naught."

"Really, Watson?" he said, looking surprised.

"Yes. Having to wait so long for that necklace to come up, I nearly fell asleep. You are lucky that someone's impudent child kicked my chair and woke me up."

Holmes laughed. "I know my Watson well. That was one of Wiggins' newest recruits. I knew you had been up late with Hopkins and would have probably allowed yourself a wine and brandy. I left nothing to chance. Young Perkins was tasked with making sure you played your part."

He headed off to look for a cab. Leaving me open-mouthed in his wake.

The Adventure of the Brandon Park Bench

(Early 1882)

T was in the spring of 1898 when I came across a distressing notice in *The Times*.

"Holmes," I said.

"Yes, Watson."

"I have just come across a sad article. Lady Jane Rosewood and her husband have been killed in a tragic accident."

My friend was buried in a chemistry book and lifted his head from its pages much like a person forced to get out of bed. "I pride myself on my memory, Watson, but that does not immediately recall anything to my mind."

"That is because your mind is highly selective, Holmes," I replied. "You will more likely remember her as Miss Jane Willow."

"Oh yes. Brandon Park. To be fair, Watson, it was sixteen years ago. How did they die?"

"They were passengers on the steam ship *Achilles*. It seems it sank in the Indian Ocean, under mysterious circumstances, a week ago."

"She was a stoic and intelligent woman," said Holmes. "She leaves an impressive legacy."

This was an understatement on Holmes's part. Lady Rosewood, assisted by her husband, Sir Alexander, had greatly increased access to education for the disadvantaged of the nation. Their lead had allegedly influenced government policy.

"Did they have any children?" asked Holmes.

"No," I replied. It was rumoured that Lady Rosewood could not have children but, understandably, the couple had refused to confirm or deny this.

"In that case," said Holmes, "the answer to your question is yes."

"My question?"

"Watson, you have been seeking to tell that story ever since and I forbade it for reasons you understand well. I know that Lady Rosewood's older relatives have passed away so there is no one to be distressed by your account emerging now."

"I shall write it up, Holmes," I said. "But I will wait until the new century before I present it to the public."

He rose from his seat and returned his book to the shelf. "As you see fit, Watson."

Sixteen years earlier, Sherlock Holmes had been standing at the window looking down onto Baker Street. At the time, we had been sharing rooms for little more than a year. I was still very much getting to understand the man and my initial list of his characteristics had gone through several revisions.

"When I retire, Watson," said Holmes suddenly, "I have been giving thought to taking myself down to Sussex."

"You are rather young to be contemplating retirement," I suggested. "Surely, you will never be able to tear yourself away from London and its diversity of crime?"

He smiled and walked away from the window towards the

mantelpiece. He removed his jack-knife from the pile of unread correspondence, permitting a couple of envelopes to fall to the floor, and toyed absentmindedly with the blade before thrusting it back into the stack of paper. "Watson, I am finding a dearth of enterprise in the London criminal classes. Increasingly the unusual is to be found outside our great metropolis."

"But why Sussex?" I asked.

He removed a piece of paper from his dressing gown pocket. "The notion was brought to mind by this telegram from a certain Miss Willow who will be calling upon us shortly. She hails from that county and has, according to this, a problem for which our services appear to be the only remedy."

Suitably intrigued, I asked when the lady was due to arrive. "She is due anytime in the next hour," said Holmes as he returned to the window, and his thoughts, leaving me to my newspaper.

About thirty minutes later, there was ring at the bell, and Mrs. Hudson entered the room with a card bearing the name Jane Willow. The young lady swiftly followed and Holmes directed her to the settee. She had dark hair, bright blue eyes, and an air of confidence beyond her years. I was immediately struck by her beauty and grace.

"I must beg your forgiveness, Mr. Holmes, for my intrusion upon your time but I could think of nowhere else to bring my problem."

"That is quite all right, Miss Willow," said Holmes. "Pray tell us about yourself and the nature of your difficulty."

"I am twenty years old, live in Sussex, and am a reluctant teacher of English."

"And the reason for your reluctance?" asked Holmes.

The lady sighed. "My family has determined that I should undertake such a path but I am less enthusiastic as time passes. I feel I should be allowed to find my own way in life."

"And you reside at Castleway School," said Holmes, brandishing the lady's card.

"Yes. It was founded by my aunt and uncle who run it to this day. It is a school for the disadvantaged."

"Disadvantaged how?" I asked.

"In any way, Dr. Watson," she replied. "The blind, the deaf, and any children whose requirements cannot be met by our conventional schools."

"I take it your family works at the school?" said Holmes.

"Yes. My Uncle John teaches biology. My Aunt Susan handles the administration. We have other tutors for the other subjects. It is with the other tutors that my story begins."

"Indeed?" said Holmes. "Please explain."

Miss Willow took a deep breath, as if she were about to dive underwater. "One month after my twentieth birthday, our teacher of geography, a lovely old man by the name of Latimer, was dismissed for reasons that were never explained to me. One day he was there and the next day I witnessed him leave with his belongings. My aunt and uncle advertised for a replacement with all the reputable agencies. They saw a good many candidates but none seemed to impress my uncle who prided himself on being an excellent judge of both ability and character."

"Presumably you did engage someone eventually?" asked Holmes.

"Yes. A man by the name of Thomas Buckley. He was a much younger man than Mr. Latimer. I believe he was twenty-five at the time he was offered the position on a three-month trial. I was surprised at their choice."

"Why?"

"All the other tutors at the school are middle-aged and I had every reason to believe that my uncle and aunt engaged tutors of that age in order to ensure a level of experience not found in the more newly qualified."

"So how did this Mr. Buckley fit in?" asked Holmes.

"He was a breath of fresh air, Mr. Holmes. He would often seek me out when he was not teaching. He told me that it was because we were of similar ages and he lacked much in common with the other tutors who tended to be a little dismissive of him. I did not complain as I greatly enjoyed his company and I too found little in common with others in the school.

"One day, when I was going about my duties, I heard raised voices coming from my uncle's study, and I recognised one of them as being Mr. Buckley. My uncle clearly was not happy with his performance as the one sentence I discerned was my uncle telling Mr. Buckley to 'knuckle down' and do the job he was being paid to do.

"I had crept towards the study to hear more so when Mr. Buckley abruptly exited the room he nearly ran into me. Although clearly flustered, he apologised before excusing himself. As he exited, I looked into my uncle's office. He sat calmly behind his desk busy with some paperwork. I lingered a little too long and he became aware of my presence. He looked up and sternly asked me to shut the door. The contrast between his demeanour and that of Mr. Buckley could not have been starker. This was to be the first of many times when my uncle upbraided Mr. Buckley for his performance. He has high standards so it did not surprise me that he would be so demanding even though Mr. Buckley seemed a perfectly capable teacher and the pupils seemed genuinely fond of him.

"Uncle John regularly takes pupils on nature walks. He would take several pairs of field glasses and encouraged the pupils to study the wildlife. He subscribed to Mr. Darwin's teachings and encouraged this in his pupils.

"A day or so after one of the arguments with Mr. Buckley, he went on one of these walks. Not long after he had left, Mr. Buckley asked for an interview with me. I accepted, assuming it was related to school matters. As soon as we were alone, it all came out. He expressed his fervent admiration for me, that it had been the reason he had sought so much time with me and proposed marriage there and then. It was quite the shock."

"How did you react?" asked Holmes.

"Much to my surprise, it was only when he proposed to me that I realised that I felt the same. I accepted but I wanted my uncle's permission to wed."

"And your uncle's reaction?"

"He seemed pleased, gave his permission, and said we should not delay in making the proper arrangements. I must confess to being surprised that my uncle would raise not a word of objection given his apparent dissatisfaction with Thomas's performance at the school. But I was happy so I decided not to question it."

"Delightful," said Holmes, with about as much sincerity as he could muster for matters of the heart.

Miss Willow continued, her eyes now becoming moist. "Then it all went wrong, Mr. Holmes. I was away from the school for a few days and, when I returned, I could find no trace of Mr. Buckley. I asked my aunt what had happened and she informed me that he had been dismissed. Shocked, I naturally asked why and my aunt said that Mr. Buckley had withdrawn his offer of marriage and my uncle had therefore felt it was not appropriate for us to remain in contact under the circumstances.

"I was distraught. How could Thomas do such a thing? I was angry and desperate for some kind of explanation. My uncle refused to let me have any information that would enable me to contact Thomas. He told me that Thomas was clearly a dishonourable man. I responded by saying I was determined to find him."

Miss Willow paused at this point, clearly a little overcome by the events she was reliving. I offered her a glass of water which she accepted and took a few sips from. My friend, while tactful, was clearly impatient for her to resume her story. The drumming of his fingers on the arm of his chair brought Miss Willow back to the matter in hand. She returned her glass to the table and mopped below her eyes with her handkerchief.

"A few days later, my uncle informed me that a letter had arrived for me from Thomas. Given his objection to me communicating with my former fiancé, I was surprised that he shared this news with me. He saw this in my face and said he had read the letter and, under the circumstances, he was more than happy for me to see it. I was obviously angry that he had read a private letter but I feared any argument on that point might cause him to retract his permission."

"And what did the letter say?"

"It was shocking, Mr. Holmes. In his typed letter, which added to the sheer coldness of the situation, Thomas chided our entire family for his treatment and asserted that he had secured a fortunate escape."

"'You see, Jane,' said my uncle. 'I told you his character and here you have proof in black and white.'

"As you can imagine, I struggled to believe what I was reading. My mind was in a whirl."

"Where was the letter sent from?" asked Holmes.

"I am afraid I don't know," said Miss Willow. "No address was written upon it."

"But the envelope, Miss Willow," said Holmes with some frustration. "The postmark would have given some indication."

"I understand, Mr. Holmes, but I did not see the envelope because my uncle had already thrown it away."

Holmes was clearly disappointed. The young lady continued.

"A few days later I was with my uncle and aunt when one of

the other tutors approached us. He informed my uncle that he had been in the village and had learned that Mr. Buckley had been seen in the area."

"How was this news received by you all?"

"I was not sure what to make of it. If he were so averse to us now, why come back to the area? Something did not seem right. My uncle was angry and my aunt suggested that contact be made with my Uncle Harold for advice."

"Your Uncle Harold?"

"My Uncle Harold is the former army officer and policeman, Major Harold Willow, who rose to be chief superintendent in the Sussex Constabulary. However, contact with him could not be made."

"Why not?"

"Since he had retired from the police, he had gone abroad. He had been game-hunting in central Africa and on a tour of Europe. My Uncle John sent a telegram to where we believed him to be but we were not surprised when no answer was forthcoming."

"So, what happened next?"

"For a few weeks, absolutely nothing. Then word reached us from Amberley that Mr. Buckley had been seen again in the area and we were further informed that he had been asking after my health."

"That must have been confusing?"

"More so for my aunt and uncle judging by their reaction to the news. I was not afraid of encountering Mr. Buckley. I still yearned for answers."

"What precisely has happened to bring you to me today?" asked Holmes.

"About two weeks ago, I was in the village to pick up a few items for the school. I had travelled in with my aunt and we had separated to run our respective errands. We had arranged to meet in a charming tea room in the High Street. I completed my errands and made my way there. As it was a fine day, I elected to sit at one of several tables outside the front of the establishment. I ordered some tea and cakes and settled down to await my aunt.

"I admit that I got lost in a world of my own when I suddenly heard a voice."

"Mr. Buckley's, I presume?" said Holmes.

"How did you know?"

"I sensed that was where this would go."

"Well, Mr. Holmes, your senses are acute. It was indeed Mr. Buckley. He hurried over and took a seat at the table."

"What did he say?"

"He made no reference to his past conduct but instead told me that he needed to discuss an urgent matter with me. I was naturally on my guard but I felt relatively safe in an open and populated area."

"So, what did he have to say?"

"Nothing."

"Nothing?"

"Well, there was clearly something but he did not get the chance. There was a sudden cry, and I looked up to see my aunt fast approaching. She admonished him for daring to approach me and made such a fuss that a crowd soon began to gather. Mr. Buckley looked startled and made off in the direction of the railway station.

"My aunt lost no time in getting me back to the school and explained things to my Uncle John. He forbade me from leaving the school grounds until such time as we were satisfied that Mr. Buckley had left the area."

"Interesting," said Holmes.

Miss Willow's expression became rather stern. "I will confess that I was angry that Mr. Buckley's reappearance should result in my activities being curtailed. I felt as though I were the one being punished.

"Some letters arrived at the school a day later. Over breakfast, my uncle was opening each in turn and suddenly said, 'What the devil!'

"I asked him what had upset him. 'That Buckley fellow has written to you again.' Without a further word he scanned the letter. 'Damned impertinence,' he said and threw both letter and envelope into the fire."

"He read a letter addressed to you and threw it into the fire without letting you so much as glance at it?" asked Holmes.

"Yes."

"Very strange behaviour. If you were banned from leaving the school grounds, how did you manage to keep this appointment?"

"I naturally chaffed at the restriction on my movement. I said to my Uncle John that I wanted to go to London for some new clothes. I expected a refusal but was pleasantly surprised when he agreed. A carriage was arranged to take me to the station but I must be back by six o'clock."

"When you leave here," said Holmes. "I strongly suggest you purchase some clothes otherwise there may be questions asked."

"I have already done so," said Miss Willow with a satisfied smile. "They await me downstairs in your hallway."

"How do you wish me to act?" asked Holmes.

"I simply need answers, Mr. Holmes. I am hopeful that you can trace Thomas and obtain them. I just want to know the truth as it feels as if it is being kept from me for reasons that I do not understand."

I felt sure that Holmes would dismiss Miss Willow. I could not see what there was for him in this matter of an extinguished love. Nothing interested him less in my experience.

Holmes sat and pondered. Much to my surprise, he said "I will make some enquiries, Miss Willow."

The young lady looked relieved. "Thank you so much, Mr. Holmes. Now I must be going if I am not to arouse suspicion. If you send any enquiries to the Amberley Post Office, I can pick them up there without my family intercepting them." She rose and headed for the door.

Before she placed her hand on the handle Holmes spoke again.

"Apologies, Miss Willow. I have three questions and a request."

"Yes, Mr. Holmes?"

"Firstly, how did your aunt and uncle come to found the school?"

"My aunt is deaf, Mr. Holmes. Deaf since the age of eight. My uncle is devoted to her and learned of her struggles with education growing up. He started the school to help other children avoid the struggles my aunt went through. The school is their whole world."

"Secondly," said Holmes, "you earlier spoke of your reluctance to remain in the teaching profession. Are your aunt and uncle aware of this?"

"Oh yes, I mentioned it shortly after my twentieth birthday. They were clearly disturbed by it and suggested I think about the matter carefully. It sometimes feels as though I started something that day as it was only a few weeks later that Mr. Latimer left and Mr. Buckley came into our lives."

"Thirdly," said Holmes without a pause. "You have mentioned your aunt and uncles but you have not mentioned your parents. Where are they?"

Miss Willow's face took on a melancholy expression. "They died in a carriage accident when I was but two years old. I have no memory of them and my Uncle John and Aunt Susan were appointed my legal guardians."

"Thank you," said Holmes. "I will contact you if I make progress."

"What was the request, Mr. Holmes?" she asked.

"Would you be so good as to send me the letter Mr. Buckley wrote to you?"

"Certainly, if you believe it will be of value." With that remark she was gone.

"You surprise me, Holmes," I said.

"I realise that," he said. "However, there is something about our young client's situation that I find sinister."

A day later Miss Willow supplied the letter from Buckley. Holmes read it repeatedly and held it up to the light. "Odd don't you think?"

"What is odd?"

"It is odd that John Willow let his niece keep this letter and burned the other without permitting her to see it. Then there is the letter itself. As she told us, it is typed but Mr. Buckley has signed his first name. It is cold, lacking the emotion that you would expect in the circumstances."

A week passed with no further word from Miss Willow. Holmes was juggling a few cases, and it was often hard to ascertain which was occupying his time at any given moment. One afternoon he returned having been absent since the morning. He disposed of his hat and gloves before filling a pipe and seating himself in his chair.

"Well, which case have you been looking into today?" I asked.

"Just the two, Watson. I cleared up that little matter of the town hall clock that went backwards and have passed the details to Bradstreet. For the last few hours, I have been occupied with the matter of Miss Willow."

"And?"

"I have been looking into the school. It truly is a passion of the family. They have run it since before our client was born. John Willow is a man on an educational crusade. According to press articles, the school used to take predominately fee-paying pupils. It seems to have been particularly popular with the aristocracy who were prepared to pay well to hide their problematic offspring away from prying eyes. Other pupils, from more modest backgrounds, are funded from a charitable foundation set up by our client's late father who, it would appear, strongly supported his brother's zeal.

"The other brother, Major Willow, enjoyed a reasonably successful military career in the infantry before resigning his commission to join the Sussex Constabulary. He rapidly rose to chief superintendent and retired in high-esteem to pursue a passion for hunting game, and other leisure pursuits."

"Any trace of Mr. Buckley?"

"None. And when I say that, I mean it. I can find no trace of him whatsoever. If it were not for the fact that he has been seen by our client I would be tempted to assert that he did not exist. I need to smoke a few pipes and ponder this one, Watson."

"Before you do so," I said. "You may want to read this letter. It arrived just after you left and I assume it comes from Miss Willow judging by the postmark and the feminine hand." I held out the envelope which Holmes took and proceeded to open.

"Well, well," he said. "Miss Willow has succeeded where I have failed."

"What do you mean?"

"She has managed to encounter Mr. Buckley and wishes us to come down as soon as possible. Be a good fellow, pop down to the telegraph office and wire back that we will be there tomorrow."

Mid-morning the following day, Holmes and I found ourselves in Amberley. It was a charming village which appealed to me but it did not appeal to my friend whose love of Mother Nature was largely limited to her poisons.

Following directions from Miss Willow, we had walked past a variety of charming, ivy-covered, cottages, and more modern dwellings. We had directions to a quiet street where we were to wait for Miss Willow outside a since-closed tavern which I noticed, upon our arrival, was now marked for demolition. It soon became clear why she had chosen this spot. It was out of sight of other buildings and would afford privacy. She joined us a few minutes after we arrived and showed us an entrance into the now deserted establishment.

We negotiated our way around discarded bottles, tankards, and other relics of the tavern's happier days, to a dusty table near the bar. The place seemed nicely situated and I did allow myself to wonder why it had failed as a going concern. Miss Willow's voice brought me back to the matter in hand. "I apologise for meeting here, gentlemen," she said as she took a seat. "If we met more openly word would get back to my uncle, and I do not wish to be put into the position of lying to him if it can be avoided."

"I quite understand," said Holmes as he swept dust off a chair before seating himself. I did likewise. "Now tell us of recent events."

"It began with one of our older boys named Simon Coyle. Unlike many of our pupils he does not board at the school but lives here in Amberley. One day he was required to stay behind and undertake chores as punishment for being insubordinate in one of my uncle's classes – an accusation that he strongly denied. When he finally left it was after dark. From what I understand, he was less than ten minutes from his home when he was attacked."

"Attacked by whom?"

"He could not say, Mr. Holmes. He was shocked and could not be sure of how many people attacked him or what they looked like. He suffered bruises and, most shockingly, a broken leg. He distinctly remembered that his attacker or attackers focused on his legs. The local doctor ordered him to rest and not travel."

"My uncle was determined that Coyle should not fall behind in his lessons and arranged, with the boy's parents, for him to continue his studies from home. There was some resistance to this from both Coyle and his parents, but my uncle convinced them. The decision was made that I would visit him at his home in order to supply him with the materials he needed to keep up with his fellow pupils.

"My uncle was eager that this special arrangement did not disrupt the education of the other pupils and wanted me to be away from the school as briefly as possible. To that end, he instructed me to take a specific route to young Coyle's house. The route surprised me."

"Why?"

"It goes through Brandon Park."

The way in which Miss Willow named the park indicated that she expected it to be understood. She was not wrong as a look came across Holmes's face. The name clearly meant something to him.

"Is it familiar to you, Holmes?" I asked.

"Only by reputation, Watson," he replied. "The crime with which it is associated occurred several decades ago and remains unsolved. It was the scene of a brutal murder and later it acquired a reputation for being haunted by the victim. The curious connection is that the victim was a teacher."

I looked at Miss Willow who seemed surprisingly unmoved by this coincidence.

"The result of all this," she said, "is that it is seldom used by anyone local. The Parish Council is required to go out of the county to find people willing to maintain it."

"You are an educated young woman, Miss Willow," said Holmes. "I do not imagine you share these superstitions?"

"Naturally not, Mr. Holmes, but my uncle has never encouraged me to enter the park before. There were rumours that criminal elements made use of the park knowing that the law-abiding did not. He saw the confusion on my face and explained it was the most direct route to the lad's home. In this he was quite correct so a lesson plan was worked out and times and dates for my visits were drawn up. The first of these was two days ago.

"In order to reach the lad's house by two o'clock, I needed to leave the school by no later than one-thirty. The park is roughly equidistant between the school and the Coyle house, and I arrived in it by quarter-to-two. The park is surrounded by trees and contains a few benches. You can imagine my shock when, as I entered the park, I heard some violent coughing. I turned in the direction of the noise and I saw Mr. Buckley seated on one of the benches."

"Go on."

"I felt a mixture of fear and excitement, Mr. Holmes. Perhaps this was motivated by the location but, nevertheless, I decided to approach him.

"He saw me immediately and I could see that he was decidedly uncomfortable. Clearly, he was not expecting to see me and feared a confrontation. To his credit, he made no attempt to avoid the situation which he could easily have done."

"What happened?"

"When I was about fifteen feet from him, he asked me to stop. He did not stand or ask me to sit, which I thought discourteous. I asked him what he was doing in the area and he offered the excuse that he had a fondness for Amberley and Brandon Park. He said he was working in nearby Storrington in a temporary position while he looked for something permanent.

"To be honest, Mr. Holmes, it did not seem credible, but I was more concerned with getting answers to my questions about the ending of our engagement."

"And how did Mr. Buckley explain that?"

"He said that he had realised that he had acted rashly with his proposal and that we had nothing in common. He said he had explained this to my uncle who had promptly dismissed him. He added that I was too young for him and that he found my family unpleasant. In short, he was quite insulting. I was upset, as you will imagine, and got closer to him with every intention of striking him."

"His reaction?"

"Mr. Buckley had never struck me as a coward, Mr. Holmes, but as I strode up to him, he slid along the bench to put distance between us. I adjusted my position, as I wanted to face him directly, but each time I attempted to do so he would slide away from me along the bench. He also could not bear to look at me. Even when he was speaking to me, he would look straight ahead avoiding my gaze. After going through this charade twice I decided I was wasting my time with him. With as much pride as I could muster, I wished him well in his life and left.

"After a few dozen paces I turned to look back. He was still there and appeared to be sobbing. I went on my way and later reported back to my uncle about the encounter. He appeared angry at first but expressed the hope that this would draw a line under the matter. 'Perhaps you will not seek to rush so quickly into matrimony in future,' he said. 'Do not worry uncle,' I said. 'It is highly likely that I will never marry if that is what young men today are made of.' He smiled and said he was proud of me."

When Miss Willow had finished her account, Holmes expressed a desire to see the tea room where she and Buckley had met earlier. We left the tavern and she led the way, maintaining distance from us.

"Thank you, Miss Willow," Holmes said as the tea rooms came into view. "Dr. Watson and I will take tea here and play the part of tourists. This will ensure that any gossip about strangers that reaches your uncle will not alarm him. If you would be so good as to describe how we get from here to Brandon Park, we will let you get on your way."

Miss Willow provided the necessary details. "Thank you, Mr. Holmes," she said. She was about to move away when her face paled. We turned to look behind us and could see a lady of about fifty heading towards us at some speed. She was about fifteen yards away but reached us swiftly. "Jane," she said, "what are you doing here and who is this Mr. Holmes and this other gentleman?"

Miss Willow seemed at a loss. "Aunt Susan, I did not realise you were coming into the village today."

"Good day, madam," said Holmes. "My name is Richard Holmes and this is my colleague, Henry Simpson. We are visitors to this delightful village and this young lady was kindly offering us directions."

"To Brandon Park," said Mrs. Willow. "I cannot imagine why that would interest you."

Holmes smiled and turned to face Miss Willow. "Good day,

Miss Willow. I will say that your aunt has questionable taste when it comes to shoes." As Miss Willow and I looked aghast, Holmes turned back to Mrs. Willow who appeared completely impassive. "Good day, madam. We are sorry if we have incommoded you." With that remark, he walked off in the direction of the park. I made my farewells and hurried after him. "Holmes?"

"Not yet, Watson," he said. He turned a corner and stopped.

"Why did you say something so rude?"

"You do not understand?" asked Holmes, genuinely surprised. "We must get to the park."

We retraced our steps to the tea room to be certain that the ladies had left the area. We then followed the directions to the park. It was an unsettling place. On the surface it seemed pleasant enough and would have struck me as charming if I had been unaware of its history. Knowing something of the crime that had been committed within its verdant borders gave it a different feel and I could understand why it was shunned by local residents.

The trees that surrounded it shielded anyone inside it from the gaze of anyone outside. It was not hard to see the various benches of which Miss Willow had spoken. At each of the four compass points of the park there was a large bush.

"That one I think," said Holmes pointing his cane to one of the furthest benches. He advanced toward it and I followed.

Holmes stopped a few feet short of the bench and motioned for me to do the same. He studied it and the ground surrounding it. "It is fortunate that the populace bypasses this park. It means these traces are almost certainly those of Mr. Buckley." He pointed some footprints. "Having made a discreet study of our client's attire, I can see that these are her boot marks and the position of the man's footprints bears out the story that she told us of Mr. Buckley adjusting his position on this bench twice. He went from his starting position on the left of the bench, over to the right and back again. He was clearly here for some time as on the left there are the remains of five cigarettes. All mostly consumed apart from the last which is barely a third smoked. Notice that there is some soil on top of all the cigarette ends."

"And what does this tell you?"

"It suggests he entered the park, took a seat on the left side of the bench, and smoked continuously. Miss Willow made no mention of cigarettes so we need to ask ourselves did Buckley smoke before or after his interview with her."

"Surely we cannot tell that," I said.

"I think we can. I would strongly suggest that it was before."

"Based on what?"

"Two things. Firstly, the soil that covers the cigarettes was almost certainly the result of Mr. Buckley attempting to conceal them. This suggests that Miss Willow disapproves of smoking and he was aware of that fact."

"Secondly?"

"Secondly, that the fifth is not fully consumed. It suggests that he put it out when he saw her enter the park. This is also borne out by the coughing Miss Willow heard when she entered. If the smoking had been after their interview Buckley would have had no reason not to finish the fifth cigarette entirely.

"I would also draw the conclusion that Mr. Buckley is still very much concerned with what Miss Willow thinks of him and perhaps cares for her more than his other actions would suggest."

"How on Earth do you come to that conclusion?"

"The attempt to conceal the smoking. If he no longer had any regard for her, he would not be motivated to conceal a habit of which she disapproved. Her good opinion clearly matters to him. It might also explain his tears after their interview."

Holmes proceeded to sit on the bench and study the park.

"Now that is interesting."

I followed his gaze back to where we had come from. Straight ahead of the bench, at the park's perimeter, and just in front of some of the surrounding trees, was one of the large bushes.

"It is certainly a sizeable bush, Holmes," I remarked.

"Indeed, it is," he replied. He suddenly got to his feet. "Ha. I think we have learned all we need to for the moment. Back to Amberley station and from there to Victoria. We need to locate Mr. Latimer."

"The school's former geography teacher?" I exclaimed.

"Yes. I believe what he has to say will confirm my working theory."

The next day Holmes was up and out before I rose for breakfast. He returned by eleven and asked me to accompany him. Moments later we were in a cab heading east.

"Where are we going?" I asked.

"I have spent the morning visiting the various agencies to which tutors go in search of a situation," said Holmes. "I began with the most prestigious and worked my way down. I was surprised to find Latimer on the books of some of them but I was told that none of them was presently acting for him. I managed, not without difficulty, to secure an address for him and that is where we are heading."

Before long we found ourselves in the Bow area. We pulled up alongside an impressive row of terraced houses. "We want number fourteen," said Holmes as he alighted.

I paid the fare and followed him. He rang the bell and the door was opened by a man in his early sixties. "Mr. Latimer?" asked Holmes.

"Yes, sir," replied Latimer.

"I wonder if you might spare me a few moments to discuss

Castleway School?" Holmes handed over his card.

Latimer looked at the card and frowned. "I knew it was too good to be true. Come in, gentlemen."

He led us along the hall to his front parlour and asked us to sit. "Ever since that odd day, I have been waiting for the school's name to come up again."

"Why is that, sir?" I asked.

"Well, it is not every day that a school close to bankruptcy pays you a significant sum of money to leave."

"Could you explain?" asked Holmes.

Latimer sat. He looked sad. "Well, gentlemen. I taught at that school for some twenty years. When I first began there, most of the pupils were from wealthy families with a few others supported by the Willow Foundation. Over time, however, Castleway ceased to be the only school offering such special tuition and the wealthy families started to send their children to similar schools further north where the fees were lower and privacy superior.

"The Willow Foundation is funded through shareholding and some high interest accounts but the money it was able to generate was at the mercy of the markets. For the past five years or so the school has only just about been able to fund itself. The spending habits of the Willows do not help."

"Have they been living a lifestyle off the back of this foundation?" I asked.

"Not as far as I know," said Latimer. "But they value reputation above all. Appearances must be kept up. So, they paid the best salaries, above market rate, purchased the best equipment, and insisted on retaining the current grand building when they could have so easily moved to somewhere more modest."

"I begin to see," said Holmes. "Are you aware that Miss Jane Willow believes you to have been dismissed?"

Latimer flushed red. "The hypocrisy," he exclaimed.

"I beg your pardon?" said Holmes.

"Hypocrisy, sir," he repeated. "They go on about the importance of reputation and besmirch mine." He rose and moved to his window. Without turning back, he continued. "Mr. Willow offered me early retirement. I was only a year or so away from my official retirement and he explained that he had finally come to realise that economies had to be made.

"To that end he had decided to abolish geography as a subject and offered me the salary I would have earned had I stayed on, but all at once. Under the circumstances, I took it."

"And yet," said Holmes. "The moment you were gone they looked for another geography teacher."

Latimer spun round with a speed that I would not have given him credit for. "He did what? What could be the purpose of such a deception?"

"At this stage," said Holmes, "all I have are theories. However, you may be able to help me."

"Gladly, if I can," said Latimer.

"Do you by any chance have the details of the Willow family solicitor?"

Latimer left the room and returned with a pencil and paper. He wrote a few lines and handed the sheet to Holmes. "I am very much of two minds, Mr. Holmes," he said. "I am angry about the deception, and want it exposed, but cannot say that I have been badly treated financially."

"I understand your dilemma," said Holmes. "Rest assured that this is the best way forward for the school and all connected to it. Good day, Mr. Latimer."

Back on the street, we strolled in search of a cab. Eventually one presented itself and, before long, we were heading back westwards.

"So, we are going to see the solicitor now?" I asked.

"Not we, but I," said Holmes. "Latimer was not the only person whom I sought at the agencies today." He handed me a piece of paper. I read it. "Who is this, Holmes?"

"Do not worry about that," he replied. "Send this note by telegram to the gentleman whose details you hold in your hand." He pulled two other pieces of paper from his pocket. "Send this to Miss Willow and this to her Uncle John."

I read all the pieces of paper. I was filled with foreboding. "If I am reading this correctly, Holmes, something bad may happen."

"Miss Willow will ensure that does not occur," said Holmes. "As long as she plays her part, I am confident I have read this correctly. I merely need the solicitor to confirm aspects of which I am already firmly convinced."

"What makes you think he will talk to you?"

"When he understands what is at stake, he will fall into line."

Holmes dropped me at the nearest telegraph office before heading on his way. As I was making my way inside, I could not help but wonder how the next day was going to play out.

The following day, at two o'clock, Holmes and I arrived back in Amberley. Holmes informed me that it was necessary to enter Brandon Park and hide in the large bush on its eastern side.

"It is highly important, Watson, that we do not move from our position until I say so. It does not matter what we may hear, we must not react until after three o'clock. By then, all the pieces will be on the board."

I nodded my assent. Upon entering the park, we made for the eastern bush and sat down behind it. I was pleased it was a warm day and the ground was not wet. I opened my mouth to speak but Holmes put a finger to his lips.

The wait seemed like an eternity. Holmes had forbidden me to look at my watch as he feared me opening and closing it would make sufficient noise to give us away. Instead, he had brought a watch of his own with an exposed face. He had lain it on the ground so we could consult it at any time.

At about twenty to three, he grabbed my arm. I could hear what sounded like two people enter the park. They walked the path, going by the sound, and we heard rustling. A short while later, all sound stopped.

"Two pieces are on the board," whispered Holmes.

We resumed our vigil. Ten minutes later we heard footsteps pass close to our position. They began to fade in sound. "Piece three," said Holmes. "One more to go."

Precisely at three o'clock we heard a voice. It was Miss Willow.

"I am glad to see you again," she said.

"I do not know what I can add to our last meeting," said a man's nervous voice.

"You can add the truth," said Miss Willow.

"I am not certain that I can," came the response.

Holmes got to his feet and, without a word, headed into the park. I swiftly followed, not knowing what he had in mind.

"Good afternoon, Miss Willow," he said. "Good afternoon, Mr. Edwards."

"Mr. Edwards?" said Miss Willow.

"Holmes turned to the south. Major Willow and Mrs. Willow. All is known."

From the large bush to the south a stiff gentleman and the woman we knew as Mrs. Susan Willow emerged. She was holding a handsome pair of field-glasses. He was holding a rifle.

"Who the devil are you?" said the man I now understood to be the major.

"Sherlock Holmes, sir."

"Good God! It is all over!" said the major.

"Be quiet, Harold," said Mrs. Willow. "He knows nothing."

"I fear, madam," said Holmes, "that there is little I do not know. Now, if you would all be so good, I think we should return to the school and meet with the elder Mr. Willow. I would much appreciate it, Major, if you would hand your rifle to my friend."

The major complied reluctantly, and I unloaded the weapon. With Holmes in front and me to the rear, we escorted the group towards the school. Miss Willow kept silent but repeatedly stared at the young Mr. Edwards who hung his head in apparent shame.

Upon our arrival we were met by an angry and confused John Willow. Holmes's commanding presence soon cowed him and we adjourned to his study where we all took a seat. At Holmes's request, mine was near to the door.

"Ladies and gentlemen," said Holmes, "this has been an interesting case but one that I believe need not have come about."

Miss Willow was the first to speak. "Mr. Holmes. Why did you call Thomas, Mr. Edwards?"

"Because that is his name," replied Holmes. "My dear Miss Willow. I very much fear that you have been ill-used by all around you. People who had so little faith in you that rather than seek your help, they chose to control and deceive you.

"I paid a visit to your family solicitor. He was very forthcoming when the situation was put before him. It seems you have never shown much interest in the workings of your father's foundation."

"No, I suppose I have not," said Miss Willow. "I always trusted Uncle John to run it."

"Well, it may interest you to know that you would have had a say in the running of it once you turned twenty-one. Furthermore, upon your marriage you would have been able to withdraw a substantial sum of money from it for your own use."

"I do not see what this means," she replied.

Holmes turned to John Willow. "I know, sir, that this school, now devoid of almost all its private pupils, is entirely dependent on the income from the shares that underpin the foundation."

John Willow said nothing and turned his head slightly to look out of the window like a petulant child.

Holmes ignored his rudeness and continued to address him. "Your refusal to compromise or economise meant that that the loss of even a few pounds would damage you. Your niece turning twenty-one and marrying were the biggest dangers you faced."

"How, Mr. Holmes?" asked Miss Willow.

"Under the terms of your late father's will, control of the foundation stayed with your uncles until you reached twenty-one. After this, you would have had voting rights on how the foundation was run. Separately from this, as I have just outlined, in the event you married you would be able to take an income from the foundation that, at today's prices, would be worth about two hundred pounds a year. A substantial sum.

"That would not have changed anything, Mr. Holmes," said Miss Willow. "Castleway is as important to me as it is to the rest of the family. I would not have taken the money away from the school."

"I have no doubt of that," said Holmes. "And I believe your family also shared that belief. You only began to unnerve them when you talked about walking away from teaching. I believe this prompted your family into a damage limitation plan. They were confident they could control you but, were you to marry, could they control your husband?"

The look of confusion on Miss Willow's face was shared by me. Holmes continued. "Were you to marry, under the law, your husband would take control of your income and be in a position to divert it away from the school whether you wanted him to or not. Your family feared the arrival of a husband who would encourage you to leave the school, and exercise his legal right, which would have tipped the school into bankruptcy and closure. Your uncle's life's work and reputation destroyed.

"They were intelligent enough to realise that they could not stop you marrying at some point. They therefore decided to find you a husband."

Miss Willow looked at young Edwards. "Is this true?"

The young man looked at the floor, shook his head from side to side, and said nothing,

"The plan," said Holmes, "began with the exit of Mr. Latimer. Contrary to what you were told, he was paid off. Early retirement. Your uncle, as you know, approached an agency for a replacement. You remarked that he hired a man much younger than he would normally do. He was using his judgment of character to find a young man whom he could control. When Mr. Edwards here came along he saw at once that he was perfect. Meek, in need of money, easily controllable. He was offered money to court you."

Miss Willow was demonstrably shocked. "Uncle?" she said, looking at John Willow. Her uncle said nothing.

"The solicitor showed me a draft of a document, which I have no doubt Mr. Edwards here would have been required to sign, that would, in return for a sizeable payment, give control of your shares, post-marriage, back to your uncle. Leaving you financially dependent on them rather than the other way round.

"The plan worked but not as fast as your uncle hoped. You told me of the arguments between the two men where your uncle chided Mr. Edwards here for not doing his job. That job was not teaching. It was courting.

"Mr. Edwards eventually succeeded in gaining your affections and your acceptance of his proposal. Your uncle was pleased as well he might be. It was all set. The two of you would marry. Your new husband would sell your shares from under you to your uncle thus going some way to ensuring the continuance of the school. You would be left virtually penniless and dependent."

Under the circumstances, Miss Willow appeared to be taking it well. She smiled. "I cannot accept this, Mr. Holmes. Thomas here would have been stuck in a false marriage."

"It is quite easy for a man to secure a divorce, Miss Willow," said Holmes. "I have no doubt your uncle and family would have assisted him in this. Am I incorrect, sir?"

Still, the Willow family said nothing.

"Then the problem. Mr. Edwards here, under the name Buckley, actually fell in love with you. He could not bring himself to go through with the deceit. He had signed nothing yet and announced he would marry you and not follow the plan."

For the first time, Miss Willow looked at Edwards with some fondness.

"Your uncle found himself in a corner. So, I suspect, he made a threat on your life. Not one he would have gone through with but it was enough to scare Edwards here who left believing himself to be saving your life."

"But the letter, Mr. Holmes?" said Miss Willow.

"Thank you for bringing me to that. Clearly it was not from Edwards. When you told your uncle that you were determined to find your fiancé it worried him. He was concerned you might succeed and learn all. So, he fabricated a letter. He had a copy of Mr. Edwards' signature from his employment contract. He could not hope to fabricate an entire letter by hand so it was typed and concluded with a forgery of Mr. Edwards' first name. You found the letter cold but were convinced of its authenticity because it was signed. Your uncle desired to turn your love to hate. It would stop you seeking answers and perhaps even delay or prevent you considering marriage again."

"Holmes," I said. "Why did Buckley, or Edwards, come back to the area?"

"Guilt," said Holmes, looking at the young man. "Perhaps he started to doubt the threat against Miss Willow. He knew he could not come to the school so he asked after her in the village. Word of this got to the family and they saw the danger. Contrary to what Miss Willow believed, they made successful contact with the major here whose lifestyle is, to an extent, funded by the foundation. He wrote back with a plan. That, Miss Willow, was the letter your uncle pretended was from your fiancé and threw into the fire after reading it. It is also why you never saw the envelope."

I looked at Miss Willow. She was justifiably sad and angry but clearly wanted to hear more.

"Mr. Edwards here spotted you at the tea room by chance and tried to explain but was frustrated by your aunt. The major here, who had arrived from Europe in the meantime, was informed and he tracked Edwards down. Edwards was left in fear for your life and his own. He may have doubted the threats from your Uncle John. He did not doubt those of the major whose comfortable lifestyle was in danger."

"Very well, Mr. Holmes," said Miss Willow, whose eyes were moistening. "Why the meeting in the park?"

"Your family was determined to turn you against not only your fiancé but all men. At the very least you would not think of marriage for some time and they would have the opportunity to come up with other strategies. They needed to engineer a meeting that achieved that goal. Their desperation resulted in the darkest acts. The unfortunate Coyle lad was delayed at the school and sent home in the dark. The major here brutally attacked him. He was chosen because he lived away from the main building. Your uncle coerced his parents into agreeing to a continuation of his studies at home. You were told that you would be delivering his lessons.

"A route was chosen for you to take that he knew would be little travelled. Edwards was told precisely when to be there and what to say. He was warned that he would be watched and both your lives were in danger if he did not comply. The major and your aunt took up a position in the large bush to the south. He trained a rifle on Mr. Edwards. Your aunt used her excellent field glasses to see what Edwards said. She can lip-read of course and this is why Edwards kept sliding away from you, Miss Willow, and did not look at you. He knew it was vital that his face and lips could be read at all times. He feared if that view were blocked, even for an instant, one or both of you might be killed.

"He played his part and insulted you. He hated it because he still loves you and knew it was wrong. That was the reason for his tears.

"Dr. Watson and I met with you as you know. When your aunt approached us, she already knew my name because she had lip-read you saying it. I had to satisfy myself that she was not faking her disability. So, I insulted her with my back turned. The lack of reaction was indicative of either genuine deafness or formidable restraint. The good doctor here, at my request, arranged the telegrams that brought you all to Brandon Park and from there to this room."

Holmes paused. For a few moments no one spoke. John Willow got to his feet. "So, Jane. What do you propose to do?"

Miss Willow stared at him. "Uncle, I cannot forgive you for what you have done but there is no reason the school and its pupils should suffer for your deceit. We will run the school as I wish. You will all sign statements confirming your involvement along the lines described by Mr. Holmes. In return, you will not be exposed and the school will continue."

She turned to the major. "You deserve jail, uncle, for what you did to that poor boy. I would not hesitate to expose you but everything Mr. Holmes has described would come out. I must put the school and its pupils first. You will leave this country never to return, and we will pay for the best medical care for young Coyle."

She turned away from the major, who had gone red with anger, in order to face Edwards whose expression was a mixture of hope and fear.

"You, sir, toyed with my heart for your own gain. It matters not that you developed genuine affection for me. Your initial motives are more important than your later ones. You will leave here at once. Your reward for your few noble acts is not to be punished for your ignoble ones. I wish to never see or hear from you again. All I will say to you is that you have not destroyed my faith in all men. Just that which I had in you."

Holmes and I supervised the statements Miss Willow had demanded. He undertook to hold copies that would be sent to the police in the event of anything untoward occurring later.

Back at Baker Street I gladly took a seat by the fire. I was worn out and longed for nothing more than a hot meal. Holmes went directly to the window and looked down on the hustle and bustle outside. "If I ever had doubts about the dangers of matrimony, Watson, this case has underscored them."

"If Miss Willow does marry," I said. "The man in question will be very lucky to have her in his life. I thought her a formidable young woman with a bright future."

"Yes, indeed," said Holmes. "On that we can agree."

The Adventure of the Feuding Baronets

(Late 1897)

T might surprise readers of my accounts to hear that, despite his success and discretion, there were some people averse to the services of Sherlock Holmes. Because of my friend's habit of allowing Scotland Yard to take credit for his cases, many people believed the official force to be more successful than it was. This has constantly frustrated me, but Holmes would wave a dismissive hand whenever I raised the matter. For him it was all about the challenge rather than the acclaim.

One such believer in the competency of Scotland Yard was Sir William Parker. The noted politician and maritime businessman, granted his baronetcy by Her Majesty in recognition of his many and varied services, had suffered the theft of several items from his Mayfair home. His home was well-known for its formidable security, and it had resisted countless break-in attempts over the years, yet it had been penetrated twice in as many weeks. He had informed the press that the criminals had obtained nothing of value on the first occasion as they had been forced to flee by his formidable hounds. Clearly, this had not put the criminal world off as a second, successful, raid had taken place three weeks ago and valuables were successfully spirited away.

Among the many items taken was a valuable diamond pendant. Gossips had long wondered why the unmarried Sir William had purchased such a feminine item. He had obtained it ten years previously at a heated auction in London where he had outbid five competitors, many of whom were from wealthy and powerful families across the Continent. The pendant was valued at £3,000, and Sir William had ultimately paid double to secure it – much to the chagrin of his opponents. Naturally, the society pages of the day had been full of theories as to why he had purchased it and for what purpose. What intrigued them even more was the fact that following the purchase nothing more was heard of the pendant.

When news broke that it, and other items, had been stolen, it generated a lot of column inches. When there was no news of any progress in the investigation, Holmes sent a note to Scotland Yard offering his services. Inspector Gregson, who was in charge, had courteously called upon us that evening to inform us that Sir William had expressly forbade Holmes's involvement. To Sir William, Holmes was superfluous.

My friend was more curious than affronted by this rejection. He left the feelings of affront to me. "What can I do, Watson?" he said. "If Sir William prefers insurance money to his property, who am I to tell him otherwise?"

To distract me rather than himself, Holmes reminded me that he had tickets for that evening at the Royal Opera House. I recalled that this was to be followed by supper at Simpson's. It succeeded in banishing the subject of Sir William from my mind.

In the evening we made our way to Covent Garden. As usual, it was busy with shoppers, revellers, and passers-by enjoying the various street entertainments. As we wandered through the piazza, I saw small groups of street urchins milling around, often being shooed away from the front of the shops and public houses when they begged for coins or, frequently, purloined them.

Holmes and I had arrived in plenty of time for the performance and made our way inside. Holmes liked to indulge my habit of a pre-performance brandy while he preferred to smoke. As we waited to deposit our hats and overcoats in the cloakroom there was suddenly a commotion. Due to the number of people in front we could not see clearly but a male voice was screaming in a manner approaching hysteria. There were no intelligible words, just wailing. A voice called out in desperation for a doctor, and with Holmes's help, I forced my way towards the front of the queue.

At the entrance to the cloakroom, we found a man lying on the floor, surrounded by coins and other personal effects. He was now unconscious and appeared peaceful. Around him were members of opera house staff, along with a few patrons. I announced myself and they retreated to give me space explaining that they had been endeavouring to restrain the man prior to his loss of consciousness. He did not seem physically injured so I had him conveyed to the manager's office. As the staff began to bear him away, I heard a lady whisper to a friend that it was only a matter of time before this happened to him. She seemed to be relishing the moment, wearing a barely concealed smile. One of the men who had risen from the floor when I approached, who had been waiting, like us, to deposit his overcoat, turned and headed for the exit with a look on his face that was between frustration and contempt. I despaired at the lack of humanity. Holmes instructed the cloakroom staff to gather the man's belongings and bring them to the same office.

Upon reaching the manager's office, the staff lowered the man onto a settee before withdrawing. Holmes closed the door after them before turning to look at our supine companion.

"Did you hear what that lady said?" I asked.

Holmes shook his head sadly. He walked over to the manager's desk, perched on the end of it and took out his cigarette case. "Some people thrive on gossip, Watson. It is like oxygen to them. Sadly, our unconscious friend must take a good deal of the credit for that."

"You know who this is?"

He selected a cigarette, replaced his case, and took a match from the striker on the manager's desk. He struck it and applied it. "Yes. It is Sir Enoch Hughes, the shipping magnate."

"What makes you say he contributed to his present situation?" I asked.

Holmes looked again at the baronet as he drew on his cigarette and exhaled. "You should keep more of an eye on the society pages, Watson. He recently let it be known that his wife, Lady Florence Hughes, had left him after a decade of supposedly happy marriage." The last three words were uttered with distinct cynicism. "In fact, the newspapers had been suggesting for some time that the marriage was in trouble. There was gossip to the effect that Sir Enoch was an unpredictable man, prone to violent outbursts, although, to be fair, no evidence for this was produced. They took a holiday to Italy a month ago, which was painted by the press as a marriage-saving trip, from which Sir Enoch returned alone. Upon his arrival in Portsmouth, he managed to elude the press for twenty-four hours before they caught up with him at his house in Chelsea. He gave a brief statement to the effect that his marriage had broken down and promptly went into a form of seclusion. His business was left in the hands of his deputy."

I felt for Sir Enoch. It was all too easy for Fleet Street to paint a man as a brute or philanderer and for an audience to be all too ready to believe it.

Holmes continued. "The problem with feeding the fire of gossip is that it yearns for more fuel. Sir Enoch was clearly distraught at the separation and his willingness to admit to it openly made the suspicious believe there was more to it. This was not helped by the fact that Lady Hughes has not been seen since his return. He has been hounded by the press for more details and his servants, past and present, have been offered money for insights. This is arguably one of his first social engagements since his return."

Holmes stubbed out his cigarette and proceeded to select and light another. I turned my attention to Sir Enoch. He was breathing steadily and I contemplated seeking smelling salts.

"There is a connection here to Sir William Parker," said Holmes.

"Really? What is that?"

"The two men loathed each other, Watson, and appeared to be in perpetual competition. They both had shipping businesses although Sir William divided his time between that and politics. Both were known to be diplomatic, courteous, gallant, and generous donors to charity. Each trying to outdo the other with the causes they championed or the donations they made. While Sir William has largely maintained this reputation, Sir Enoch's has been somewhat tarnished by the events I have just described.

"Sir William made no secret of his amusement at Sir Enoch's plight and Sir Enoch spoke in a similar vein when approached for comment on the burglaries at Sir William's house. Prior to these events, they had been regular sparring partners in the pages of the broadsheets. They clashed on almost every subject from the arts to politics. Whatever position one adopted; the other would take up the opposite.

"They have hated each other for as long as anyone can remember and, intriguingly, no one seems to know why. It has long been presumed to be a business rivalry, but it is the one thing both men are tight-lipped about. Now, Doctor, is your patient well enough for my examination?"

I nodded. Holmes stubbed out his cigarette and approached the baronet. He knelt to examine the man's shoes and made notes in the notebook that was never far from reach. Sir Enoch was still wearing his coat having not completed his cloakroom transaction. Holmes gently opened the coat to examine Sir Enoch and his clothing. "Most strange," he said.

"Why strange?"

"He is minus his hat, gloves, and cane. We must assume that those will be brought to us shortly. His watch is hanging loose rather than being in his waistcoat pocket and all his pockets, bar one, are empty. In said pocket is a card for Simpson's with the word 'Booth' and the numbers nine and thirty written in pencil on the back. He appears to be missing his pocket book as well."

At that moment, there was a knock at the door. Holmes opened it and a young man entered carrying a tray with various items on it. Holmes took the tray and the young man backed out of the room, stealing a glance at Sir Enoch as he did so.

Holmes carried the items to the manager's desk. There, he spread them out and I joined him. "So, we have a pocketbook containing bank notes totalling fifty pounds. There are a few shilling pieces, pennies, and a couple of guineas. Presumably for cab fares and tips." Holmes picked up a silver case and opened it. "We also have a handsome cigar case containing the best Cuban cigars. Finally, we have a handkerchief, opera hat, a pair of white dress gloves, and one rather handsome cane. In short, he appears to have all the items one would expect of a gentleman attending the opera."

"Perhaps the poor man simply had a turn?" I suggested. "From what you have described he seems to have undergone more than his fair share of woe."

"Perhaps," said Holmes. "Ah, he is coming to."

I turned to the settee and could see Sir Enoch's eyes were beginning to open. "Where am I?" he asked as he looked around the room and at each of us.

"You are in the manager's office of the Royal Opera House and I am a doctor," I replied.

Sir Enoch's face went bright red. "I am sorry to have been a nuisance, Doctor. I have been under a lot of stress. If you read the papers, I am sure you know why."

"My friend here is not a devotee of the society pages," said Holmes from behind a cloud of fresh cigarette smoke. "My name is Sherlock Holmes. Is there any way that I may assist you?"

"The detective?" asked Sir Enoch, his eyebrows raised.

"The same, sir," replied Holmes.

Sir Enoch straightened up and adjusted his clothing. "No, thank you, Mr. Holmes. My situation does not require a detective. Regrettably, my wife abandoning me is not a crime." He stood and endeavoured to muster some dignity. "May I offer you something for your services, Doctor?" He reached into his coat for his pocketbook.

I gestured towards the desk. "Your pocketbook and other effects are on the desk, Sir Enoch. I thank you, but I require no payment."

"Most gracious of you, sir," replied Sir Enoch. "If you will excuse me, gentlemen." With that, he collected his belongings and swiftly exited.

"Well," said Holmes, as the door shut behind the baronet, "that is twice that my services have been spurned. It is getting dangerously close to a regular occurrence. Shall we take our seats? I believe there is still time before the performance commences. Regrettably, you will have to forego your small vice."

For three hours we were absorbed by the performance. From time to time, I would look at Holmes, who sat, eyes closed, but evidently with his attention focused on the music. The cold logician was never further from sight than at these moments. At the conclusion we collected our coats and made our way, across the piazza, towards Simpson's.

Upon our arrival, we learned that, due to an uncharacteristic error on the part of that venerable restaurant, we were not able to have our usual booth. Holmes always favoured a booth as he preferred to study others rather than be the object of study. With copious apologies, the staff seated us at a more central, exposed, table and offered us complimentary drinks to ease the discomfort.

When the waiter attempted to present us with the menu, Holmes waved it away and delivered his order from memory. I did the same and the waiter left us. Holmes watched him go before turning back to me. As he did so, his face took on an expression of surprise. "Well, well."

"What is it?"

"Our friend, Sir Enoch, has chosen to dine here also. That would explain the card."

I turned. In our usual booth, at the side of the restaurant, sat the baronet. He was attempting to eat but was doing so without any conviction.

"Do you notice something, Watson?"

"No."

"Although he is alone now that was not always the case."

I peered as subtly as I could manage. The table was indeed laid for two people. While Sir Enoch was eating, the other plates appeared unused. "Holmes," I said. "Perhaps his guest failed to appear or is still to arrive?"

"Your eyesight does not do you credit, Doctor," Holmes replied. "There is a used second wine glass. Appearances suggest that his guest did attend but chose merely to drink. The fact that the empty glass has not yet been removed by the, usually efficient, staff suggests that said guest has only recently departed."

Suddenly, Sir Enoch looked up and was in time to see us staring at him. Holmes smiled and nodded. Looking more alarmed than annoyed, the baronet summoned a waiter, settled his bill, and made his way out, giving us a brief nod of acknowledgement as he passed.

"That was embarrassing, Holmes," I said.

"More for him than us, it would appear," said Holmes.

After supper Holmes announced that he would like to walk to Baker Street. The route he chose took us back through Covent Garden. By now the piazza was a lot quieter. As we walked past the Punch and Judy public house, Holmes put a restraining hand on my arm bringing us both to a halt.

"What is it, Holmes?" I asked. Without turning towards me, he placed a finger on his lips and looked ahead.

I followed his gaze. About twenty yards away we could see Sir Enoch. He was walking slowly, his cane held behind his back and his head bowed. As we watched, one of the street urchins approached him, clearly trying to get something from him. He appeared to speak briefly with the lad before giving him some money.

"He will regret that," I whispered. "Word will be passed and they will descend on him."

"As Sir Enoch desires no connection with us, I suggest we maintain our distance," whispered Holmes.

Sure enough, my prediction came true. Sir Enoch was approached by a further half-dozen young boys over the next ten minutes. He took time to speak with them all and they all departed with coins. His reputation for charity was clearly well-deserved.

As we watched, one final boy approached the baronet. As before, they spoke, perhaps slightly longer than the others. Coins were handed over and, as the boy ran off, Sir Enoch watched him leave. He looked around, caught sight of us, and departed the piazza, his pace considerably quicker.

"He will begin to think we are being paid to follow him," said Holmes.

The next day, the ever-efficient press was reporting on the unfortunate Sir Enoch's opera experience. As always, they had sought the opinion of Sir William Parker but reported that the long-standing rival had refused to pass comment. Instead, the Telegraph's representative had reported on how Sir William had his butler slam the door in his face.

That evening, I remarked on this to Holmes who showed little concern. For him neither man held any further interest. "Time to turn our attention to more worthy matters," he said, without elaborating on what those were.

A day later, the afternoon newspapers were carrying the story that Sir Enoch had boarded ship for the Continent that morning. It was suggested by some that he was going abroad until the talk about his recent embarrassment was forgotten. Others suggested it was a forlorn quest to Italy to win back his wife's affections.

I had just finished reading the article when Holmes wandered into the sitting room. He had gone early-morning to the British Museum to conduct some research which, when I questioned him, he explained would bore me.

"Afternoon, Watson," he said.

"Afternoon, Holmes," I responded. "Was your excursion fruitful?"

He seized a pipe and flopped into his chair. "The museum? Yes, I suppose so. Is that a telegram I spy on the dining table?"

"Yes. It arrived about an hour ago."

He sprang out of the chair and seized the envelope. He tore it open, liberated its contents and dropped the envelope on the floor as he returned to his seat. As he read, a smile crossed his face. Knowing Holmes, this did not bode well for someone.

"There has been a body found at the docks, and Lestrade invites us to take a look."

Moments later we were in a cab rattling our way east. "What can you tell me?" I asked.

Holmes stared straight ahead. "Nothing of substance. Lestrade was a little cryptic. I got the distinct impression that it does not interest him but he thinks it will interest me."

In just under an hour, we reached the location. Several warehouses were lined up only a stone's throw from the river. In front of all but one stood crates and barrels containing imports and exports. Dockworkers were milling about occasionally throwing suspicious looks at the police stationed outside.

We alighted from the cab and approached the warehouse with the police presence. It looked a little more dilapidated than its neighbours and was clearly in need of maintenance. A modest sign pinned to the door carried the name of Windsor Auctioneers. As we approached, Lestrade came out to meet us. "Good afternoon, gentlemen," he said, with a grin. "Nice day for it."

Holmes overlooked the tasteless remark. "What is so special about this one and why don't you concern yourself?"

Lestrade, having shaken hands with us both, thrust his into his pockets. "Because a criminal has been killed, Mr. Holmes, and that is always a little better than someone innocent. When you see who it is you will be surprised."

He gestured towards the open door, "Gentlemen."

We stepped inside. The interior was even less impressive than the exterior. Cobwebs could be seen in abundance and various types of debris were strewn across the floor. We made our way towards an office at the rear of the building. The constable on duty stepped to one side and permitted us to enter. It was a perfectly ordinary office with one exception. In the corner, on the floor, surrounded by loose papers, was the body of a young man who had clearly been stabbed or shot through the chest going by the blood-soaked shirt he was wearing.

"After you, Doctor," said Holmes.

I advanced carefully and knelt next to the unfortunate young man. He was no more than twenty, perhaps even as young as sixteen or seventeen. I briefly mused that there is always something additionally tragic about a life cut so short. There were flecks of blood on the wall behind him and in his hand was a tiny scrap of white paper. On one of his outstretched legs was some dried mucus and he was missing his shoes. He had clearly had shoes when he arrived as his sockless feet were clean. You did not need Holmes's powers to see that. The desk alongside where his body lay had been ransacked. Drawers were half-open and papers were everywhere, some resting on the body itself. On top of the desk, amongst other paperwork, was a half-empty whisky bottle. One or two of the scattered papers had the outline of a shoeprint on them. Others had evidence of minor water staining.

I completed my examination and stood up. "He has been dead for around ten to twelve hours so somewhere between eleven last night and one this morning. It looks like this young man was searching for something judging by the papers. It seems he has been run through with a long blade but he may have been struck first going by the marks on his face."

Holmes nodded.

"I thought you would be interested," said Lestrade from the doorway.

"What does he mean?" I asked.

"This is Stephen, or Stevie, Williams," said Holmes. "A prolific petty thief and opium addict. He was the latter first and turned to crime to feed his addiction when his family cast him out. He was only fifteen."

"Older, surely?" I said, looking at the body.

"Watson," said Holmes, "he tried to pick my pocket in Leicester Square about a year ago. I introduced him to Wiggins in the hope that we could channel his skills, but he was not really one for teamwork. I assure you that he was that age."

"How sad," I said.

"He has been the bane of my life," said Lestrade. "The number of times I have been asked to investigate stolen property that this ragamuffin had lifted would make your head spin."

I turned to Holmes. "I can see why Lestrade is of two minds about this. But why does he want us here?"

"It is a question of location. Stevie had no business here. His patch was the West End. The gangs that work this area would be decidedly hostile to his presence. He would not come here lightly."

"His addiction?" I suggested. "As you well know, Holmes, there are plenty of such dens around here."

"True, but they also exist far closer to Stevie's usual patch. He would have no reason to head out here for that. The chaos here in this office is interesting."

"It seems clear to me," I said. "This Stevie came here to steal. He went through all the drawers and was interrupted and killed. Perhaps by one of the rival gangs you just mentioned."

Holmes was clearly not convinced. "But why, Watson? He would not come here on the off-chance. He would need to have a strong motive. Did someone tell him there was something special here? If so, who, why, and what?"

The question was clearly rhetorical as he did not wait for an answer. "If Stevie was interrupted by another individual, also bent on stealing something, or someone angered by his intrusion onto hostile turf, it could have taken the form of a territorial dispute. The problem with that is the manner of death. The local criminal fraternity prefer short, concealable, blades to overt ones.

"What is your theory?" I asked.

Holmes approached the body, taking care not to disturb the scene. He lent down to the dead boy's face. "Stevie clearly had some of that whisky. The bottle is new, and a cheap brand commonly purchased by his ilk, so we can infer that he brought it with him given that everything else here is old and the place largely abandoned. This whisky also stands against the idea that he came here to steal."

"It does?" I said. "How?"

Holmes ignored the question and turned to Lestrade. "This warehouse seems very much abandoned but is it guarded in any way?"

"It was occasionally patrolled by a retired soldier named John Castle," replied Lestrade. "They are often employed in that kind of capacity."

"How often would this John Castle check on the warehouse?"

Lestrade frowned. "Twice a day. First thing in the morning and in the evening. Normally he would not enter the building. He would merely check the locks. He overslept this morning, arriving just after eleven. He only entered and found the body, when he discovered the place was not locked and a ground floor window was open."

"Was the lock forced?"

"Yes."

Holmes nodded and began to examine the scene around the body. He paid attention to the many papers. When done he appeared unsatisfied.

"None of these papers are torn," he said. "Whatever Stevie was holding onto it is no longer here." He reached into his pocket and withdrew a small leather case. He opened it and produced a pair of tweezers. With them, he lifted the small piece of paper from the dead boy's hand and placed it in an envelope taken from the desk. "Quite thin. Thinner than pretty much all the other papers here. That suggests one strong possibility."

"I will take that, Mr. Holmes," said Lestrade. Reluctantly, Holmes handed it over. "How do you plan to proceed, Lestrade?"

"My men will go over this area and we will question everyone in the vicinity."

"I doubt you will get far."

Lestrade shrugged his shoulders. "I realise that, Mr. Holmes, but it has to be tried."

"I will do my best to assist. I will return to Stevie's usual haunts and make enquiries there. Before I do that, is it possible to speak to Mr. John Castle?"

"He is just outside, Mr. Holmes," said Lestrade. He turned his head to the open door. "Stretcher!" he barked.

Before leaving we watched as Lestrade's men came in to remove Stevie's body. They gently lifted him, leaving a macabre silhouette where his body had been.

As we left the warehouse, Lestrade pointed out the guard to us. Holmes and I approached him. "Good afternoon, Mr. Castle."

Castle, who was around forty-five to fifty, did not get up from the barrel he was sitting on. "Who's asking?"

"My name is Sherlock Holmes and I am working with the police regarding the dead boy you discovered."

Castle shrugged.

"Perhaps you would like a cigarette?" said Holmes.

Castle grunted his agreement and Holmes offered one from his case. Castle took it and accepted a light.

"Can you tell me why you were late to the warehouse this morning?" asked Holmes.

Castle smirked. "I bumped into an old army mate after I checked the warehouse yesterday. We decided to go for a drink and talk about the old days. My head was a bit sore this morning, so I was late."

"At what time did you check the warehouse before meeting your friend?"

"About ten. I was away by half-past as it does not take long to check the doors and windows."

"Did you see anyone suspicious?"

Castle laughed. "Everyone 'round here is suspicious."

Holmes frowned at him. Castle got the message. "No, sir. When I left, I saw no one nearby. Can I go?"

Holmes nodded and Castle shuffled off.

Holmes rubbed his hands. "That was more useful than I anticipated."

"It was?"

"Mr. Castle's recollection chimes with your estimate of death. We now know that this warehouse was secure thirty minutes before the earliest time you believe Stevie could have met his maker. Furthermore, no one obviously suspicious was visible in the immediate area."

"Meaning?"

"One of three scenarios. Stevie was either inside the building already and laying low; he was outside hiding and waiting for a chance to break in; or he came along later. The fact he was not seen implies either luck or a knowledge of Castle's routine."

He marched off in search of a cab. I ran to catch up.

"Earlier you said Lestrade would struggle with his enquiries here. Why?"

"Aside from his usual incompetence?" said Holmes with a smile.

"Yes."

"He will struggle because the denizens of the docklands are not on the best of terms with the police. Many dip their fingers into the world of crime and will not want to be seen helping the authorities."

As he had stated, Holmes asked our cabby to take us back to the West End. "Stevie mostly operated alone but sometimes he would attach himself to some of the gangs that work the West End. He learned his trade from these gangs – mugging, pickpocketing, card tricks – Stevie learned it all."

We alighted in Covent Garden and spent ten minutes walking the piazza looking for anyone whom Holmes recognised. Failing in this, Holmes suggested we walk to Trafalgar Square. We walked the perimeter three times before Holmes moved on. Finally, we ended up in Leicester Square.

"At last," said Holmes as he spied a small group of boys. One of them spotted Holmes but too late. Holmes seized his collar. His fellows scattered.

"Settle down, Joe," said Holmes.

The boy stopped struggling. "Oh, it's you, Mr. Holmes. I ain't done nothing."

"We've spoken about double-negatives before, Joe," said

Holmes. "They can get you into trouble."

Holmes steered the boy to one of the benches in the square's centre and sat him down. He released him and showed him a shilling. The boy stared at it as if mesmerised.

"Now, Joe," said Holmes, "I have some bad news for you. Stevie is dead."

"People die in our game, Mr. Holmes."

I was staggered at the level of indifference in someone so young.

"Do you know of any reason someone would wish him harm?" asked Holmes.

Joe laughed. "'alf of the West End, sir. Stevie stole from people from Piccadilly to Fleet Street."

"But had he acted out of character lately?"

"He was a bit odd the other day," said Joe. "We'd seen him at the beginning of the night. We usually met either 'ere or in Trafalgar Square before headin' off. I bumped into one of the other lads around 'alf-seven. He said he'd seen Stevie by the river looking shaken. Stevie wouldn't say what had upset him and we assumed he'd had a scrape with the Peelers."

I watched Joe during this speech. Except for an occasional glance at Holmes, his eyes rarely left the shilling.

"Anything else?"

"I decided to go to the river and see if I could find 'im. On the way I bumped into another lad, Tully we call him. He was headin' towards Covent Garden in quite the 'urry. I asked if he'd seen Stevie, as they were close. Tully said he had just left him at the river close to the needle."

"Did you find him?"

"Yes, Mr. Holmes. He was staring across the river and jumped when I called out."

"What did he say?"

"Not a lot, sir. 'is answers to my questions were short. He started to get angry and told me to go away. He wanted to be on 'is own. That was the last time I saw either of 'em."

"You are telling me that this Tully is now also missing?" asked Holmes.

"Dunno, sir. Me not seeing him and him being missing ain't the same thing."

"What does Tully look like?"

" 'bout my height, short black hair, skinny. Oh, and a birthmark under his chin."

Holmes nodded and flicked the shilling to Joe, who caught it deftly. "Now, Joe," said Holmes, "there is another shilling for you if you bring me any other information. Ask around. If you find Tully let him know I wish to talk to him. A further shilling for you both if you bring him to me."

With a brief salute, Joe vanished into the crowd.

"I do not see how that information was worth a shilling, Holmes. Where does it get us?"

"With a little imagination," said Holmes, "there is a theory that works. However, I currently lack the facts to support it."

We returned to Baker Street where I was able to have a sandwich while Holmes went through his files. About an hour later we were joined by Lestrade. His face showed how successful he had been with his enquiries.

"No luck with the dockland denizens?" asked Holmes.

"None. You?" asked the detective.

"Nothing solid," said Holmes. "It seems Stevie was on edge about something in the days before his death but that is all."

"Well, I am not going to miss the oik," said Lestrade. "That said, I do not like having this on my books unsolved."

"What more do you know about the location?" asked Holmes.

Lestrade smiled. Presumably this was an area in which he had made progress. "The warehouse is, or was, the head office of the Ferguson shipping company. It was in a sorry state, bankrupt. An auction for its assets is due in the next few days."

"I see. Anything else?"

"The auctioneers informed us that they had approached certain individuals about the pending sale in order that they might view the property in advance."

"Do we know who has expressed an interest?"

Lestrade flicked to another page. "I have the names of the approached here. All of them quite well known in the industry."

"Can you copy down the list?"

"I suppose so," said Lestrade. He took a seat at our dining table and tore out a sheet from his notebook. He scribbled down some names and handed it to Holmes. "Anyone there catch your eye?"

Holmes scanned the page. "Well, I can see the names of Sir William Parker and Simon Harper. They are the two most interesting."

"Why so?" I asked.

"As you know, Watson, Sir William has an interest in shipping. Mr. Harper is Sir Enoch's deputy who has been running his business since Sir Enoch's marriage fell apart. It was mentioned in the newspaper reports."

Lestrade scratched his head. "I see nothing unusual in two shipping magnates showing an interest in the assets of a shipping company." He stood and walked to the door. "Do let me know when you have something useful."

"Lestrade," said Holmes. "Find out what you can about the names on that list please."

Lestrade looked at me, rolled his eyes, and left.

Holmes took his seat by the fire. "Interesting, isn't it?"

"What is?"

"We now have a link, albeit a tenuous one, between our warring baronets and the death of Stevie."

"It is a bit of a leap, Holmes," I replied. "What you have is a tenuous link between every name on that list and Stevie's death."

About an hour later we were sitting down to dinner. Mrs. Hudson had prepared a most excellent fish pie. Holmes ate enthusiastically which was a relief to see as he would often abstain while working. His conversation largely avoided the current case and focused on several more modest ones he had undertaken, without my assistance, many of them purely through correspondence.

"I thought your pile of letters was smaller than usual, Holmes."

"Thanks to your powers of selection, Watson, your readers remain ignorant of exactly how many puzzles are put before me. Alas, one of the reasons I sought to get involved in the matter of the missing pendant was the simple fact that our postman has brought me very little of interest in the last few weeks."

"Which of these cases has presented the greatest challenge?" I asked.

He smiled. "Let me tell you about, what the local newspapers called, the Helmsdale Horror."

Before I knew it, it was past two in the morning and I had worn down two pencils taking notes. I realised how tired I was and turned in, leaving Holmes smoking by the fire.

A little after nine the next morning, I descended to the sitting room to find Holmes eating a boiled egg and looking at a letter that lay alongside his plate. I was not entirely sure he had bothered to sleep.

"What is that?" I asked.

He looked up. "Morning, Watson. It is a note from Gregson. He is cock-a-hoop as he has discovered Sir William's stolen property."

"A feather in his cap," I observed.

"To a point. He has not recovered the pendant which remains missing. Also, my choice of wording was poor. He did not discover the items. They were brought to his attention by an honest labourer who found them discarded in a vacant shop near Kingly Street. Sir William has already handed over a substantial reward."

"So, why are you wearing that quizzical expression?" I asked.

"Something does not quite sit right," he said. "I think we should pay Sir William a visit."

"I do not imagine he will welcome that," I said.

"I fully expect a frosty reception, Watson."

Much to our surprise, we were admitted to Sir William's Mayfair home. The stories about its security were well-founded. The front door had multiple locks and, when we were removing our coats, we could hear the deep barking of more than one dog elsewhere in the house. In response to our questioning, the butler informed us that the dogs roamed the house freely at night and were kept hungry.

We were shown into the study where we found Sir William writing at his desk. He did not immediately acknowledge our presence and I took the opportunity to look around. I noticed formidable locks on the windows and assumed the house was probably similar throughout. My thoughts were interrupted by the baronet. "I have admitted you as a courtesy, Mr. Holmes," he said, without rising or putting down his pen, "but I thought I had made it quite clear that your services were not required. Scotland Yard has done its job."

"We appreciate you receiving us," said Holmes. "It is not the theft of your property nor its recovery that brings us here."

Sir William seemed relieved to hear this. He put down his pen and waved us into seats. "Then what may I do for you, gentlemen?"

"I believe," said Holmes, "that you have shown an interest in the auction relating to the Ferguson Shipping Company?"

Sir William frowned. "That is true but forgive me if I fail to see how that is a concern of yours."

"It is a concern because of a boy found murdered there recently."

"A death is always tragic, Mr. Holmes," said Sir William. "I have seen my fair share of death at sea. I still fail to see why that should bring you here."

"I am trying to ascertain a motive for the murder and wondered if your knowledge of the company might offer a clue."

Sir William leaned back in his chair and smiled. "The company overstretched itself trying to increase market share. It happens to many businesses."

"I understand that you viewed the property," said Holmes. "Was there anything that you saw that might be worth stealing?"

"Not on site. Much of their cargo was perishable and passed being of any value. My interest was the building and I think that would be rather hard to steal. If a young boy was able to break into it, its security was clearly not as good as I was informed."

"You were aware of the security of the building?"

"Up to a point. The auctioneers informed us that all the windows had locks, that the main door was secured with a sturdy padlock and that the building was checked twice a day – first and last thing. Naturally, when I viewed the building, it was accessible."

The clock chimed the half-hour and Sir William checked the time against his watch. It was clear we were keeping him from other business. He stood and we did likewise.

"Now, I think it is time to bid you good day as I cannot add anything further."

"May I ask if you have filed an insurance claim for your pendant?" asked Holmes.

Sir William flushed red but maintained his composure. "That is impertinent, Mr. Holmes. That subject is closed to you."

"May I see where the items were taken from? It may assist in the recovery of the pendant."

"No sir. You may not. I have been perfectly clear that I will not have you involved in that matter. Good day, sir."

Sir William's butler escorted us to the front door with effectiveness.

"We went from a frosty welcome to an equally frigid farewell," observed Holmes with a smirk.

"I do not see what good it did you to anger him," I said.

"It was instructive. Sir William is a man possessed of above average self-control. Useful for a man in business, politics and, possibly, murder. We also know that anyone who viewed that warehouse may have been informed, as Sir William was, of its security arrangements.

"It may also interest you to know that he was in the process of writing to his insurance agents. Reading upside-down is a skill all detectives should cultivate."

We secured a cab in the next street. Our destination, I was surprised to learn, was the vacant shop where Sir William's stolen property had been discovered.

"Why the interest in this theft, Holmes? Surely, we should be focusing on the death of Stevie?"

"At the moment I have made all the enquiries I feel necessary and we shall act on any further information we receive. As intriguing as Stevie's murder is, Sir William's determination to keep me at a distance is, at least, equally so. Why buy a pendant ten years ago for double the valuation, proceed to hide it from the world, procure some of the city's best security for it and then be so blasé about its loss?"

He paused and smiled. "Also, his lack of faith in me has dented my pride a little."

Fortunately, several labourers were present, one of whom had been responsible for the discovery. Some coins changed hands and we were led to a yard at the rear of the property.

"Tell me, Mr. Wood," said Holmes, "how did you come upon the items?"

The labourer scratched his head. "We were booked to start work on this shop next month but finished our last job early. We're getting it ready for the next tenant. Early this morning I came into this yard with some rubbish we had cleared and noticed a large sheet that was covering something. I was nosey, sir, so I lifted it to find an old tea chest in which were several silver plates and candlesticks."

"And you reported this to the police?"

Wood seemed affronted. "Yes. I'm an honest man. I had read about the theft and saw that the items I'd found matched the description." He paused, "Also, there was the reward."

"I understand," said Holmes. "So, you cannot be sure how long the items had been there?"

"Sorry, no, Mr. Holmes. They may have been there a day or weeks for all I know. We'd had no reason to enter the yard before today. I am worried for the owner though."

"Why so?"

"The owner of this building is Sir Enoch Hughes, Mr. Holmes. It occurred to me straightaway that someone was trying to pin it on him. Everyone knows how he and Sir William Parker don't get on."

"You do not seem ready to consider the idea that Sir Enoch could be responsible," I said.

Wood turned to me. "Not him, sir. He has always struck me as an upstanding gentleman. Funny in his ways, wears his heart on his sleeve if you know what I mean?"

Wood had nothing to add so we left. "Well," said Holmes, "our friend was more educated than I gave him credit for. I believe

Othello is the source for that expression. Is this theft just the latest round in their feud? If so, things have gained a pace. Assuming Sir William knows where the items were found he must have concluded that Sir Enoch could have had a hand in it. Given their long-standing dislike of each other I am surprised he has not pressured Scotland Yard into making an arrest.

"We should pay a visit to Sir Enoch's company and talk to his deputy. Before that, we should stop by Baker Street in case Lestrade has left any information relating to Stevie."

On our arrival at Baker Street, we learned that Lestrade had indeed dropped a message off. Holmes, without removing his overcoat, seized the envelope from the dining table and tore it open. As he read, he smiled.

"Good news?" I asked.

"Of a kind," he replied. "It seems that, of the people approached by the auction house, only three paid a visit to the warehouse. Sir William, Simon Harper, and a Mr. Roger Jones who, it seems, has been abroad since before the murder."

We turned to leave and the bell rang. We headed downstairs as Mrs. Hudson opened the door. It was our young friend, Joe. At Holmes's invitation, he stepped into the hallway. "I found Tully, Mr. Holmes. He's in a right state and wouldn't come with me."

"I quite understand," said Holmes. "Tell him I can help him."

"He won't believe that," said Joe. "He is scared for his life."

"Very well, Joe," said Holmes. "Tell Tully that he will have to help me if he wants to be safe. You can reach him if needed?"

Joe nodded.

"When the time is right, I will ask you to find him again. He needs to trust me, he really does, or the danger will never go away. When he agrees to do this, tell him to bring anything that he has that will be useful." Holmes tapped his nose as he said this.

Joe nodded again. "Right you are, Mr. Holmes." With that he dashed off.

"What's that about, Holmes?" I asked.

"A piece of the puzzle falling into place. One I expected based on the murder scene."

We were soon in a cab heading for Sir Enoch's office not too far from his Chelsea home. "To me, Holmes," I said, "that news from Lestrade doesn't seem helpful."

"How helpful it is," said Holmes, "depends on what we learn from Simon Harper."

Mr. Harper greeted us warmly upon our arrival. He was a soberly dressed man in his late thirties. He exuded a level of authority that I would have normally associated with a teacher or clergyman. We were shown into his rather spartan office. "It is an honour to meet you both," he said. "How can I assist you?"

"We are here in connection with two matters," said Holmes. "Firstly, the theft of the property of Sir William Parker and, secondly, the murder of a young boy at the Ferguson Shipping Company."

Mr. Harper sank into his seat. "What can I have to say on those matters?"

"Something instructive, I hope," said Holmes. "A fact which you may be aware of is that Sir William's property has been discovered at a building owned by Sir Enoch. A vacant shop near Kingly Street."

"Yes. I know it," said Harper. "The workmen started on it early. I gave them permission and the keys."

"You must see how it looks?"

"I must disagree, Mr. Holmes," said Harper. "One of the reasons the previous tenant vacated the premises was that it was not secure and had been broken into in the past. The lock was poor and the building was accessible via its rear yard. Addressing those two concerns is one of the jobs for the workmen."

"Was this weakness widely known?"

"That I do not know." Harper rose and walked to the window. He resumed speaking whilst looking down onto the street below. "I run most things these days, and it is hard to keep abreast of it all. Sir Enoch has been little more than a figurehead for years. He attended board meetings and took the big decisions but had little interest in the day-to-day. With the end of his marriage, he stepped back further still. Even the fall of the Ferguson Shipping Company failed to interest him. Normally he would have sought to purchase its assets if only to annoy Sir William.

"I considered his lack of interest foolish and took it upon myself to go in his place. I gave him a summary report on my return but he responded that the warehouse was too small and would cost too much to make secure. I did not agree but finally decided to drop the matter. Now he has gone to Italy and I have no idea how to reach him, should it prove necessary. The situation is intolerable."

"Do you, by any chance, know the reason for the enmity between the two men?" asked Holmes.

Harper turned back to face us and rolled his eyes. "No. I believe it would make Sir Enoch easier to understand if I did. All I know is that it dates back a good decade. A time when they were both on the brink of their present success. I did wonder if it was a financial motive."

"What makes you say that?"

"Sir Enoch inherited his business from his father. He built it up from where it had been but he undeniably had the advantage. At the time, Sir William, who was not yet titled, was struggling, and Sir Enoch managed to undercut him on quite a few contracts. It is my belief that this lay behind their feud."

"How well do you know your employer?" asked Holmes.

"I thought I knew him very well," said Harper. "He was always the most predictable of men. Aside from his refusal to pursue the Ferguson auction, he has only done one other thing that surprised me."

"And that was?" asked Holmes.

"Shortly after his return from Italy, and the public failure of his marriage, Sir Enoch announced his intention to visit Sir William."

We were both surprised by this. "Details please, Mr. Harper," demanded Holmes.

Harper took a deep breath. "I had met Sir Enoch's ship in order to escort him back to London. He had not asked me to but I thought he would appreciate the company. Understandably, he was not in an amiable mood. I recall that there was trouble almost immediately when a porter at the station tried to load Sir Enoch's luggage onto a trolley in order to take it to the train. Sir Enoch snapped at the poor fellow when he picked up a Gladstone bag and snatched it back from him. He insisted on carrying that one piece of luggage to the platform personally. We boarded a train bound for Waterloo and paid the guards to keep the, ever-present, press at bay.

"About twenty minutes into the journey he told me that he needed to see Sir William. It was vital that the press did not know. He told me it was his intention to leave the train at Clapham and take a cab to Sir William's house from there. It was my role to ensure the press did not follow him."

"How did you manage that?" I asked.

Harper smiled. "It was all rather clever. Sir Enoch knew how desperate the press was for a story. So, he had me head to third-class and inform them that he would give a further statement after the train had passed Clapham. Naturally, they were keen to hear it. Sir Enoch quietly exited the train at Clapham, taking his bag with him, and, as soon as the train continued, I led the press to our compartment. When they discovered him absent the reporters were less than pleased."

"How did the meeting between the two men go?" asked

Holmes.

"As I understand it, not well," replied Harper. "Sir Enoch told me that he had extended an olive branch to Sir William. He explained about the end of his marriage and how he wanted no further conflict. By way of proof, he assured Sir William that he would be unchallenged at the Ferguson auction. It seems this did not move Sir William who had Sir Enoch escorted to the street within five minutes. Can you believe that, Mr. Holmes?"

"Having met Sir William, I can indeed believe that."

"I must confess that I hope Sir Enoch gets more involved again," said Harper. "This is a big business to run alone."

We left Mr. Harper to his paperwork. As we waited for a cab, Holmes lit a cigarette. "I wonder why Sir William omitted to tell us about Sir Enoch's visit."

"Well, Holmes," I said, "he did not seem keen to talk to you about any subject."

Holmes nodded.

For a few days no progress was made. Sir William let it be known through the press that he considered the matter of the theft closed. Most of his property had been returned, and he was planning on filing a claim for the pendant saying that it had no sentimental value and the money would do just as well.

I read this to Holmes as he sat smoking in his chair. Through the silvery curtain of smoke Holmes responded. "For a man as controlled as Sir William that seems entirely in character. That said, I do not believe him to be sincere."

I read on. "Holmes!" I exclaimed.

"What is it, Watson?" he said, with a weary tone.

"It says here that reporters in Italy have seen Sir Enoch and Lady Hughes together in Rome."

Holmes put down his pipe. "So, he has effected a reconciliation?"

"That is what is being suggested. The article paints quite the picture. They were seen together near the Pantheon. The reporter has quite the turn of phrase. He likens Lady Hughes to the goddess Venus in the painting by Botticelli. He adds that that she looked rather pale. The couple are due to return to England in a week."

"That is excellent news," said Holmes. "This reporter seems to share your love of lurid detail, Watson. On this occasion it is suggestive. Their return will offer me the chance to test a theory that I have been building for some time. We must meet whatever ship they arrive on and have Lestrade on hand."

We later learned that the ship upon which Sir Enoch and his wife would be arriving was due into Portsmouth six days from the date of the article. Holmes made the arrangements to meet it. On the day, Holmes declined to travel with me saying he had last-minute matters to attend to. He insisted I travel with Lestrade and he would follow on in time for the arrival.

Lestrade and I obtained some food at a hostelry upon arrival in Portsmouth. It was a quiet affair as we had little in common other than Holmes. An hour later we found ourselves waiting in the harbour with several reporters. It was not long before the ship came into view. "Holmes better get here soon," said Lestrade. "I am taking a risk with this."

"Do not fret, Inspector."

We turned to see Holmes. "How long have you been here?" I asked.

"Around fifteen minutes. I had to attend to a few matters. We had better board the ship when it arrives. If they get onto dry land things will be more difficult."

Lestrade made himself known to the port authorities and

secured permission to board the ship on arrival.

This was duly done and we were shown to the dining room. After a few minutes Sir Enoch and Lady Hughes were brought in by the captain. Lady Hughes was an arresting sight. The look on her face was that of someone fearful but it was offset by her beauty and her equally exquisite hair that cascaded down onto her shoulders like a golden waterfall.

My reverie was broken by Sir Enoch. "What is the meaning of this?" he demanded.

Holmes nodded at Lestrade. The inspector stood forward. "Sir Enoch Hughes, I am here to arrest you for the murder of Stephen Williams at the warehouse of the Ferguson Shipping Company."

Sir Enoch paled and his wife looked on wide-eyed in horror. "Rubbish," said Sir Enoch. I have never even been there."

"Not true," said Holmes. "You were there just under two weeks ago where you murdered a boy in cold blood. I accept you did not go there with that intention but you did it nonetheless."

"Enoch, what have you done?" asked Lady Hughes.

"Nothing, my dear," replied the baronet. "These gentlemen have no idea what they are talking about."

"I fear that we do," replied Holmes. "Lestrade, pull out a chair for Lady Hughes for I think she is going to need it. I suggest you also take a seat, Sir Enoch."

"I will have you prosecuted for slander," said the baronet.

"That would be foolish," said Holmes. "Now, sir. May I see your pocketbook?"

"What on earth for?"

"If you are able to produce it, it may prove your innocence."

Sir Enoch smiled. "Very well, sir. I will indulge you before I destroy your reputation." He reached into his coat and pulled out his pocketbook. Lestrade took it and handed it to Holmes.

"Very nice. Italian leather. Evidently purchased about a week ago. No evidence of the wear and tear associated with an item possessed for longer. Perhaps I can help you?"

Holmes reached into his own pocket. From it he produced a top quality but well used pocketbook. I recognised it at once from the Royal Opera House. Sir Enoch was silent.

Holmes opened it and extracted the bank notes. He singled out one and laid it on a nearby table. "Inspector?"

Lestrade removed an envelope from his pocket and handed it over. Holmes tipped out the contents and positioned it next to the bank note. "An exact match."

"Holmes," I asked. "Is that the scrap of paper Stevie was holding?"

"It is."

"That proves nothing," said Sir Enoch. "It was stolen from me some time ago."

"Not that long ago, Sir Enoch," said Holmes. "You had this at the Royal Opera House. You are correct about one thing. It was stolen from you. May I introduce you to its thief?"

A door opened and a boy walked in. I say walked but shuffled would be more appropriate. His feet barely left the floor as he moved to stand just to Holmes's side. He was thin and I could just see a birthmark on his throat. It was clearly the elusive Tully.

It was equally clear that Sir Enoch recognised him. "This young lad did not steal my pocketbook. I gave him money the same night I met you, gentlemen."

"That is quite true," said Holmes. "We witnessed that. But the next day he stole it from you. After you murdered Stevie."

Sir Enoch appeared to be growing in confidence. "Nonsense."

"It's true, sir," said Tully as he stood shaking.

"I am sorry, gentlemen," said Sir Enoch as he stood up, "but you are wasting my time. No jury would believe this boy. I intend to return home with my wife. If you would be so good as to return my property." He advanced, holding out his hand.

"I am afraid not," said Holmes. "Your deputy will attest that you told him that the Ferguson warehouse would cost too much to secure and you would not therefore buy it. He had made no comment to you on its security. You would only know that it was insecure if you had been there."

"I was told by the auctioneer."

"They have already confirmed to me that their only contact was with your deputy. We also know that their comments about the building's security were somewhat embellished. Again, something you would only know if you had been there after it had been locked up."

Sir Enoch spluttered. Holmes continued.

"Your pocketbook was taken from you outside the warehouse. A ten-pound note that matches part in the dead boy's hand was inside this very pocketbook."

"That means nothing. You could have placed it there?"

"To what purpose?" said Holmes, incredulously. "Finally, I have convinced Sir William to speak against you."

Sir Enoch snorted. "That is all he has done for ten years. People would be surprised if he did not."

"About the fraudulent theft and the reasons for it?"

Sir Enoch was still unmoved. "I will contest anything that man says."

Holmes sighed. "I had hoped you would not force me to do this." He rose from his seat and advanced towards Lady Hughes. Sir Enoch moved to intercept him but Lestrade manoeuvred himself between them. "I would not get in Mr. Holmes's way, sir."

"Thank you, Inspector," said Holmes. He positioned himself behind Lady Hughes. "I am truly sorry for this, madam." Before anyone could react, he gently lifted her hair.

It was a horrendous sight. Lady Hughes' right earlobe had been cut off. The injury was healing but was clearly recent. She began to sob and Holmes moved away. Sir Enoch rushed to sit at his wife's side. "Very well, gentlemen," he said. It was clear that the fight had gone out of him.

A few minutes later Lestrade, Holmes and I were alone in the dining room. Young Tully had been taken into custody. He was going to be a vital witness. A distressed Lady Hughes had been taken to a nearby hotel. Sir Enoch was on his way to a cell in Portsmouth Police Station.

"Come on, Holmes," said Lestrade. "How did you put it all together?"

Holmes smiled. "The moral of this story, gentlemen, is how destructive love can be and what men and women will do for it. Love is what is behind all of this.

"The final proof had to be obtained from Sir William by appealing to his worst nature. I am not proud of my methods in this case but I feel the end justified the means.

"It all started with the beginning of their feud ten years ago. Two things happened at that time. Sir William purchased the valuable diamond pendant and Sir Enoch married Lady Hughes.

"Why does a man normally purchase such a piece of jewellery?"

"To give to a lady," I suggested.

"Exactly. It was hardly for himself and was not the kind of item one would buy for one's mother or sister. You will always go a little bit further for your love.

"I concluded that Sir William loved Lady Hughes. He admitted this to me in our most recent interview. That was the reason I could not accompany you today, Watson. They courted in secret as her family did not approve. He was not yet titled and was seen as inappropriate for her. His career called him away to the United States. He was there for almost three years and Lady Hughes, or Florence Richards as she then was, had written to him repeatedly requesting his return. She cared little for her family's objections and was convinced she could overcome them. Despite this, Sir William had declined because, he told me, he wanted to prove his worthiness. Faced with his refusal her love faded and she turned to Sir Enoch who was equally in love with her and met with her family's approval.

"When she wrote to inform Sir William, he at last realised what he risked losing. During his time away he had made a lot of money. He returned to England and, in an effort to secure her affections, purchased the pendant at auction. The fierce bidding was well reported at the time. Little did Sir William know, that some of the people he had outbid were not content to leave the matter there. A certain Italian family was determined to secure the pendant and its members were behind the many attempts to steal it."

"But Lady Florence married Sir Enoch," I said.

"Yes. Sir William's actions were too late. Lady Hughes had become engaged, and later married, to Sir Enoch. Being spurned enraged Sir William, despite it being his own fault, and he directed his fury at Sir Enoch because, despite everything, he still loved Lady Hughes. Hence his decision to retain the pendant. If he had sold it none of this would have happened."

"How do we get from there to here?" asked Lestrade.

Holmes smiled. "You will recall that there were two attempts to burgle Sir William's house recently. He said that the first attempt had failed because his dogs had scared off the intruders. That was a lie. They had indeed been scared off but not before they had secured several letters. Amongst them was some of the correspondence between him and Lady Hughes which he had foolishly retained.

"The gang immediately realised that Lady Hughes was Sir

William's weakness. By sheer good fortune, Sir Enoch and his wife took a holiday in Rome, where they had previously honeymooned, and this fact was reported in the press. Not long after they arrived in Rome, Lady Hughes was abducted."

"Good Lord," I said.

"The price of her release was the pendant."

"They were expecting Sir Enoch to steal it?" asked Lestrade.

"Not at all," said Holmes.

"What then?"

"The gang told Sir Enoch precisely what to do. He returned to England and made use of the many unjust rumours about his marriage to tell a lie that the press was all too willing to believe. Lady Hughes's disappearance was consequently not given the attention it deserved. With the aid of his deputy, he eluded the press on the train and went straight to Sir William's house.

"I am sure the conversation was hard to get started but Sir Enoch got Sir William to listen long enough to understand his wife's plight."

"But why would Sir William believe his long-standing enemy?" I asked.

"You already know," said Holmes. "The gang understood that Sir Enoch might not be believed so they sent him to Sir William with grisly proof."

"The earlobe," I exclaimed.

"And a letter in her hand," added Holmes. "This horrific piece of proof was almost certainly contained in Sir Enoch's Gladstone bag and was the reason he refused to be parted from it – even for a few minutes. The gang was clever enough to injure Lady Hughes in a place that could be covered. I had theorised some time ago that the lack of sightings of Lady Hughes might be due to an abduction. You will recall that more recent article, Watson, where Lady Hughes was compared to that famous painting of Venus. It was unlikely that Lady Hughes was unclothed so the other striking feature of that painting was the long flowing hair. Ladies of marrying age do not wear their hair in such a fashion so there had to be a reason for it. We now know what that was.

"Sir William, still in love with Lady Hughes and faced with the horrific evidence of her predicament, agreed to hand over the pendant to save her. The two men concocted the second theft, the one later reported in the press as successful, just in case the pendant was to surface in the future and cause questions. Of course, more than the pendant had to vanish so various items were removed from the house by the two men and placed in an empty shop owned by Sir Enoch. Sir William staged the break in. At the risk of flattering myself, this was why he did not want me involved. He probably rates me higher than he would admit and feared my involvement would reveal the deception."

Lestrade snorted. "If I had been on the case rather than Gregson, I would have seen it."

Holmes made no comment. "Who knows how they planned to recover the other items but that was taken out of their hands when the items were discovered by Sir Enoch's own workmen when they began repair work a few weeks early."

"But Holmes," I said, "how do we get from there to Covent Garden?"

"This is more speculative but I trust I will be proved correct. Sir William's part was over. He played no further role beyond sticking to the story they had concocted. Sir Enoch had the pendant and was desperate to recover his wife. A representative of the Italian family made contact, upon learning of the theft, and demanded an exchange in London. Of course, there was the risk that the pendant could be handed over and Lady Hughes not released but Sir Enoch was too blinded by fear to consider that.

"One party or the other suggested the Royal Opera House. I

suspect the gang but it does not really matter. Sir Enoch attended, carrying the pendant in his overcoat. I imagine it was the intention to perform the exchange in the bar prior to the performance.

"When he got to the cloakroom, he checked his pocket, probably not for the first time, for the pendant. To his horror, he found it was no longer there. In a panic, which you and I heard Watson, he went through every pocket, dropping whatever he found onto the floor in his fruitless search. What we know is that his contact was right there."

"We do?" I asked.

"Yes. You saw him yourself, Watson. We got to the scene and had Sir Enoch carried away. You remarked upon the gossiping lady."

"Not her, surely?"

"No. You and I both noticed that man who had been near Sir Enoch, who left soon after. That got my attention. Why leave before the performance had started unless you were not there for the opera. Before we got to Sir Enoch, this man slipped the Simpson's card into his pocket. He had likely dined there beforehand and thus obtained the card. We can surmise all this because if Sir Enoch had been carrying the card on arrival it would most likely have found its way onto the floor along with everything else.

"After Sir Enoch recovered and left us. He discovered the card. He understood and went to Simpson's for the time on the back. He probably spent the intervening time scouring the piazza and other places for the pendant in the forlorn hope of finding it. Ultimately, he keeps the appointment and informs the contact what has happened. The contact does not eat because he has recently done so. Sir Enoch is told that the loss of the pendant is his problem and he knows what is at stake. The contact was almost certainly already booked onto a ship for the Continent so could not remain in London.

"I suspect Sir Enoch was told that he would now need to make his way back to Rome to conclude the exchange once the pendant had been located. I am sure his wife was threatened with further harm.

"The contact left the restaurant probably moments before we arrived. I suspect the last-minute arrangement to meet was the reason we did not get our usual table that evening. If we pressed the staff, we would probably learn that pressure was applied to obtain our table. We had our uncomfortable meeting with Sir Enoch, who promptly left. He returned to the piazza and started searching the ground again. What else could he do? He could not report it to the police and no doubt remembered where he was when he last had the pendant. We later saw him doing this Watson. He was not head bowed in sadness or embarrassment. He was head bowed studying the ground. He was pestered by urchins after money but one got his attention. That was our friend Tully."

"How do you know that?" asked Lestrade.

"I did not until I had a description of the boy from one of his fellows."

"What did he have to say to Sir Enoch?" I asked.

"I put my theory to Tully and he confirmed almost all of it. Think back to Joe. He told us that Stevie and Tully were close. It is not a leap to suggest that Stevie was working the piazza that evening and saw Sir Enoch. Stevie deftly picks his pocket and secures a lot more than he bargained for.

"He is initially delighted and then sad as he realises this is too big to move without attracting attention. He goes to Cleopatra's Needle to think and is later met there by Tully. He confesses all to Tully and between them they come up with the idea of selling it back. They know what it is as even those boys see an occasional newspaper and this story had been in all of them. So, they also know that Sir Enoch will not involve the police.

"Intelligently, they realise that Sir Enoch will look for the pendant where he last had it. Tully returns to the piazza to wait and eventually finds Sir Enoch based on Stevie's description. He tells him the situation and makes it clear the pendant can be brought to him for the right price.

"Such an exchange needs privacy and, in the heat of the moment, Sir Enoch thinks of the Ferguson warehouse which his deputy had been advising him to purchase. He knows it to be vacant. He says to Tully that someone can sneak in during the day, when it is open for viewing, and hide. When the building is later closed, he can wait there to let Sir Enoch in.

"On the appointed date, Stevie and Tully made their way to the warehouse. Stevie asked Tully to keep watch in case anyone else came. He sneaked inside and, after the guard had been round to lock up, he let himself out through the window. He forced the inadequate padlock so it would be easier to admit Sir Enoch.

"Stevie was no stranger to violence so he realised that he should not keep the pendant on him. He went into the office and hid the pendant in one of the desk drawers. If he were assaulted the pendant would not be found in his possession. To pass the time before Sir Enoch arrived, Stevie drank some of the whisky he had brought to steady his nerves.

"Sir Enoch arrived and was seen entering the warehouse by Tully. The baronet went to the office and had his interview with Stevie. He clearly produced some notes from his pocketbook based on the price told to him by Tully. Stevie took them but, feeling overconfident in the face of Sir Enoch's desperation, likely demanded more. Sir Enoch lost his temper and punched Stevie in the face. Stevie did not fall but held his ground saying that he had not brought the pendant so it would be unwise to harm him.

"Sir Enoch was in a blind rage by this point. He drew his swordstick and ran poor Stevie through. I suspect he punctured a lung and Stevie began to choke on his own blood and was therefore not able to call out.

"Sir Enoch realised what he had done but, in a clear-headed moment, surmised that Stevie would have kept the pendant close. As Stevie sank to the floor, it was Sir Enoch who proceeded to ransack the office. He hurled papers everywhere in his search and eventually found the pendant. We know it was that way round as there were no papers under Stevie's body when it was removed.

"Sir Enoch pulled the banknotes out of Stevie's hand, leaving that small scrap, and left the warehouse. Tully told me that Sir Enoch tripped and fell over in his desire to get away. Tully helped him up, stealing the pocketbook as he did so. Now it is possible Sir Enoch did not recognise him in his panic; he had what he wanted and left.

"Tully was very pleased with himself and went into the warehouse to find Stevie. We know what he found. Stevie was still just about alive. Tully was distraught and tried to help him. His sobbing is what led to that mucus on Stevie which dripped from Tully's nose in his distress. It was also Tully's footprints that appeared on some of the papers. Having already measured Sir Enoch's feet at the Opera House I knew there had been a third person there. Stevie died soon after and Tully took his shoes. The same shoes you saw him wearing a moment ago."

Lestrade spoke up. "So, are you saying that Sir Enoch calmly got the first ship to the Continent?"

"Those were his instructions. He headed for Rome as fast as he could. Eventually he was recognised and the transaction took place. He had missed his pocketbook by then but waited until after he had rescued his wife before securing a replacement."

I was stunned by what I had heard. Lestrade made his excuses and headed to collect Sir Enoch. Holmes and I left the ship.

"Sir Enoch could still get away with this," I said. "A jury will likely not believe Tully's testimony."

"Possibly not," said Holmes, "but they are very likely to believe it partnered with that of Sir William and the evidence of the banknote which I will present. I think even the dullest jury is not going to believe that Tully killed Stevie with a swordstick after giving him ten pounds."

"How did you convince Sir William to testify? Surely, he will be prosecuted for fraud if he admits to faking the theft."

"He may be able to use his influence to minimise any punishment. This is why I am not proud of my actions. I hinted that Sir Enoch would likely face the rope for murder. In that event, who would Lady Florence turn to for comfort if not the man who always loved her and sacrificed a fortune and his own reputation for her?"

"Oh, Holmes," I said. "That leaves an unpleasant taste."

"It does not mean that I am wrong, Watson."

It later emerged that Sir William would face prosecution for wasting police time. His influence, and the fact that he had not yet filed any insurance claim, helped him to sidestep a fraud charge. The Italian authorities were given full details but failed to track down those responsible for Lady Hughes' abduction and assault.

There has been no further news of the pendant. Holmes believes it is now sitting in the private collection of a certain prominent Italian family and will likely not be seen again.

Sir Enoch was sentenced to hang for the murder of Stevie and is presently in prison waiting for the sentence to be carried out. Lady Hughes has seldom been seen.

It remains to be seen if she and Sir William will join forces once the state enacts its punishment.

The Adventure of the Hirsute Intruder

(Mid-1896)

UMMER was giving way to autumn and the sun was retreating earlier each day. Sherlock Holmes was buried in his latest experiment which, although it was offensive to almost all the senses, was preferable to him dealing with his boredom via other, even less desirable, means. About an hour previously, I had moved around the sitting room, turning on the lights, and treading on many a discarded newspaper as I did so. All the while, I hoped not to disturb his formidable concentration.

Before he had immersed himself in his test tubes and chemicals, Holmes had reminded me that Mrs. Hudson was preparing one of her succulent meat pies for dinner and that prospect had helped me endure the less than aromatic results of his experiments. I had eventually returned to my chair, picking up one of the newspapers on my way, and sat down with my only desire being to read the leading articles before the arrival of the pie.

My hopes of a relaxed dinner were dispelled by a frantic ringing of the doorbell which caused Holmes to lift his head from his test tubes and gaze reproachfully in my direction as if I were personally responsible for the interruption.

From the sounds below, it was clear that a put-out Mrs. Hudson had opened the door and barely got a word in edgeways before our visitor had begun to ascend the stairs. The rapid footsteps had successfully secured Holmes's attention and we both waited with bated breath.

The door flew open, without even a knock, and a young woman stumbled into the room. Her clothing indicated she was a servant and was spattered with mud and water. Having found herself at her destination she seemed at a loss. She was panting in a manner which suggested that her entire journey had been on foot and at considerable pace. She looked from one to the other of us.

"My dear young lady," said Holmes, "are you in need of a doctor or a detective?"

The young woman appeared too exhausted to speak and her recovery was not being aided by the smell from Holmes's many test tubes. I stood and pulled out a chair for her at the dining table. She lowered herself into it, her eyes conveying the gratitude her speech could not, and continued her laboured breathing. "Give the lady a moment, Holmes," I ordered, as I filled a glass with water and placed it before her.

Having had his experiment interrupted, Holmes was not in the mood to be patient. "What brings you here?"

"No time," came the breathless response. She drank deeply from the glass. "I need you to come with me now, sir."

"Out of the question," said Holmes. "You have interrupted an important experiment to which I am keen to return."

"Please, sir," replied the young woman. "My mistress needs you urgently."

"Your mistress needs my help but will not come in person? I am not a doctor to be called out."

"She couldn't leave the baby, sir."

I looked at Holmes, my chivalrous side roused. "Come now, Holmes. This young lady has clearly hurried to get here. It must be urgent."

Holmes sighed. "Very well, Watson. But we will go in a less energetic way than this young lady arrived." He returned to his desk and put out his Bunsen burner. "I will leave you with the unenviable task of explaining our departure to Mrs. Hudson."

Moments later, we were in a four-wheeler heading south. I sat alongside our nervous visitor and Holmes across from her. Holmes rapped his fingers on the handle of his cane. It was an act that seemed to intimidate the lady and caused her to fall largely silent. As a result, we had only elicited two things from her. Her name was Sarah Mackie and we were heading for Clapham.

Holmes abruptly stopped tapping his cane and leaned forward so he could address the young lady. "So, Miss Mackie, I do not like to arrive unprepared. Please give us whatever information you possess."

The poor woman found her voice. "Well, sir, I act as maid and cook for Mr. and Mrs. Harvey who live in Stansfield Road. I have worked for them for about eight months. Mr. Harvey is an accountant and he and his wife had a baby just before they engaged me.

"Mr. Harvey does the accounts for a few businesses and individuals. He is much sought after and counts the likes of Sir Alan Smithie amongst his clients." She delivered this name as if it should mean something. To me it did not but Holmes's expression suggested that it meant something to him.

"Mr. Harvey would usually leave the house at eight each morning and return by five in the afternoon. I would prepare dinner for seven o'clock."

Holmes held up his hand. "Interesting as this is, could you come to the events that led to you being sent to my door?"

Miss Mackie looked a little irritated at the interruption but complied. "Mr. and Mrs. Harvey take the baby out in his pram for about an hour, returning just in time for dinner. On this occasion, Mrs. Harvey sent me to a shop two streets away to get a bottle of wine to go with the meal. We all left the house at the same time, them heading one way and me the other.

"On my way I met another maid, who works in the next street, who was on a similar errand. We stopped to chat for about half an hour until I realised how late I was. On my return I found Mrs. Harvey on the doorstep looking deeply distressed. The baby was crying and from inside the house I could hear shouting, barking and the smashing of crockery. In short, sir, it sounded like a fight.

"She was frozen to the spot, sir, so I went inside. It suddenly went quiet with only the occasional sound of growling. I could see nothing odd so I slowly made my way down the hallway. Halfway down was the rear parlour. I looked in to see Mr. Harvey. He was knelt over the body of a frail looking man. A couple of feet away from him was a poker and all around were broken ornaments. Their pet mastiff, which they also took on these walks, stood just behind Mr. Harvey and was still growling."

"Who was this man?" asked Holmes.

"No idea, sir," said Miss Mackie. "He looked old, and had a bushy beard. His arms were above his head and his overcoat was in a right state. You didn't need to be a doctor, sir, to see that he was dead.

"Mr. Harvey looked up and said 'It was self-defence, Sarah.' He was upset, shaking, and barely managed to get the words out. Without a further word he stood up, unsteadily, walked past me out of the room and headed for his study at the far end of the hallway. As I watched, he went in, closed the door for a few moments, and came out again."

"What happened next?" asked Holmes.

"He ran back up the hallway to the front door and tried to calm Mrs. Harvey who was holding their son, tears rolling down her face. I think she thought Mr. Harvey had been hurt and was relieved when he appeared to calm her. He had started to tell her what had happened when a constable turned up. He said he had been alerted by a neighbour. Mr. Harvey told him where to go. The constable emerged a few moments later and directed them all into the front parlour. He sent me to the local station to fetch the inspector on duty. This turned out to be an Inspector Foy."

"I know of Inspector Foy," said Holmes with a slightly pained expression. "He was a sergeant until a year ago." He looked at me and raised his eyes heavenwards. "He is a protégé of Lestrade."

Miss Mackie continued. "He and some other police took over the house while they examined the room where the fight had taken place. After about thirty minutes he emerged and arrested Mr. Harvey for murder."

"Murder?" I said.

"The Inspector said that he did not accept the claim of self-defence. The bearded man had no weapon, and was no match for Mr. Harvey. He was convinced that Mr. Harvey had killed the man deliberately although he did not give a reason.

"They took him away, sir. Mrs. Harvey was distraught and didn't seem to know what to do. After about half an hour she sent me for you. I couldn't pay for a cab the whole way and had to cover the last half-mile on foot."

Holmes sat quietly, digesting the information, his hands tightly grasping the end of his cane. It was not long after this that we arrived at the address. It was a typical suburban house at the end of a terrace. It was probably not more than twenty years old. One of countless similar properties built to house the growing professional classes.

A constable was on the door. Fortunately, he recognised us and let us inside, informing us that he would make sure the inspector was told of our arrival. As we stepped inside, we could see another constable, a few feet down the hallway, at the door to what was presumably the scene of the confrontation.

Directed by Miss Mackie, we turned immediately right into the front parlour. There we found Mrs. Harvey. She was a striking lady not much older than her maid. She had evidently composed herself in anticipation of our arrival. Given what she had been through so recently, I was impressed at her apparent stoicism. Her son was sleeping in his pram, which had been wheeled into the room for that purpose. Her face was red from her earlier sobbing.

"I am so pleased to see you, Mr. Holmes, and I apologise for calling you here in such a fashion. Do sit down."

"No matter, Mrs. Harvey," said Holmes, taking a seat. "We have heard some of the events from your maid. Could you please give us your account?"

The lady took in a breath and began. "I had asked Sarah to go and get a bottle of wine. We do not normally keep drink in the house, but my husband had said tonight was a cause for celebration."

"And what were you celebrating?" asked Holmes.

"Oddly enough, I do not know," replied Mrs. Harvey. "David had been in a gloomy mood for some five months. Ever since he lost Sir Alan Smithie as his principal client."

"And why had that happened?" asked Holmes.

"I do not know, Mr. Holmes. David was clearly hurt by it but would not discuss it. It cut our income quite severely but David did have other clients. All he would say was that things were looking up. He also described it as a cloud that was about to lift.

"With Sarah on her way for the wine, David and I turned our attention to our walk. We had been taking one ever since we got Conan, our mastiff. David purchased him only a short while before he lost Sir Alan as a client. He is too big for a house of this size, Mr. Holmes, but, at the time, David would not entertain the idea of any other breed. We walked him every evening to burn at least a little of his energy. I would push the pram and David would take the leash. We walk a route that takes us about a mile from the house. Just over half-way into the walk David said that he had come round to my way of thinking regarding Conan and that he would soon look into finding a more suitable home for him. I was about to ask what had led to this change of heart when we met one of our neighbours, Mr. Fitzsimmons, a surveyor.

"When he saw us, he looked concerned. 'Is your maid doing some work outside your house?' he asked. It was an odd question. We answered in the negative and he responded by informing us that he had passed our house some time earlier and had noticed the front door was ajar.

"David's face startled me. He went as white as a sheet and lost hold of the leash. Conan ran off and David, clearly in a panic, ran after him."

"In the direction of home?" asked Holmes.

"Yes," she replied. "Conan, if left to himself, heads home like a pigeon. The last thing I saw was the two of them disappearing around a corner in the direction of the house. Mr. Fitzsimmons, seeing what effect his news had had, offered to escort me back. He is not a fit man so I was forced, despite my worries, to walk quite slowly. After a little while I begged him to excuse me so I could speed up and hasten my return home. He was averse to this, but I gave him little choice.

"It took me about ten further minutes to get to the house. The door was still open, and I could hear Conan barking and my husband shouting at someone. I did not dare go inside, and abandon William, so I waited and shouted for my husband from the door. He did not answer me but continued to shout at whomever he was confronting. As this was going on, I looked around to see various neighbours either on their doorsteps or looking through their windows. A few moments later

Sarah returned and she ventured inside. No doubt she has told you what she found?"

Holmes said nothing for a moment then looked up. "Where is the dog now?"

"Inspector Foy demanded that he be shut in the kitchen. He does not like strangers and the inspector and his men felt in danger."

At this, Holmes permitted himself a brief smile. "Does he respond well to commands?"

"Sarah here is good with him. He is muzzled now so will not be too dangerous."

This news gave me very little comfort. Holmes stood. "Good. Let us go and meet him."

I followed Holmes out into the hallway. He turned and called back into the parlour. "I understand the room at the very end of the corridor is your husband's study?"

"That is correct, Mr. Holmes. To the left of that door is a door to the basement where the kitchen is."

We walked down the hallway, past the rear parlour where the constable stood guard. Holmes nodded as we passed. He also studied the floor as we walked. I followed his gaze and could see a lot of scratches that seemed to run from the front door for the entire length of the hallway. Reaching the study door, we turned left and descended to the basement with Sarah leading us. We entered the kitchen to the sound of growling. Conan was standing in what was clearly his bed in the corner. Thanks to his impressive size, he dominated the room. He was on the small side for a mastiff but still a formidable animal. Upon seeing Miss Mackie, he calmed down but continued to focus his eyes on us.

Holmes studied the dog, staring at Conan with an intensity equal to that which was returned. "Thank you, Miss Mackie," said Holmes. "I have seen enough." He turned, left the room, and climbed the stairs with me in pursuit.

"Watson, would you be so good as to fetch Mrs. Harvey?"

I went up the hallway and requested Mrs. Harvey's presence. Her son asleep, she was willing to leave him for a moment. We joined Holmes at the study door.

"I understand, Mrs. Harvey, that, after the confrontation, your husband left the intruder's body and entered this room. May we?"

Mrs. Harvey nodded. Holmes turned the handle and pushed the door open.

Inside we found a charming but modest study. It was just the kind of study you would expect for a middle-class accountant. Comfortable but not ostentatious. A window faced south onto a small garden. To one side of the window was a bookshelf, and a desk was roughly in the middle of the room with an oil-lamp upon it. In another corner of the room was an empty valet stand that seemed rather more luxurious than the other items in the room. Once we were all inside, Holmes asked me to shut the door.

"Now, Mrs. Harvey. Does everything look in place here?"

The lady looked carefully. "Yes, I think so. I do not come in here often so I would not know all that well." She turned right round to take in the entire room. "The only thing I would say is that David's smoking jacket is usually on the stand rather than the back of the door. He would usually hang his hat there. The stand was a gift from Sir Alan. David really prized it."

Holmes looked impatient. "Do the desk and bookshelves look as they should?"

Mrs. Harvey looked tense. "I do not know what you want me to say, Mr. Holmes. All looks as normal as I can recall."

She headed for the door, clearly a little upset by my friend's line of questioning. I followed her as she turned the handle. "It looks like you will need some repairs there," I said.

She followed my gaze to the wall near the door. The wallpaper was scuffed and slightly torn between three and four feet down from the ceiling. She gave me a look of reproach and I fell silent. Her husband was in a police cell for murder and I was commenting on their décor.

She left the room and headed back to the front parlour and her son. We followed, me still feeling tactless. She resumed her seat next to the child and gently rocked the pram. "Can you help me?" she asked.

I waited for Holmes to speak and when there was silence, I turned to see he was not there. I was about to return to the hallway when he joined us.

"I plan to pay a visit to Inspector Foy now, Mrs. Harvey," he said. "Before I do, is there anything that you desire to add?"

Mrs. Harvey's lip started to tremble as she thought. The effort in maintaining her composure was clearly becoming too much. "I just remember the shame as David was led out to a carriage in handcuffs. Our neighbours were all looking on as he walked out of the gate. Even a man just passing by stopped and stared as David was put into the carriage. I think even David noticed him as he seemed to look in his direction briefly. It was only after the carriage had left that I had the idea to send Sarah for you, Mr. Holmes."

Holmes gave Mrs. Harvey as much reassurance as he could before we took our leave. Miss Mackie was loitering in the hall, clearly not sure what to do with herself.

"Tell me, Miss Mackie," said Holmes. "When did you last varnish this floor? One or two days ago?"

"Close, Mr. Holmes," she replied. "Three days ago. Why?"

"No matter," said Holmes as he let himself out.

I joined my friend on the pavement. Plenty of curtains were still twitching. There is nothing like a crime to get the attention of your neighbours. I could feel eyes watching us as we headed back to the main road in search of a cab. We secured one swiftly enough and headed to Clapham police station. When we arrived, it was clear we were expected. We were shown into Inspector Foy's office to await his return. About five minutes later he arrived and shook our hands warmly. In my opinion, he was rather old for a recently promoted inspector. "Good to see you, gentlemen. Although I think you are wasting your time."

"Lestrade has said that more than once," said Holmes. "Usually, he was wrong."

Foy swallowed, recognising the rebuke. He invited us to sit, and took his seat behind his desk, lowering himself into his chair slowly almost as you would for a hot bath. "Look," he said, "it seems simple enough. The family and maid leave the house, not locking the door properly. While they are gone our intruder enters and begins ransacking the rear parlour looking for easy pickings. Unfortunately for him, a neighbour of the Harveys sees the open door and becomes suspicious when he later encounters the couple on the street. Mr. Harvey runs back to the house with his dog and finds the intruder still there. A confrontation ensues, Mr. Harvey seizes a poker and strikes a fatal blow."

"You forget, Inspector," said Holmes. "We have not been fortunate enough to see the body."

"Ah. Well, you are welcome to it when you are ready. You will find a blow to the forehead consistent with a poker which, according to the police surgeon, was the fatal blow. There is also a secondary, and superfluous, wound to the back of the head as a result of the intruder falling back against the wall or similar surface."

"Do the circumstances not strike you as odd, Inspector?" said Holmes. "How did the intruder know nobody was home?"

"Could have been lucky I guess," said Foy.

"Or he knew their routine?"

"I think that unlikely, Mr. Holmes."

"Were any of the rooms disturbed apart from the one where the body was found?"

"They did not appear to be," replied Foy. "Everything was neat and tidy. All the action was centred on the rear parlour."

"Was there anything of value there?" asked Holmes.

"No," said Foy. "But an opportunistic intruder was not to know that."

"Surely, Inspector," said Holmes, "an intruder seeking to steal would target a room where valuables were more likely to be? The bedrooms, the study? He would at least be methodical about it. Why start in a room in the middle of the house?"

Foy looked irritated. "He may not have done. The rear parlour is where he was confronted. It may not have been the only room he entered."

Holmes abandoned the line of questioning. "How is Mr. Harvey?"

Foy frowned and stood up. He began to pace up and down behind his desk, hands clasped behind his back. "He is sticking to his story. He admits dealing the killer blow but insists it was in self-defence."

"Why do you not believe him?" I asked.

"Because the dead man was no physical match for him and was not armed. He was shorter than Harvey at around five feet ten and Mr. Harvey, aided by an aggressive dog, was never in any danger from him."

"So, what is your thinking, Inspector?" asked Holmes.

"I have given it some thought and have come down to two possibilities. This was either excessive force delivered in the heat of the moment, or this was a man Harvey knew and had good reason to want dead."

"I struggle to picture an accountant moving in such violent circles," said Holmes. "It also means that you are, in fact, entertaining the idea that this could be someone familiar with the Harvey household rather than a more opportunistic crime."

If the situation had not been so serious, I would have laughed. Watching Foy's range of facial expressions as he analysed Holmes's reasoning was amusing. He sat back down. "Yes. That is a good point, Mr. Holmes. I seem to recall Inspector Lestrade once telling me that theories need to be bent to suit the facts rather than the other way round. I am much obliged to you for the perspective."

Holmes and I exchanged amused glances. Foy was not yet finished. "One last thing I will say is that Harvey's solicitor clearly shares my negative view of his client's situation."

"How so?" asked Holmes.

"He turned up about an hour after we brought Mr. Harvey in. Sent for by Mrs. Harvey, I assume. After the usual formalities, we let him into Harvey's cell. They were in there for less than thirty minutes."

"That does seem rather short for such an occasion," I remarked.

"To be honest," said Foy, "I think he could see how hopeless it was. The constable who let him out commented on how frustrated he looked. It was the look of a solicitor who sees no way to save his client. We will hear from him again before the trial, of course."

"Do you mind if we see the body now?" said Holmes.

"Not at all. I will have a constable escort you."

About five minutes later we were standing by the body. The police surgeon had shaved the back of the head so the wound there could be examined. It was relatively minor compared to the shocking wound at the front which had clearly been delivered with considerable force.

The police surgeon took us through the report, not that there was much to say that could not be readily seen. While this was happening, Holmes stared at the face of the body.

"Doctor, would it be possible for you to shave the beard off?"

The police surgeon looked perplexed. "Why, sir?"

"I believe I know this man but need to see him clean-shaven to be sure."

The surgeon looked hesitant. "I shall need to speak to the Inspector." He left the room.

"What is it, Holmes?" I asked.

"If this is who I think it is," said Holmes. "It will add a new dimension to this case." He whipped out a tape measure and proceeded to check the height of the body.

"Always wise to confirm these things. Our intruder is, in fact, five feet, eleven." He put away the tape and scribbled the information down in his notebook.

The surgeon returned. "The Inspector was rather amused and said he can see no reason why not as we have already taken photographs."

He proceeded to shave the face. As he progressed, Holmes looked more and more content.

"As I thought," he said, and left the room.

We returned to Foy's office. "That was an odd request, Mr. Holmes," said Foy, his amusement fully on display. "Were you enlightened?"

"Very much so, Foy," replied Holmes. "Can I have your permission to interview Mr. Harvey?" Foy nodded.

"Can I also see the room where the death took place?" Foy nodded again and wrote out a note for Holmes to give to the constable on duty.

"By the way," said Holmes as he took the note and headed for the door, "your dead man is Arthur Cooper." As I followed him, I took one last look at Foy. He was clearly surprised.

"Who is Arthur Cooper?" I asked as we headed to the cells.

"Not here, Watson," replied my friend.

In a few moments we stood in the cell of David Harvey. He was a sorry sight, as would be any man in his position. He knew of us and seemed unnerved at the idea that his wife had engaged us. I could see that this struck Holmes as odd as much as it did me. People were usually grateful to see us – unless they had something to hide.

"I do not know what to say, Mr. Holmes," said Harvey.

"I do not have your version," said Holmes. "If you wish to avoid the rope you would do well to tell me all."

Harvey swallowed. "It was old Mr. Fitzsimmons who told us that our house was apparently open. My first thought was that Sarah had returned early but there was no reason for her to leave the door open."

"Your wife remarked that you went pale," I said.

"She has a tendency to exaggerate," replied Harvey, dismissively.

"But you lost control of your dog," Holmes reminded him.

"Yes, that is true and I ran after him. He was quite some way ahead but I felt sure he was heading for home. Even if he had not been, my priority was to get to the house. I found the door open and I heard Conan growling and barking inside. I was about to go in when another neighbour, an old lady named Mrs. Johnson, called to me from across the street and said that a constable was being looked for and I should wait. I thanked her but headed inside anyway.

"I immediately realised the noises were coming from the rear parlour and ran in to find a man trying to fend off Conan with our poker. The room was a mess with drawers open and a few ornaments on the floor. I challenged the man and he demanded I call Conan off and permit him to leave.

"I knew Jane would soon be back with our son and I did not want her to encounter this man. I also had no idea how long it would be before the police arrived. I called Conan to heel and stood to one side, telling the man to drop the poker and get out before the police arrived."

"He started to head towards the door but showed no inclination to drop the poker. Conan was still growling and as the man got near to the door he decided to strike out with the poker. I grabbed his arm and we struggled together. I was surprised to find him rather weak so we knocked into things sending more ornaments crashing to the floor. I punched him in the stomach and he dropped the poker. Conan went for him but I called him off. I just wanted this man to leave. To encourage him, I picked up the poker and pointed it at him. 'Get out,' I said."

"And then your wife arrived," said Holmes.

"Yes. I heard her call out. I was going to tell her to get out of the way so this man could leave. Instead, he charged at me. In a panic, I lashed out and hit him in the head. He fell to the floor and was still. I assumed he was merely unconscious. I bent down to check and that is when Sarah appeared in the doorway, and the constable arrived soon after."

"The inspector did not believe your story?"

"He did up to a point but he could not believe that the man would stay and fight after learning that police were on their way. He told me, pretty much there and then, that he believed that, blinded by anger, I killed the man as soon as I had control of the poker."

"Why did you go to your study immediately after striking this man?"

Harvey swallowed. "I keep a bottle of brandy in there and needed a drink."

"Your wife stated that you do not keep alcohol in the house."

"She did not know about the brandy. I kept it in a drawer. I found it a restorative on late nights working."

"She also told us you were going to be celebrating. What about?"

"I had secured some new clients so our money worries were going to ease."

"On that subject, what was the cause of your falling out with Sir Alan Smithie?"

Harvey looked at the ground. "I cannot answer that, Mr. Holmes. As much as it wounded me, the details would violate Sir Alan's privacy."

Holmes did not seem too irritated by the lack of cooperation. "Perhaps Watson and I should go and talk to him?"

Harvey managed a smile. "You could try, sir, but Sir Alan is fussy about whom he meets. He will not see you without good reason and my name will not be viewed as a good reason."

"Any message for your wife?" asked Holmes.

"Just tell her I love her and I hope to be with her soon."

We left the cells and headed out of the station. Holmes was lost in thought so I kept silent. I managed to attract the attention of a passing cab which overshot us and had to turn round.

"It is always easier to hide a lie amongst the truth," said Holmes as he climbed in. "Stansfield Road, Clapham, please, cabby." I was barely in before the cab began to move.

"What do you mean by that?" I asked.

"I mean that a good deal of what Mr. Harvey just told us was true but a portion was not."

I put this to one side as I had a more pressing question. "About this Mr. Cooper?"

"Apologies, Watson. Arthur Cooper is, or rather was, a man in a similar line of work to myself."

"A private detective?"

"Of a sort. He was also willing to break the law in the service of his clients."

"How reprehensible," I said.

"Hypocrisy does not suit you, Watson."

The blow was justified as I recalled the times Holmes and I had done the same.

"So, why was he in the Harvey house?"

"An excellent question, my friend," said Holmes. "His services were not cheap. Well beyond the purse of your average person."

"But not beyond Sir Alan Smithie?" I asked.

Holmes smiled but did not reply.

Back in Clapham, the note handed over, we stood in the rear parlour. The room was in a state of chaos. "It bothers me, Watson," said Holmes.

"What does?"

"The breakages."

"Well, it happened in the struggle."

"Not all of it. Mr. Harvey said there were broken items when he challenged Cooper. Now why would Cooper break anything?"

"Clumsiness?"

"That will not do, Watson. Cooper was not clumsy. He was a professional. He was not a thief. He was a seeker of things."

"What do you mean?"

"People hired Cooper to find things. If you were in the nobility, you might hire him to find information about a lady your son wanted to marry, for example."

"How horrible," I observed. "Raking through people's private lives."

"Just one of his many talents, Watson," said Holmes with a subtle smile.

He studied the carpet. "You can just make out where the body lay. Close to the door but not too close. That casts doubt on what we have been told."

"It does?"

"Yes. How, after receiving the blow to the head, does Cooper fall back and hit a wall or the door. He was too far away from anything that would deliver such a wound and there is no sign of such a collision."

It was a sound observation to which I had no answer. We learned from the constable that Mrs. Harvey had retired and Miss Mackie had done the same. With the constable's permission, Holmes made a second visit to the study, tape measure in hand. He was but a moment and then we left the house and headed back to Baker Street. It was, after all, nearly midnight and we had packed a lot into the last few hours.

As I ascended the stairs to my room, Holmes called after me. "Be up promptly tomorrow, Watson. We are going to visit Sir Alan Smithie."

"Unannounced?"

"Unannounced, Watson."

The next morning, we were on a train to Canterbury where Sir Alan Smithie had his country home. I was troubled by Holmes's decision not to wire ahead. It seemed the height of bad manners not to request an interview more formally. Holmes, who despite his bohemian attitude, liked and observed many of society's conventions, appeared untroubled, even amused, at my discomfort.

At Canterbury station we hailed a cab. As soon as we announced our destination the cabby asked, "Guests of Sir Alan, gentlemen?"

I thought it impertinent but Holmes replied in the negative.

"You'll be lucky guv'nor," the cabby said. "I'd best wait for you as you'll be needing a cab back pretty sharpish. He's been known to fire a shotgun at unwanted visitors."

"You can rest assured that we will be admitted," said Holmes. "Stay on hand anyway as we will want to return to the station once our audience has concluded."

The cabby's disbelieving chuckle echoed in my ears for the remainder of the journey.

After about ten minutes he informed us that we were approaching the house. The word house was a decided understatement. We passed through an impressive gatehouse which, the cabby informed us, was home to Sir Alan's gamekeeper. Beyond it was an immaculate road lined with gas-lamps. The journey from the gate to the front door seemed almost as long as the journey from the station to the gate.

Holmes gave me a potted history on the way. Despite being imposing, the house was not a long-held family seat. It was little more than one hundred years old and had been purchased by Sir Alan within the last ten years. Holmes also explained that Sir Alan had been a diplomat in the Far East, for which he had been knighted, and was the second son of an earl. His elder brother was now the incumbent earl with a family seat in Lincolnshire. One thing was abundantly clear. Sir Alan had the kind of money to hire one of the country's best investigators.

We arrived at the front door and alighted, our feet sinking into the gravel. The cabby, as Holmes handed him his fare, said, "I'll be ready when you need me." It was uttered in such a way that it was clear he expected us to require him sooner rather than later.

We advanced to the front door. It was a sturdy, studded door that would have looked more in keeping in a church or castle. As we neared, I looked up to make sure that there was nowhere from which defenders could pour boiling oil onto us. It was silly but, at the same time, instinctive.

In response to our ring, the door was opened by a stern butler who, in answer to our greeting, said we were not expected and would not be seen. Holmes took out his notebook and scribbled down a few words. He handed his card and the note to the butler who proceeded to shut the door.

"It should not be long, Watson."

In less than two minutes, the door opened and we were summoned inside. As he entered, Holmes turned to look at the cabby. The man was plainly astonished.

With the door closed, the butler took our hats, coats, and canes. We followed him down a long corridor before he indicated a door. The room we entered was a magnificent study. The walls were covered in oil paintings. Every surface had vases and plates of an oriental design upon it. There was a lot of money in the room.

"What is the meaning of this?" uttered a booming voice.

I turned to see a formidable man holding Holmes's note. He was over fifty, probably nearer sixty, lean, over six feet, balding and bespectacled. "I repeat," he said. "What is the meaning of this?"

"Just three words that I knew would get us into this room," replied Holmes.

"I do not associate with detectives," said Sir Alan, dismissively.

"And how would you classify the late Mr. Arthur Cooper?" asked Holmes.

Sir Alan paused. "Late?"

"Yes," said Holmes.

"I would classify him as a trusted friend," came the reply.

"A friend who happened to be a detective," I said.

"Are you the author of this note, sir?" said Sir Alan to me, waving the paper.

"No," I replied.

"Then be so kind as to remain silent."

I could feel myself redden with anger and clenched my fists.

Holmes remained calm. "I take it you still do not know where it is?"

Sir Alan said nothing.

"Thank you," said Holmes, apparently satisfied. "How do you feel about Mr. Harvey facing the rope?"

"It is no concern of mine."

"Despite him being an equally trusted friend?"

"He was. No longer."

"Mr. Cooper died whilst on your commission."

"You cannot prove that, Mr. Holmes."

"Not yet."

"Get out," barked Sir Alan.

"What if I can find it?" said Holmes, his feet rooted to the spot.

Sir Alan fell briefly silent. "Do you have information, Mr. Holmes?"

"Perhaps."

Sir Alan marched up to Holmes and thrust the paper back at him. Holmes took it. "If you do, present it to me and you will be rewarded."

We heard a small cough and turned to see the butler. Without ceremony we turned and followed. At the front door we were hastily reunited with our belongings and found ourselves back on the front step.

"You were longer than I thought you'd be," said the cabby.

Back in the cab, Holmes handed me the paper. "You were bound to ask."

I opened it. It simply read "The Sapporo Pearl."

"What's this?"

"Three words that gave Sir Alan pause for thought. The Sapporo Pearl was sold to Sir Alan at auction in Japan some years ago. He found himself in a bidding war with an Arab noble named Sheikh Abadi who was most displeased not to secure it. Said Sheikh even tried to buy it from Sir Alan and threatened dire consequences when he was rebuffed. You know what it is like to be rebuffed by Sir Alan."

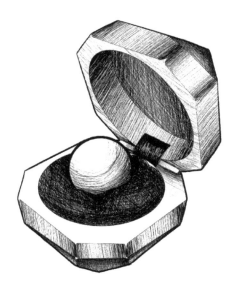

"Subsequently some doubts were raised about the legality of the auction. By this time Sir Alan was back in England and rejected all approaches on the matter from the Japanese authorities. You have seen his study. He has a passion for the Orient and its treasures; the Sheikh equally, if not more, so."

"I do not see the connection," I said.

"About six months ago the pearl vanished. It was leaked to the press but Sir Alan said nothing and refused police involvement. It was suspected that Sheikh Abadi was connected to the matter and Sir Alan was embarrassed to be outsmarted by him. I think it is too much of a coincidence that he dispenses with Mr. Harvey at around the same time, don't you?"

At Canterbury, we boarded the first available train back to London. Upon our arrival we passed a newsagent. Outside was a sign with a worrying headline which read, "Burglary at Clapham Murder House."

Needless to say, we headed directly back to the Harvey house. We found Inspector Foy at the scene. "It never rains, Mr. Holmes," was all he could say.

"What happened?"

"Mrs. Harvey's maid dragged my constable into the house a little after eight o'clock. It seems that she woke to find Constable Morris unconscious in the hall with big knock to the head. He later admitted to having fallen asleep so did not see the attack coming. Mrs. Harvey entered her husband's study to find it in complete chaos. It had been torn apart methodically, perhaps over a couple of hours. A professional job."

"No other room?"

"Just that one."

Holmes smiled. "I think we should speak to the lady of the house."

We found Mrs. Harvey, as before, in the front parlour. As we entered, she looked up. "I am not sure I can take much more of this, Mr. Holmes."

"Rest assured it is almost over," said Holmes. Foy and I exchanged bemused glances. "I have one question."

"Yes?"

"Did you send for your husband's solicitor after his arrest?"

"No," she said. "We do not have a regular solicitor. We have not needed one since we bought this house."

"That is what I suspected. Thank you, Mrs. Harvey."

Inspector Foy and I followed Holmes back onto the street.

"What on earth was that about, Holmes?" asked Foy.

"The solicitor question was the final piece of the puzzle," said Holmes. "I am confident I have the sequence of events."

"You know how the murder was done and who keeps breaking into the Harvey house?"

Holmes turned to look at Foy. "There was no murder, Inspector."

I might have taken some pleasure at the inspector's confusion if I had not shared it. We got into Foy's carriage and Holmes asked to be taken to the Northumberland Hotel. Foy was too perplexed to object. Upon our arrival Holmes entered the foyer alone and emerged a few minutes later. We headed back to Clapham police station.

With the two of us in tow. Holmes headed down to the cells.

We were admitted and Harvey rose to his feet.

"It is all over, Mr. Harvey," said Holmes. "If you will excuse the expression, your employer will not get his prize."

Harvey sank back down and placed his head in his hands.

"Jane and William are doomed," he said, beginning to sob.

"I do not believe so," said Holmes. "I have sent a message that I am confident will be received. The Inspector here will ensure your family are guarded in the meantime."

Harvey did not look convinced.

"Now when were you approached to steal the pearl?"

"What pearl?" said Harvey.

Holmes sighed and reached into his pocket. "This one."

Between his fingers was a beautiful pearl. Foy and I audibly gasped. "How long have you had that?"

"Since my second visit to the Harvey house," replied Holmes.

"Where was it?"

"In Mr. Harvey's desk."

Before we could say anything, Harvey spoke. "Seven months ago."

"Please continue."

Harvey wore the look of someone now pleased to confess. "I was at a party arranged by Sir Alan in London. I am not good at that sort of thing so was lingering on the edge. A man sidled up to me and introduced himself as Mr. Stephens."

"A false name of course," said Holmes.

"If you say so," said Harvey. "He calmly told me that he represented powerful men who wanted property of theirs returned. They had been watching me and said I was perfectly positioned to retrieve it for them. If I did not or if I involved the authorities, my wife and new-born child were in danger."

"You should have spoken to the police," said Foy.

Harvey looked up, wide-eyed. "And risk harm to my family? I knew this was no joke. Stephens quoted my address to me, my routine, and even presented me with details of the layout of my house. The danger felt real. He went on to say they wanted the Sapporo Pearl. They told me Sir Alan kept it at his Kent home and I was to steal it as soon as possible.

"As it turned out, I managed it surprisingly quickly. Sir Alan loved to occasionally show off his oriental treasures to his inner circle, which I was proud to be a part of. On one such occasion, when I was there with his solicitor, his extended family, and some business associates, he produced the pearl. When he later put it away in his study, I followed him quietly and saw where he kept it. As I watched him, I thought my heart would come out of my chest. About an hour before I left, at a time when his guests were scattered throughout the house, I crept in and stole it. I also broke a small window so it would look like someone came in from outside.

"I was shaking for my entire journey home. On the one hand, I knew my life was over if what I had done came to light. On the other, I was protecting my family. I brought the pearl into the house and placed it in a secret compartment in my desk. I placed a lamp in an upstairs room one night as a pre-arranged signal that I had the pearl. At work the next day I received a note to the effect that I had to hold onto the pearl as Sir Alan had discovered its loss. It was considered dangerous to move the pearl until the matter died down.

"I was terrified. I had hoped to pass it on quickly to remove the threat from my family. Now it was hanging over my head like the sword of Damocles."

"You were dealing with patient and dangerous people," said Holmes.

"Imagine my terror," said Harvey, "when a week or so later Sir Alan invited me back to his home. All kinds of fear went through my mind. Did he know it was me? I also knew I had to go to avoid raising suspicions.

"The journey down was not good for my nerves. When I finally arrived, I saw I was not the only guest. Everyone I saw had been at the earlier engagement. We were invited to assemble in his dining room where he introduced a Mr. Cooper to us. It was explained that he was an investigator of some kind that had been tasked with locating the pearl. Sir Alan came right out and said he was not fooled by the broken glass and knew it had to be one of us. Everyone was shocked but before anyone could protest, he had us all shown out."

"This is when you were dropped from Sir Alan's employment?" asked Holmes.

"Yes. He severed contact with everyone who had been at the

party with, I believe, the exception of his solicitor. If you ever meet him, you will see how ruthless he can be."

"We have had that pleasure," I said.

Harvey nodded. "The loss of income was nothing to the terror I felt every night that pearl was under my roof. I could not dispose of it without endangering my family. Yet it was the only proof I had committed the crime. Then, recently, the good news came."

"The gang was coming to collect," said Holmes.

"Yes. I had another note to say that a man would call at the house, two evenings from that date, posing as a salesman. He would announce himself as Mr. Collier and I was to hand him the pearl. I was so relieved."

"So relieved that you decided to announce a celebration which prompted your wife to seek wine to toast it," said Holmes.

"Yes. When the day came, I was so nervous. I tried to conduct myself normally but it was difficult. I had been instructed not to act in any way that might draw attention so I did my best to adhere to the normal routine. I returned home from work and went on the normal walk with Jane, William, and Conan."

"The oversized dog you had bought out of fear not long before the theft?"

"Yes. But the fear had largely left me at that point. It had been replaced by a kind of excitement. When we ran into Mr. Fitzsimmons, and I learned the house was open, I feared the worst. I lost control of Conan who headed back to the house at speed. I followed as fast as I could but he arrived far ahead of me. What I found terrified me."

"What you found was a strange bearded man dead in your study."

"How did you know, Mr. Holmes?"

"The evidence was there if you knew how to read it. Your wooden floored hallway that runs from your front door all the way to your study had been recently varnished, we had that from your maid. Conan had charged home into that hallway and saw a man emerging from your study. He dislikes strangers and charged towards this unknown figure, leaving copious scratches in the fresh varnish. These ran all the way to the study door proving that was where the stranger was or headed to. That stranger was Arthur Cooper, Sir Alan's investigator, hiding behind a newly grown beard. I knew Cooper and he was not a brave man in the face of certain danger. He was probably several feet up the corridor, on his way out with the pearl when he encountered Conan. Terrified, he fled back into the study with every intention of fleeing out of the window there. First, he had to shut the door, but was not fast enough. Conan, slid on the new varnish and slammed into the door with all his might. The hook on the back of the door, which would usually have your hat on it, was bare and slammed into Cooper's head killing him. His body was also thrown into the wall behind the door accounting for the wound there. He slid down the wall and onto the floor where you found him."

"Good God," said Foy.

"You did not want any attention on your study. You searched Cooper and found the pearl. You returned it to its hiding place and dragged Cooper's body to the next room along the hallway, your rear parlour. You pulled him by his feet which is why your maid reported to us that his arms were above his head when she later saw you. Drag a body in that fashion and the arms will do that.

"But you now had a dead body with a head wound. You had to invent a way to account for that. You quickly settled on the poker. You smeared it with Cooper's blood before breaking some items in the parlour. At the same time, you shouted in order to suggest a confrontation. My suspicions were aroused by the fact that both your wife and maid attested to hearing only your voice but you told us that Cooper was making loud demands for you to let him pass which your wife would have heard had he really been alive. Miss Mackie prevented any further stage management by her appearance. But you remembered one thing."

"What was that?" asked Foy

"The hook on the back of the door. He did not want any chance of it being noticed and the police making a connection. All he could do, in the time available, was cover it. He had lost his hat in his race to get home. So, he rushed past his maid into the study."

"The smoking jacket," I exclaimed.

"Bravo, Watson. Mrs. Harvey told us it usually hung on his valet stand, a prized gift from Sir Alan. With the door briefly shut, he transferred it to the hook and left probably not noticing the damage to the wall."

Harvey looked both amazed and dejected. "I ran out of energy at that point. I knew it was vital that the police did not search the study. If they did, and found the pearl, my family was lost."

"That was another mistake," said Holmes. "When a man tells me a tale that I consider false and risks the rope in doing so, I know he is protecting someone more important than his own life."

Harvey nodded. "When the police later charged me and took me away, I noticed a strange man in the street amongst all my curious neighbours. He was carrying a case and it occurred to me that this might be Mr. Collier who had come to collect. I locked eyes with him and mouthed the word, 'Help.' I did not know if it would do any good but I had to try."

"I presume," said Holmes, "that he later turned up at the police station posing as your solicitor?"

"Right under my nose," said Foy.

"When we were alone," said Harvey, "I told him where the pearl was and asked him to get it out of there. He said he would and left."

"I am afraid to say," said Holmes, "that he was too slow. In the elapsed time I had already worked out much of your deception. I just did not have a reason. When I understood the timing of the split from Sir Alan, in relation to the disappearance of the pearl, and the identity of your intruder, it was too much of a coincidence. In that second moment alone in your study I located the pearl. Those desks are manufactured to a standard design with which I am familiar. The secret compartments are nothing of the kind.

"Cooper had presumably been busy all these months investigating those who might have taken the pearl and was now focused on you. He had worked out your routine and was waiting for his opportunity. He entered and began in your study. He knew the desks as well as I do and found the pearl. The only mystery to me is why he left the front door ajar. Perhaps he assumed he would be in and out fast enough. He had grown a beard as a disguise which I have no doubt he planned to shave off within hours of retrieving the pearl. Then events got out of his control, courtesy of your mastiff, and he lost his life."

"But what about the later break in?" asked Foy.

"Mr. Harvey's 'solicitor,' or an associate, entered through his study window and headed to where they had been told the pearl was. When they did not find it immediately, they knew they had to search the whole room. They crept out, stunned your sleeping constable, and spent their time searching to no avail. Hence our trip to the Northumberland Hotel."

"Come again?" said Foy.

"One of the pageboys there runs occasional errands for me. I asked him to place a personal ad in all the evening papers to say that the pearl is back with its owner and that the Harvey family is to be left alone. It is phrased more covertly than that but that is the message. If they fail to heed it, I will tell you enough to locate them."

"It is against the law to withhold information from us, Mr. Holmes," reminded Foy.

"There is no information, Inspector. It is a bluff but hopefully one they will heed. Sir Alan's ongoing safety is far from guaranteed but that is the concern of the Kent police. In the meantime, Foy, you had better take this."

Foy took the pearl from Holmes's outstretched hand. "I will get this back to Sir Alan," he said, transfixed at the shiny bauble he now held.

A few days later we were able to read in the papers that Mr. Harvey had been released on the grounds of self-defence. Cooper was not identified as the victim. In the later *Evening Standard* Holmes drew my attention to an ad. It simply read "To SH. Bluff, but we know when to leave the stage."

"Can we trust that?" I asked.

"I think we can," said Holmes. "Organisations like that move onto their next objective. It would be a waste of resources to do otherwise."

"But who is running it?"

Holmes picked up his pipe and began to fill it. "Who indeed, Watson? Who indeed?"

I do believe it was the happiest I had seen him.

This is volume one of a planned series. To keep up -to-date with all that is going on, please visit my blog

https://caidencoopermyles.blogspot.com/

Or scan the below QR code:

To Mum

I am sorry it took me so long